Benedict Fitzsimmons, the reclusive fourteenth Duke of Ashington, nurses a secret desire for his own sex he'd much prefer nobody ever found out about. Indeed, having only ever given in to his urges as a youth—and with disastrous consequences—he never imagined they would. Preferring the company of his race-horses to people, Benedict spends most of his time working on estate matters, longing for a lost love he can never have.

When an anonymous letter threatening to expose Benedict lands in his lap, he's shocked to the core. He doesn't have any enemies; why would anyone want to destroy him? Terrified, and with his family's impeccable reputation at stake, Benedict joins forces with loyal friend, the Earl of Rossingley, to track down the culprit.

Risen from poverty and with a sordid past he'd rather forget, Tommy Squire has a mind dedicated to growing his business ventures and a heart shaped from stone. When the man who once broke it in a life-changing betrayal requests Tommy's help to avoid a scandal, he finds himself embroiled in a daring scheme to bring down a blackmailer. As their plot unfolds, Tommy realises it's more than his former lover he's endeavouring to protect, it's his battered heart.

This second book in the Rossingley Regency romance series turns to friends of the fourteenth earl of Rossingley, Lando Duchamps-Avery, who once again has a hand in the shenanigans set in London's wealthy Ton society. This book can be read as a standalone.

TO DEFEND A

DAMAGED DUKE

REGENCY ROSSINGLEY, BOOK TWO

FEARNE HILL

A NineStar Press Publication

www.ninestarpress.com

To Defend a Damaged Duke

First Edition, June 2025

ISBN: 978-1-64890-878-1

Also available in eBook, ISBN: 978-1-64890-877-4

CONTENT WARNING:

This book contains sexually explicit content, which may only be suitable for mature readers. Discussion of past trauma (recounted).

Prologue

London, 1813

AT THE BACK of the fruit and veg market in Convent Garden, a showman scraped a living. Every Tuesday and Friday, for more years than Tommy Squire had been alive. Same patch, same old rickety stall, same old rickety routine. Same anticlimactic finale. Declaring himself the world's greatest magician, he'd hold aloft a playing card, purse his wrinkled, whiskery lips, and pretend to blow the spots off it. Tommy had watched him fumble the cards up his sleeve hundreds of times; seen him drop them on occasion too. And yet, on his mother's grave, even as he wriggled a grubby knave down from his elbow to his wrist, the old sot still swore it was magic.

Tommy was reminded of that showman whenever the lord-ling's black eyes, like two jet pearls, fluttered closed. Usually, the memory came seconds after the lordling's throat made a helpless little whine, speaking its own language, directly into Tommy heart. It heralded the shortest sliver of time before he spilled into Tommy's mouth and then pressed his lips against Tommy's, tasting himself on them. Whispering sweet nonsense.

Those were the times Tommy remembered that old showman and his frayed cards, and it was only years later he understood what he meant. The daft sod had spun the story to himself so many times, believing in the magic of it, he ended up fooling himself.

*

"OUR YOUNG LORDLING'S here, Tommy. Waiting in the best room." Ma Duggan's expression soured, matching the sallow hue of her downturned sneer. "Taken off upstairs already to get hisself ready. He's asked for you."

Fancying himself as a bit of an actor—he had to be in this business if he wanted paying right—Tommy pretended not to notice young Dickie flouncing out of the parlour. Nor Sidney's jealous sulk. After all, who could blame them? The handsome lordling had caught everyone's eye.

"I'll be there when I've finished me tea. Won't hurt him to wait a minute or two."

Tommy could control his face, keep it blank. And his voice flat. But the mad thumping in his chest? Not a chance. No more than he could prevent the spirited rush of joy to his head, nor the twitching of his prick. Not when his beloved raven-haired beauty impatiently paced six feet above his head.

He carried up a jug of ale, not pausing to check himself in

the glass hung at the bottom of the stairs. He didn't need to; Tommy's pretty looks hadn't waned since he examined them last. Dress him in a corset and stays, and Sidney declared he could work alongside the girls in the bawdy house on the corner. He scratched at the door, thrice, his pulse hammering.

"Tommy. At last. I was growing quite weak with want."

Already, the lordling had removed his hat and coat, all the better for Tommy to admire his raven locks curling over his stiff collar. Unfastening his cravat with an urgent flourish, he was as eager as Tommy, more so, if the swelling in his breeches was any measure. They were of an age, the raven and Tommy — Tommy eighteen years young to the raven's seventeen. Yet both so sure.

"My lord." In the demure fashion he'd perfected, Tommy bobbed his head. The lordling blushed with delight. He relieved Tommy of the laden tray, and his plump mouth twisted into a smile. His hooded eyes, dark as night, latched onto Tommy's.

"Afterwards with this, Tommy. My…my need for you can wait no longer."

The *best room* wasn't much to crow about. Nothing but a slender bed with a mean pillow, worn sheets, and a wooden chair upon which his handsome raven had tossed his coat. Around a water pitcher, his paying guest's silk cravat lay unfurled like a banner. Tommy's threadbare neckcloth joined it.

"Then you must have at me, my lord." Behind his ribs, his soft heart trembled. "I am yours."

In pulled up undershirts and pushed down breeches, they tussled on the bed. A pair of kittens let loose in the sunshine. Tommy kissed his raven on the mouth, the only madge he'd ever kissed, but then none of the other madges tasted so sweet. Or returned his kisses with such unmatched desire.

"Tommy," the lordling groaned as Tommy's hand found his heavy cock. Already, his smooth fingers gripped Tommy's more modest member with a familiarity borne of a summer of snatched rendezvous in this simple, private chamber. "Want you," he sighed, his promise slipping over Tommy like satin. "Forever."

That first release, as always, came blessedly fast. A race, a relief, a ritual. And if Tommy let his mind go there, it was an unhappy reminder of his true purpose — to let the raven pay for Tommy's clever hand, and handsomely too. The prettiest youth in the house must pleasure him as he saw fit. That the lordling only ever asked for the plainest of pleasures, and that he pleasured Tommy in return, that he whispered words of affection and held Tommy in his arms as they dozed awhile afterwards, were transactions they kept to themselves.

"Alas, I have but a few more minutes," the lordling said, wiping Tommy tenderly. Dropping the cloth to the dusty floor, he scooped him up against his chest. "Mama and Grandmama are conducting the serious business of purchasing hat ribbons at Madame Bellevue's. I am to join them. Apparently" — and at this, he blessed Tommy with a wicked grin — "I am in dire need of two new cravats."

Tommy fumbled for the one so hastily discarded earlier and pretended to examine it, rubbing the fine fabric between finger and thumb.

"Goodness, yes. This is *so* last season," he drawled in an approximation of the lordling's own cultured vowels, making the other laugh. A most joyful sound, Tommy wanted to capture it and pin it like a moth.

The lordling caught the length of silk as Tommy tossed it aside. Then, easily, because he was so much bigger than Tommy, he rolled him onto his back. Taking Tommy's slim wrist above his head, the lordling turned it over and pressed his lips to the thin skin, tracing the fragile tangle of blue veins with his tongue as if a path leading to his wildest dreams.

"You dare mock me, Master Tommy?" His scolding was ruined by an escaping giggle. "Then I shall punish you by tying you to the bed. With last season's cravat, too; oh, the shame of it."

Pouting, Tommy fluttered his eyelashes. With his fair curls and eyes the docile blue of a china doll, he was a picture of innocence. "That is no punishment at all, my lord."

"Don't be too hasty, Tommy." The lordling wound a loop of cloth around Tommy's wrist, playfully pulling it tight. "I haven't yet outlined my plans for when I have you all tied up and at my mercy."

Anything. You can do anything.

He kissed Tommy's mouth. "I shall tease you, relentlessly," he murmured, his tongue stealing Tommy's breath. "Starting here."

With his wrist now secured to the bedstead, Tommy tugged a little, sighing with pleasure as lips ghosted along his jaw. Groaning, the lordling buried his face into Tommy's neck.

"Why do you always taste so divine, Tommy?"

Tommy rolled his hips, his prick hard for his lover once more. "Perhaps because I was made especially for you."

The lordling leaned up onto an elbow. Solemnly, he studied Tommy. "I do believe you were." A flush crept up his neck. They could stare at each other all day and never grow tired of the view.

"You were saying," Tommy prompted, his need growing.

"Something about doting on me until I spend again?"

His raven grinned, showing all his beautiful teeth. "Yes! And I shall make it my life's work."

Warm fingertips glided up Tommy's thigh as the lordling came back to himself. "We shall grow old together, you and I. And I shall pass the years teasing you endlessly. Each morning, I shall touch you like this, everywhere but here." The tip of his thumb tapped the head of Tommy's swollen prick. "Until I have you begging for me." Again, his black eyes lifted to gaze adoringly into Tommy's. "As, hourly, you have me begging for you."

Lain over Tommy like a thick blanket, the lordling's body was supple and smooth. If God chose to take Tommy in that moment, he would thank Him kindly and consider it a life well lived. As they deepened the kiss, the lordling's hips ground into Tommy's. One day soon, Tommy decided, he'd suggest more; his empty hole craved it, a topic they had yet to broach. Sometimes, Tommy wondered if his lover even knew that was a thing men like them could do. He would explain it, then take the youth's innocence as tenderly as if it were his own first time.

Soft lips melded as they lost themselves to love. The lordling rubbed himself against Tommy, his teases forgotten. His eyes shuttered closed, his bottom lip trapped between his teeth, the alabaster skin of his cheeks glistened with heat. He was close; they both were. Slipperiness built between their bodies, and with his one untethered hand, Tommy clasped the lordling's tight buttock.

"I lov —" the raven began.

And never finished.

Cut off by a holler from below. Rattling Tommy's soul like a musket blast.

"Raid," Sidney screeched. "Everyone out! Raid!"

*

LOVE WAS MAGICAL. Until the moment it wasn't. Tommy knew that now. It was a lesson he learned the hard way, alone, with his wrist trapped against an unforgiving headboard and his nakedness cooling in the draught of a doorway flung wide. A lesson paraded along a dim corridor, bundled into a runner's carriage, ridden through mocking streets. Pilloried at dawn, spat on, and leered at by a hundred jeering faces.

Love. An illusion. A flimsy, sickening story made up in one's mind. There one day and gone the next. Blown away by the blast of a musket or a puff of wind. As delicate, as ephemeral as spots on a playing card. An illusory pyre on which other people could happily burn their souls. Tommy would never find himself troubled by that crushing emotion again.

Heartbreak though? That was an entirely different story.

Chapter One

Park Lane, Winter, 1823

"IT'S HIGH TIME you married."

Benedict Fitzsimmons, the fourteenth Duke of Ashington, regarded his ebullient youngest brother — by five years — over the edge of *The Times*. "Should this betrothal occur before I reach the end of this astute prediction for Saturday's race at Epsom? Am I permitted to digest my poached kippers first?"

"Oh, all right. I suppose you may." Francis grinned. "But eat up and eat well. I have a dreadful suspicion marriage to a lady of breeding will require courage and fortitude."

"So do I," Benedict agreed drily, adding his lack of both those attributes to his ever-expanding list of reasons never to marry. One of which he kept private, being more pertinent than the rest. He turned a page. "If you don't mind, I'll stick to my four-legged thoroughbreds. At the very least, they will never expect me to endure a week in the country with their parents."

"It's not me that wants you wed," said Francis. "It's Isabella. She has this crazy notion that if you marry, her father will look more favourably on allowing her to be betrothed to me."

Benedict frowned. "I don't follow."

Lady Isabella Knightley and her swooping, dizzy mind were two handfuls of trouble by anyone's standards. Frankly, if Benedict were her father, he'd have offloaded her onto the nearest suitable bachelor — such as Francis, the youngest brother of a wealthy duke — as soon as she came of age. Why her father, the Right Honourable Earl Ludham, insisted her older sisters were suitably wed first, holding off until an earl like himself or higher-ranking noble offered his hand, was unfathomable. Mind you, not the cleverest of chaps, Benedict found much unfathomable these days.

"Nor do I." Francis sounded glum. "And I'm tired of all this waiting." Though he was usually even-tempered, his mouth formed a petulant moue. "Perhaps we could elope? Not to beat about the bush, but old Lord Ludham seems to have forgotten that young men in love have certain…urges."

"Eloping won't endear you to him," rebuked Benedict mildly. "Many uncertainties prevail in this life — as this newspaper insists on reminding me — but I can assure you that isn't one of them. And the less I hear about your urges at the breakfast table, the better my digestion."

Francis heaved an enormous sigh, flopping back in his seat. "Don't you ever feel like this, Benedict? As if the…the world is conspiring against you? It's not as if I don't have money. I'm not a gambler, a drunkard, or a rake. And she's the only woman I'll ever love! Whom I've *ever* loved."

The last part came out as a wail of despair, and Benedict threw his brother a commiserative look. *Love.* Never mind the emotion behind it; even the pitiful word had no place at the duke's breakfast table. Not love of the romantic sort with its hooks in his brother, anyhow. Love *for* his brother, yes, Benedict had oodles of that. For Isabella too. Almost rivalling the love lavished on his eighteen thoroughbreds.

"It's quite clear he's keeping you in reserve," Benedict declared as if he knew the first thing about fatherhood, daughters, or, indeed, love. "Isabella might be your childhood sweetheart, but she's a diamond of the first water, and Lord Ludham is determined to find the best possible match. Trust me, if Isabella showed the slightest inclination to be falling for undesirable competition, I'd wager he'd accept your offer at the drop of a hat. As things stand, he doesn't need to."

"She doesn't want an undesirable or even a well-mannered, blameless earl! She wants *me!*"

A familiar hopeless tone re-entered his voice. From the library next door, the longcase clock chimed a solemn half hour. Pushing aside his breakfast, Benedict rose to his feet.

"The stables call," he announced. "Care to join me?"

His brother shook his head. "Can't, I'm afraid. I'm meeting some chums later. We're boxing at Jack's, then heading out to that new club on the corner of St James. Tuffy Bannister says its already quite the place to be seen. Even Lyndon's been spotted there, once or twice, losing at piquet. Squire's is the name. Have you heard speak of it?"

Squire's. Benedict frowned. That name had cropped up

somewhere else recently. Ah, yes. Plastered in bold lettering above a new betting stand at Newmarket.

"Same chap also owns a brothel or two," added Francis, "according to Tuffy."

Another topic Benedict preferred to avoid at the breakfast table. "Sounds as if this Squire has his snoot in a few businesses. No wonder his club's thriving if Lyndon's a member." He grimaced. "His coffers are being filled with Ashington money."

"I'm surprised Lyndon has any left to squander."

On that, Benedict agreed. Lord Lyndon Fitzsimmons was a thorn in anyone's side, but the side he needled the most, by far, belonged to his twin brother (by three minutes), Benedict. The duke didn't often wish his pugnacious father back from the grave, but after having all but disinherited Benedict's younger twin, their father had fallen in a dead heap a day later instead of facing Lyndon's wrath. Which was damned inconsiderate. Reluctantly inheriting the august title nine months ago, Benedict had also inherited the role of human punchbag; overnight, Lyndon had transferred his ire from his father to his brother.

"Funds miraculously appear from somewhere," observed Francis. "We must pray he's not up to something smoky. The fifteen hundred pounds you generously entrust him with per annum doesn't extend that far."

"No." Benedict frowned again. He'd been doing that a lot since taking up his title, ensuring his reputation as serious, aloof, and reserved remained as intact as ever. A useful, if somewhat lonely, shield for hiding his intellectual inadequacies, Francis and his delightful amour were amongst the very few able to penetrate it.

"You should join us," Francis suggested, perhaps witnessing the frown more frequently than he'd like. In a manner which would horrify the very proper Lord Ludham, Francis crammed a triangle of toast into his mouth, then carried on, spraying crumbs across the table. "At Squire's. Give yourself an afternoon off from all of this."

He indicated the ever-increasing pile of correspondence that inheriting a large dukedom entailed. It cast a long shadow over the breakfast table. Knowing one would someday become the duke was a different beast from taking up the title when one least expected it. Before the old duke's sudden demise, Ashington menfolk had prided themselves on longevity; Benedict had hoped to tread a path of wilful obscurity for at least another decade.

"All of this," he remarked, "won't miraculously have disappeared on my return." Some mornings, Benedict swore it would swallow him whole; a hundred years from now they'd find his body entombed within a pyramid of damned confusing foolscap. "And anyhow, I don't gamble."

"So what? Nor do half the folk in there. Even Rossingley is a member; he doesn't gamble either. Plenty of your White's crowd have joined. Decent scran, excellent port, and uncivilised conversation. Comfortable armchairs, too—and warm fires."

Benedict smiled indulgently, turning to where a footmen held his coat for him. "Comfortable armchairs? You sound older than I."

"I'm simply trying to entice you out of the house once in a while. How will you ever marry if you don't?"

"I'm leaving now! Look! Heading straight through the front door!"

Francis threw a hand up dismissively. "Only to visit the bloody stables!"

*

BENEDICT WAS RATHER fond of the bloody stables. In fact, as he pulled up in his black-liveried phaeton, he'd go so far as to boast (to no one except himself, being far from a boastful sort) that they were the finest in all of London. Eighteen thoroughbreds raced under his ducal colours, the most successful of whom poked his long snowy muzzle over the door of his capacious stall to see what all the fuss was about. Though retired now, after an undefeated career including six St Leger wins, Nimbus's successes continued unabated; last year alone, he'd made Benedict eighteen thousand pounds from stud fees.

Benedict petted him awhile, largely ignored as the daily routines of the stables clattered on around him. Now and then, he pitched in and helped; more than once, he'd been caught in rolled-up sleeves, shovelling shit. No one ever asked him difficult questions while he was shovelling shit. Some wealthy stud owners turned their visits into a spectacle, parading themselves around, demanding attention. Benedict visited so often that if he behaved in such a fashion there would be no time left for his grooms to attend to anything else. Dressed in the Ashington silks, he'd take his dear Nimbus out for a canter later. Remind him of the good old days.

With a final kiss, a whispered reassurance that he was still Benedict's favourite sugar plum fairy, and an instruction to the stable boy to saddle Nimbus up, Benedict moved on to the next stall. Ten wooden boxes lined this side of the sandy courtyard with another ten facing, some doors hanging open, others closed. Casting his gaze around the peaceable, orderly scene, Benedict breathed in the sour tang of manure mixed with perspiration, festering away under the dusty, sweet scent of hay. Rich, dense smells, combined with the earthy musk of a recent rainfall, wrapped around him like freedom itself.

A sturdy, solitary oak rose from the middle of the yard, sheltering a water pump around which one of Benedict's newer acquisitions, Ganymede, was being slowly walked, his head hanging low. He'd purchased the thoroughbred at Tattersall's six months earlier from a baronet unable to meet his debts. He'd come a respectable second at Newmarket last month, ahead of a fine field, so the groom's troubled countenance perturbed him.

"He's sluggish today, Your Grace." Alfred ran his expert hand down the horse's sleek mahogany withers. "Like he's eaten something that's disagreed with him."

Benedict pressed two fingertips under the animal's jaw, feeling the strong pulse. "Is he excessively warm?"

The groom shook his head. "Nah. He's had a couple of runny shits, but it's back to normal now." He jerked his chin. "Her ladyship over there up the corner was similar last week. After she lost at Heath."

Benedict turned to see an unfamiliar stable boy brushing down Cleopatra, his demanding chestnut mare. Surprisingly, for such a temperamental beast, she indulged him.

"New lad," explained the groom. "Knows what he's doin'." With a glance up at the leaden sky, he added, "Thought she was just sulking. But mebbe it's the changeable weather."

"Perhaps." Benedict fondled the soft crest between Ganymede's flattened ears. Possibly, the skin felt a little hotter than usual. "Keep me abreast of matters."

The horse softly pawed the ground. From a liquid brown eye, Benedict's own image reflected back at him. Tall, dark, forbidding. Diffident. But nothing seemed amiss.

"Check over his teeth and hooves," he said, "and encourage him to drink plenty. He's in the four thirty at Epsom a week Wednesday. Tipped to place."

With yet another niggling anxiety to add to his roster, Benedict walked on alone. Francis accompanied him occasionally. Though a decent horseman and kind master, when his brother swung his foot into the stirrups, it was merely for the purpose of suitable transport from *A* to *B*. Whereas Benedict would ride all day long in circles just for the hell of it. His thoroughbreds were his best friends, his equals, a means of escape. He rode swiftly, respecting every inch of the muscle, raw power, and sweat between his thighs. With the heart and dedication of a carefree lover.

And God knew those were in very short supply.

Chapter Two

SOME HOURS LATER, ensconced in the second study, the four-teenth duke was absorbed in the solitary sport of thumb twirling. Documents relating to estate matters awaited his attention, but he didn't have the inclination to unseal them.

His father had been a thumb twirler; he'd frequently prac-tised while waiting for Benedict's mother to grace them with her presence at dinner. Since she was habitually tardy, his father be-came one of those rare folks who could twirl them in contrarota-tion; whenever Benedict attempted it, his thumbs inexplicably re-verted to their former direction.

Outside his window, a carriage splashed noisily through the puddles, drawing his attention away from his wretched ennui. Though mastering his newly inherited title was a struggle, Bene-dict wasn't necessarily *sad* — he had nothing to feel sad about. He was a healthy and wealthy young duke, for goodness' sake! Put simply, he was empty, his enthusiasm for anything, except for his thoroughbreds, spread as thinly as butter. It was as though he waited, twirling his blessed thumbs, on something that might never happen.

The carriage momentarily paused, its occupants shrieking with laughter as water sploshed across the windows. He pictured the group of young, happy souls stuffed inside, taking part in a world full of people Benedict had never met, a world crammed with experiences he'd never experienced and potential lovers he'd never discover. Not if he spent every bloody evening thumb twirling.

Where was it his brother had muttered that he was off to? Squire's. That new club on St James. Could he? Should he? Reticence and the fourteenth duke lived side by side. Reflexively, he dismissed the idea. He should send for his paperknife. And get on with unsealing his papers. On the cusp of Benedict ringing for a footman, another shriek invaded the calm of his study. Francis would be there, Tuffy would be there, and no doubt a few other chaps too. He could go for an hour, he supposed. An hour wouldn't hurt.

And how bad could it be?

*

ON FIRST IMPRESSIONS, the place looked every bit as if it had occupied the four-storey building on the corner of St James and Charles Street for as long as White's had been plying the same trade at the other end of St James. The carriages lined up outside were equally as smart, as were the raucous young gentlemen of the *ton* exiting them, none of whom Benedict recognised. Feeling old and staid and wondering if it wasn't too late to turn back home, he waited behind three jolly chums divesting themselves of coats and hats and signing themselves in.

And then it was his turn.

Benedict considered himself tall, but the craggy-faced man behind the desk was taller still. He dwarfed the desk, his brawny shoulders seemingly reaching from one edge of it to the other. If he banged his fist down in anger, it might splinter. Benedict had no intention of finding out.

"Good evening, sir." The man's blunt gaze roamed Benedict's features as if committing them to memory. "May I enquire if you are member?"

Unused to being scrutinised, especially when the scrutiny ended with a curiously knowing smile, Benedict found it rather disconcerting.

"No," he admitted. "My…um…brother invited me."

"His name, sir?"

"Lord Francis Fitzsimmons."

Dampening his meaty thumb, the man flicked through a thick ledger, his expression blank. A large, rectangular gilt mirror adorned the wall behind him and, unaccountably nervous, Benedict examined himself in it. God, he looked severe. A study in black and white, as if newly risen from the dead. And so stiff; his charcoal coat and matching waistcoat could stand up by themselves. What on earth possessed him to choose such a dull waistcoat? There was once a time when he made a beeline for the most outlandish.

Hating all he saw reflected back, he dropped his gaze.

"Found him," said the man. "He's in tonight."

"Good." Benedict breathed a sigh of relief.

"And your name, sir?"

"I'm…uh…it's *duke*, I'm afraid." He always felt peculiar telling someone who he was; people tended to already know. On the necessary rare occasion, it usually elicited a change in behaviour; fawning was the best word to describe it. "I'm…um…the Duke of Ashington."

For all the effect it had on the man behind the desk, he could have declared himself to be his youngest brother's valet delivering a mislaid snuff box.

"This way, Your Grace," the giant declared.

*

PERCHED AWKWARDLY ON the edge of Francis's rambunctious gaggle of friends, Benedict sipped at his very good quality sherry. He tried not to behave like a spectre at the feast, except he didn't quite think he was pulling it off. Three of his brother's pals turned out to be the high-spirited chaps he'd followed in. Oh, they made him feel welcome, and two of them he even vaguely knew something about, through Tattersall's and the racetracks. Except, once he exhausted their enthusiasm for horseflesh (his own was inexhaustible), and their eyes began to glaze over, he realised the only reason they'd stuck with the polite conversation was due to his superior rank.

Taking pity on them, Benedict took a turn around the room, pretending to examine the sombre oil paintings of bygone bloody battles, bucolic generals, and long-forgotten racehorses. He wasn't much of a historian or scholar, but some of the racehorse oils were actually quite striking. The salon, one of three available for guests, was also impressive. At some point in time—perhaps a roof had fallen in, or a fire had broken out—the end farthest from the window had been rebuilt and now had a double height ceiling. Above a line of tall bookcases ran a galleried landing, hemmed by a thick wooden rail preventing whoever was up there from tumbling to a grisly death on the parquet below.

Benedict toured the salon a second time, dawdling at the fireplace, hoping his presence wasn't putting too much of a damper on his brother's evening. Most probably, they all thought him quite odd, a stuffy, friendless bore and with the sartorial style of a tea chest.

So it was with vast relief, just as he contemplated making feeble excuses to Francis to slink away, that two newcomers entered the room. One of whom, thank heavens, was a few years older than him. Though with his arresting white-blond hair, exquisite lilac silk costume, and ravishing features, it would be hard to convince anyone. The man at his heels, equally handsome, though a dark, brooding sort, Benedict didn't recognise.

Nonetheless, Benedict's heart lifted.

"Ashington," said the fairer newcomer at once. "Hullo, old friend! It's been too long." He strode over with a warm smile and clasped Benedict's hand in his much daintier, cool one, and beamed. "My fault entirely. I've been quite the hermit over the last few years." He cast an amused glance back at his companion. "Only recently have I been encouraged to venture from my shell."

"You're not entirely to blame, Rossingley."

"And I must offer my condolences on the loss of your dear father. Taken from us far too soon, bless his soul."

Aware of a flush creeping up his neck as he waved away

Rossingley's kind words, Benedict tugged a finger into the tight gap between his cravat and his skin. As a boy, he'd harboured a childish infatuation with Rossingley. Their mothers had been good friends, and sometimes, the older youth had been home when they paid visits. Years later, the blissfully unaware earl still possessed the power to discombobulate Benedict.

"I'm not exactly...ah...the pink of the *ton* myself."

"No," agreed Rossingley carefully, giving Benedict a shrewd look. "But that's not a crime."

Benedict had a dreadful certainty his high colour had not escaped the man. Which only made him flush more. The earl laid a hand on his companion's arm.

"Allow me to introduce my darling friend, Mr Christopher — Kit — Angel. Kit, I present His Grace, the Duke of Ashington."

"Your Grace." The man offered a small bow. His left ear held a gold loop. Benedict tried not to peer at it.

"Angel has taken over Gartside's place next to mine," explained Rossingley. "We have since become very close neighbours."

Something about Rossingley always gave Benedict a frisson of pleasure. He'd often felt a kinship towards him, though they couldn't be more different in spirit than a mule and Benedict's finest stallion. He experienced it again now, wishing he could loosen his cravat even further. There was something about the way he described his friendship with Mr Angel as *close*, as if infusing that basic geographic adjective with a hidden meaning. Or perhaps that was simply wishful thinking on Benedict's part. Privately, he'd always wondered about Rossingley. Yes, the man had once married and begat sons, but even so, he was awfully — Benedict would say gloriously — effete.

"I have two of Gartside's thoroughbreds," Benedict informed them, seeing Rossingley's pale blue eyes light up. "Purchased them back in September for a song."

His nerves eased a little. Rossingley was always happy to talk horseflesh. His excellent seat on a horse, only surpassed in recent years by Benedict's own, had occupied a younger Benedict's thoughts (and his nether regions) for many a long, dull summer in the country.

"If nothing else, that blasted creature knew his racehorses," answered Rossingley dolefully. "Horrid business. Horrid man."

Yet again, he exchanged a look with Mr Angel, whose dark gaze had hardly left the earl's slender figure since they'd walked into the room together.

"Would you care to drink with us awhile, Ashington?" Rossingley asked. "Our usual table is over by the window." Nodding his elegant head in the direction of Francis and his friends, he smiled. "These young bucks will be losing their blunt, hand over fist, to one another at basset any minute now. And I find it gets rather rowdy at this end of the room. How's your dear mother?"

Chapter Three

TOMMY SQUIRE RUBBED at his gritty eyes. After poring over his accounts for hours, the neat rows of figures had begun to zig-zag into one another. Most evenings at around this time, Sidney would suggest he employ a secretary, and Tommy had started to wonder if the man was on to something. All work and no play made Jack a very dull boy. Searching his weary brain, Tommy tried to recall the last time he'd indulged in anything remotely pleasurable. Or *anyone*, for that matter.

That was not to say he hadn't gained a modicum of pleasure from accruing great wealth. Squire's was his and Rossingley's third gaming establishment, but their first in a salubrious part of town and thus the only one to attract the *ton*. In addition to their ever-expanding portfolio of blackleg stands, two brothels, and a boxing club, Tommy's coffers and those of his silent investor were well and truly swollen. A thrill with which he'd yet to find another to compare. Well, almost.

Three rhythmic raps on the door signalled the arrival of Sidney, relieved from front desk duties to deliver his nightly report. Tommy lay down his quill pen, closed the ledger, and locked it in his desk drawer before returning the key to the thin silver chain tucked inside his undershirt. As one of his two oldest, most trusted friends (his investor, the Earl of Rossingley being the other), he paid Sidney handsomely. But even Sidney wasn't party to everything. As Tommy had found to his cost, trust and friendship were nothing but the reckless parents of betrayal.

"More in tonight than last Thursday," announced Sidney by way of greeting. "Twenty-two members and seven guests." He shrugged out of his coat and pulled up a chair, unasked, grinning when it emitted a loud creak of protest. "This fancy furniture ain't made for common arses like mine."

"Believe me, aristocratic arses aren't very much different from yours." Tommy helped them both to a snifter of brandy. "And, like yours, they don't smell of roses."

"God, no." Sidney chuckled. "Remember that old baronet used to come to the White Hart on a Wednesday? Him and the inside of a bath had never been acquainted. I used to lie there blue in the face from holding my breath. It wouldn't have been too bad if he wasn't always so leathered. It took him a bloody age to get it up."

They reminisced about the good old days for a while. Or rather, Sidney did and Tommy, always miserly with words, half listened, contributing very little except bile. Sidney had an enviable knack of only recalling the parts he wanted and helpfully disregarding the rest. Even the bad, such as the repugnant baronet, he could twist into an amusing anecdote.

"Yer mate's in tonight," Sidney informed him, realising he was holding a one-sided conversation. "The earl and his fella. I said you might pop down and say hello. Can't say 'is fella looked too delighted about it."

Tommy huffed. Famously quick-tempered, Rossingley's lover—Kit Angel—had never been quite sure how to pigeonhole Tommy, and Tommy wasn't in a rush to reassure him that ship had long sailed. He enjoyed hot-headed Mr Angel's fearsome stares far too much. Tommy and the earl shared a special relationship, that much was true, but not of the kind Mr Angel fretted about.

"Then I shall definitely pay him a visit."

"We've even got a duke in tonight," Sidney observed with a raised eyebrow, topping up his brandy. "Miserable-looking bugger, for all he's handsome-like. A guest of Lord Fitzsimmons. Yer getting very high in the instep, Tommy. It will be King George himself next."

Tommy permitted himself a rare smile. "Rumour has it he'd drink us dry. And that chair would complain even more than it's doing now. Which duke?"

"Ashington. Heard of 'im, of course, on account of the horses. Never seen 'im in the flesh before. Always had 'im in mind as old, from what the lads at the track say about 'im. Turns out he's a fairly young 'un."

Tommy made it his business to have a familiarity with all members of the *ton* and to keep abreast of their business. Especially monied ones.

"I've not met him, either. By all accounts, he lives for

horseflesh and not much else. He keeps to himself, rarely attends parties and the like. Sometimes visits White's, but never gambles. He inherited his title around nine months ago after the sudden death of his father. He's very plump in the pocket and now spends more time in town than at his Hampshire estate. He's the elder brother of Lord Francis Fitzsimmons, hence the introduction."

Sidney gave an odd laugh. "I'll wager you've got his inside leg measurement too."

"There is another brother," Tommy continued, rattling off his knowledge. It was a shame he didn't have more friends to impress with it. "The duke's twin. Lord Lyndon Fitzsimmons. The black sheep of the family. I daresay you've seen him here once or twice. Or at least heard him."

"The redhaired fella a bit too fond of the drink?"

"That's the one," Tommy acknowledged. "He's had a reputation as a troublemaker for years. The previous duke largely disinherited him due to thievery. They say he tried to pay off some gambling debts by flogging the family silver. It was the final straw, allegedly. If he starts pitching up more often, keep a close eye, and don't offer him a line of credit."

Sidney saluted him extravagantly. "I take it his wealthy brother is disinclined to bail him out?"

"Apparently so." Tommy rose to his feet and smoothed back his dark-blond hair, checking that his annoying cowlick, the only part of him not under his complete control, lay flat. He once knew a youth who liked nothing more than to curl its errant strands around his little finger as Tommy lay naked across his chest. *Spun from gold and moonlight*, he'd whisper. The romantic idiot. His hair would soon turn prematurely grey if Tommy continued working as hard as this.

"Walk the floor awhile," he ordered Sidney, wishing to be alone with his weariness. Even in this fancy establishment, it didn't harm for the punts to see a bit of muscle lurking, especially towards the end of an evening. "I may join you later. I'll observe from the top corridor awhile."

*

ONLY A HANDFUL of the regulars at Squire's had met the owner. As long as the drink flowed and the cards were shuffled and dealt, very few cared. Thomas L'Esquire had made his fortune in America, according to those who had. Others surmised him a private person, suggesting he had something to protect. Those who'd met him more than once declared him secretive, suggesting he had something to hide.

Some of the facts about Tommy were true. Others had been fabricated by himself or Rossingley. Yet the one thing everyone could agree on was that he ran a very tight ship.

Below, in the gaming lounge, the lamps were lit and the fires stoked. Red and yellow ribbons of flame danced in the hearths; crystal chinked against crystal as decanters passed around. Voices—assertive, braying ones—drifted up to the rail of the shadowy landing from where Tommy observed the room of happy patrons; rarely did anyone think to glance up.

Engrossed in a lively game of basset, Lord Francis and his chums were having a rare old time. Tommy smiled thinly. Sometimes, watching them made him feel seventy-eight, not twenty-eight. Between a childhood filled with the tensions of poverty followed by a youth spent clawing his way out of the mire, there hadn't been much room left for idle frivolity. He didn't mind them though. Harmless nobs with capacious pockets and decent manners were always welcome. The longer they stayed and supped and gambled, the more of their unearned good fortune slid in Tommy's direction.

An older circle of gentlemen, as far away from the boisterous card table as possible, were passing a snuff box around. One white-haired chap pointed out the intricate engraving to another before taking a generous pinch. Their deeper tones travelled. Tommy listened a few minutes, filtering the wheat from the chaff, before filing away some interesting facts about that morning's debate in Parliament for when it might come in handy.

He saved the view at his favourite table until last. Reserved for Tommy's business partner, the Earl of Rossingley, the cosy nook afforded him and his Mr Angel privacy, should they require it. Squeezed into a narrow corner, its armchairs were close together out of necessity, and, only lit by candles, dark enough for a hand straying to a thigh to go unobserved. The earl's silvery-white hair was easy to pick out, his low purring tones less so.

As Mr Angel leaned towards him, murmuring something, Rossingley threw his head back with laughter. Glad for his friend's happiness, Tommy enjoyed a small rush of pleasure.

They had a third with them tonight, which was not unusual. Since Rossingley had returned to society, so, like a moth to a flame, had his popularity. But what was out of the ordinary was Rossingley's own seat slightly tilted towards the newcomer and away from his lover's, as if affording him the lion's share of his attention.

The leather wing of an armchair obscured their guest's face, only the neat crown of his raven-haired head visible. He sat quite still, with his long legs stretched easily in front of him; if one could sit in a manner exuding power and wealth, then the man had mastered it. Each of his hands rested on the arms of the chair, and from the smallest finger of his left one, a fat gold signet ring glinted in the flickering candlelight.

His Grace, Benedict Fitzsimmons, the fourteenth Duke of Ashington, Tommy deduced.

Sidney had taken up a casual pose near the window, ostensibly looking out of it into the darkening night. In reality, he was watching the card game in its reflection. There'd be no sleight of hand with this crowd, though rumour had it from the doorman at Boodle's that Lord Lyndon Fitzsimmons, the duke's twin, wasn't averse to a spot of cheating if he thought he could get away with it.

A footman did his rounds, a silver carafe perched on his white-clothed tray. All very civilised, thought Tommy, amused. The lad — Mickey, Tommy's young cousin — poured and bowed, ignoring spittle flying from half-sprung lips as if he'd been born into service. No one would ever have guessed that, six months ago, he'd been plying his wares out of the same rooms above the coffee house as Tommy used to.

Rossingley acknowledged Mickey with far more warmth than an earl should, but then Rossingley was no ordinary earl. After generously topping up his glass, Mickey proffered the carafe to Mr Angel, who declined, and then to the duke, who accepted. For a brief moment, Rossingley's head and the duke's much darker one inclined towards each other. Saluting his companions, the duke raised his glass, causing his face to tilt slightly to the left and up. Enough for Tommy to snatch a glimpse of a straight noble nose, a stern profile, an angular, masculine jaw. A glimpse of a boy with eyes like glass pearls and soot limned lashes. Of last year's cravat. Of laughing ruby lips full and lush.

And while all the other hearts in the warm salon continued to beat, Tommy's cold, hateful, embittered one drew to a jagged sickening halt.

Chapter Four

THE HONOURABLE BEATRICE Hazard, Isabella's bosom friend and confidante, ought to leave the harpsichord to a person more skilled. Though, on this fine morning, her slaughter of Bach traumatised Benedict much less than usual, and for good reason. An hour earlier, he'd received word that Ganymede's temper was markedly improved and that Helios, his stablemate, had romped home in yesterday's opening race at Epsom Park by five lengths. Furthermore, his brother Lyndon's name hadn't been raised in a concerning way for over a month.

But best of all, Benedict had reacquainted himself with Rossingley and enjoyed the company of his charming friend Mr Angel. In addition, he'd found himself a discreet somewhere to while away a few hours in an atmosphere far less stuffy than the bay-windowed salon at White's and far more convivial than his own second study.

"Have you thought any more about marrying, Your Grace?" asked Isabella sweetly from her perch on the sofa, far too close to Francis than was conventional for an unwed young woman. "You aren't getting any younger."

"So you and Francis insist on reminding me." Benedict threw her a stern look. Or attempted to. The young chit had cheeked him since she was old enough to toddle around the walled garden clutching his brother's chubby hand. "I've not yet reached thirty! And the answer is still no."

She bobbed her tongue at him, and he chuckled. Why her father, currently under the impression the ladies were shopping for new silk stockings, refused to let her be betrothed to her childhood sweetheart was beyond Benedict. The man was simply pigheaded.

From the harpsichord, Beatrice regarded the canoodling couple—and really there was no other word for it—with a sigh. "I'll marry you, Your Grace, if I must. Seeing as you have such a well-stocked library." She shook her head. "It would be the most honourable thing."

Isabella chortled with delight, and Benedict smiled fondly at both ladies, his gaze lingering on Beatrice. Gentlemen weren't supposed to enjoy the company of bluestockings, known to be too opinionated, too audacious, too frightening to contemplate. Nonetheless, he found Beatrice especially pleasing.

"My laden bookshelves and I shall bear your starry-eyed proposal in mind."

"Truly perfect, of course, would be the library minus the husband," Beatrice added with a long-suffering sigh. "But beggars shouldn't be choosers."

"You're far from a beggar, my dear," scoffed Benedict.

Unlike Isabella, Beatrice had no intention of marriage. Fortunately, her frail but wealthy father liked his spinster daughter's company well enough that he was perfectly happy if she stayed that way.

"Shh." Beatrice put her finger to her lips. "Don't tell everyone, otherwise I'll have the likes of Mr Bannister coming to call. Gossip regarding my association with you is the only thing keeping them at bay. And goodness knows, I only tolerate you for the books."

Benedict threw her another smile. "Then, if we had to marry, I would be sure to apologise daily for the inconvenience of my existence."

He returned his attention to *The Morning Post* and tried to block out both Beatrice's clumsy destruction of Bach's Fugue in E-flat major and his brother and Isabella's inane doe-eyed giggling.

"You seemed to be rather enjoying yourself at Squire's the other evening with Rossingley and his pal," Francis commented. "Thinking of joining?"

"Yes," Benedict answered swiftly, surprising himself as well as his brother. "I do believe I might. Is it…ah…a difficult process?"

Francis guffawed. "For you? You're a duke, Benedict." Despairingly, he shook his head. "Sometimes, I wonder if you have any idea at all how the world turns outside of your various homes and that damned stable block."

"At the pace of a snail," piped up Beatrice, scowling. "That is, if one is expected to spend all of one's waking hours embroidering cushion covers and perfecting fugues."

"You are a long way off that, my dear." Benedict peered over the top of his paper.

Francis continued. "Joining is quite straightforward. One must simply be of good standing and a nominated member of the *ton*."

"And be in possession of a *member*, obviously," added Beatrice.

"Beatrice!" Isabella flung a hand across her mouth. "How can you say such scandalous things! Or even think them! And in the presence of His Grace too!"

Fleetingly, Benedict expected his father to appear at the door. Nearly three-quarters of a year gone, and the absurd grandeur of the thing still caught him out.

"Settle down, ladies. You've made your point, Beatrice." He shook out his paper. "If it's any consolation to you, I doubt very much you'd enjoy it in there anyhow. Although" — and he gave her a wicked smile — "a veritable cornucopia of books line the shelves."

"All of them unread, too, I'll be bound," interjected Francis. "Their spines just waiting to be cracked open. I'll nominate you for membership tonight, Benedict. Poaching a duke from Boodle's and White's? I daresay Thomas L'Esquire will bite your hand off."

Benedict frowned. It was not a name he recognised, but then, he wasn't terribly observant. "Squire's owner, I presume?"

"Yes," confirmed his brother. "According to Tuffy, he's come from abroad. Made his money there. I've only met him a couple of times, very briefly. A grim sort, he certainly doesn't give much away. Watchful and quiet, you know."

"Squabbling seagulls are quiet compared to you, Francis,"

commented Beatrice.

Francis grinned. "But sadly, your harpsichord playing isn't."

He turned back to Benedict. "Apparently, when Mr L'Esquire is not being silent and enigmatic, he's awfully fond of the gee-gees. So I daresay you'd get on splendidly."

*

BENEDICT TRIPPED UP the steps of Squire's with much more confidence than a few days earlier. His long-suffering valet had even teased him into a more form-fitting waistcoat with a black silk stripe running through the charcoal and a matching pocket square. The austere set to his countenance, his valet could do nothing about, although Benedict had practised smiling in the glass a few times as he'd powdered his teeth. For a moment, he almost glimpsed the blithe, carefree youth he'd once been. Before that dreadful, dreadful afternoon.

He wouldn't dwell on that tonight, not now he was trialling this new, emboldened version of himself. At some point, for all his fobbing off of his brother and Isabella, Benedict would have to consider marriage. Perhaps bluestocking Beatrice and her witty tongue might suit him well. She was comely enough, he supposed. If only he could somehow stir his errant body into…performing with a woman.

"Good evening, Your Grace."

The same colossus as before rose from the front desk. He bowed, somehow managing to make it both subservient and intimidating. Benedict couldn't help thinking he must be an excellent deterrent of poor behaviour. The colossus proffered an elegant swan feather quill pen.

"If one could simply sign one's name here in the ledger, Your Grace, then I shall add you to the member's list. The Earl of Rossingley has already proposed you. I shall take the liberty of addressing all correspondence from here on to your man of business so as not to concern you further."

Another little bow accompanied the last, no less off-putting than the first. "I believe Squire's owner, Mr Thomas L'Esquire, is upstairs this evening, Your Grace. It would give him great pleasure to offer you a tour. Would it trouble you too much to ask if you would spare him a moment of your time later?"

"Not at all," said Benedict expansively. "I should be delighted." He scribbled his name in a rather fetching blood-red ink before allowing the man to lead the way. Really, the whole thing had been as terribly straightforward as Francis promised.

Rossingley was absent this evening, but Benedict's favourite brother and his chums, already settled and in full flow, greeted him with much more enthusiasm than he generally warranted. Waving them away, Benedict perused the bookshelves awhile. To give him something to occupy his hands other than brandy, he selected a mercifully slim tome with a decent-sized font about the life and achievements of somebody called Major General James Wolfe. Soon, he was ensconced in Rossingley's preferred corner with the book, brandy, and a warm glow of contentment.

A shadow crossed his field of vision. Expecting a footman, hell bent on pandering to his every whim, Benedict schooled his features into polite neutrality, only for them to fall flat when his twin, Lyndon, slid into the chair opposite. His ruddy cheeks proved he'd also been at the brandy, but without a bloodthirsty description of the besting of the Frenchies at Quebec to distract him. A less agreeable man than Benedict would question the exclusivity of the place, yet even now, after all his twin's degeneracy, a masochistic part of Benedict remained pleased to see him. Was it idiocy to still hope his once biddable brother had developed a semblance of decent behaviour and returned to the fold?

"Your Grace," Lyndon acknowledged.

Never had those two words been uttered in such a sardonic tone.

"Lyndon. I am still your brother. This damned title has not altered me."

A sly smile crept across Lyndon's ruddy face. "No, I suspect not." Cocking his head, he peered bleary-eyed at Benedict. "Our innate selves, our inner desires and our passions, have an annoying tendency to persist, do they not? Regardless of external pressures placed upon them." He spread his hands wide. "Such as a dukedom, for instance. They are the very devil to quash. Wouldn't you agree?"

"Um…I daresay, yes?" Benedict floundered. Lyndon had always been a much cleverer bugger than himself—even half-foxed, such as now. "I'm still closely invested in my thoroughbreds, if that's what you mean."

His brother's peculiar smile grew wider. "I imagine you are. Have any…young colts caught your eye recently?"

"No," Benedict admitted, a little uncomfortable. Lyndon didn't usually demonstrate this degree of interest in any of his pursuits. "Not currently. Papa never warned me quite how much ducal affairs eat into one's leisure time. Though I think I'm finally getting to grips with it all. I hope to acquire one or two in the spring."

"Still not the marrying type, then."

Marriage and investing in young colts weren't mutually exclusive projects, as far as Benedict knew. Puzzled, he shook his head. "All in good time. You?"

"The aspirational fathers of the *ton* don't find me an enticing prospect for their virginal daughters. Can't imagine why," he added drily. "Can you?"

Benedict sensed an imminent outpouring of bitterness. In the main, it tended to focus on their deceased father but invariably swung in his direction, too, leaving him conflicted between his need to protect the wealth and reputation of the Ashington name and his dislike at seeing this man, whom he once loved dearly, ruin himself. Of course, Lyndon never considered pointing the needle of his hostile compass at himself.

"You could always try harder to endear yourself to them." Benedict gestured to his brother's freshly topped up glass. "Imbibing a little less of this and spending less time and money at the card tables might be a start."

"How very dull," observed Lyndon.

"But excellent for your purse," countered Benedict. Nine months into the dukedom and already he sounded exactly like their pompous father. "And for your standing with the aforementioned wealthy papas."

Should he offer to channel more funds in Lyndon's direction? Or would it simply increase the speed at which his brother's ruination would be complete? As much as Benedict hated being cast in the role of stolid, conscientious older sibling (although, to be fair, it came to him naturally), his current course of action was still best. And sensible, smart Francis agreed. Benedict braced for an unpleasant ending to their rare interaction.

"My purse," Lyndon groused, "is not empty through excess liqueur. It's empty because someone saw fit to follow our dear father's—God rest his virtuous, pious soul—orders to the letter."

How did this damned brother's snide comments always succeed in wheedling under Benedict's skin? "And someone saw fit to steal the family silver, Lyndon. The remainder of us Ashington's are quite fond of it and would wish it to remain in the family. Have you ever considered…"

A footman approached, and Benedict snapped his mouth shut. Bickering with members of one's close family in a public space was never a good look, even for a duke.

"I am terribly sorry to interrupt, Your Grace," the footman said. "But if I may be so bold, Mr L'Esquire is awaiting the honour of your acquaintance in the upstairs library."

Benedict blew out a breath. Thank heavens for Mr L'Esquire. "Certainly. The pleasure would be all mine."

Bidding Lyndon a curt adieu, he fair leaped out of his seat. Not only would he thank Mr L'Esquire for allowing him to join this excellent establishment, but he'd also thank him for an excuse to escape his damned difficult brother.

Chapter Five

OVER THE YEARS, a tiny thread of a voice—largely ignored—often hinted to Tommy that, one day, his lordling might cross his path. Back when he earned a crust treading the boards at Drury Lane, face paint so thick and voice so disguised even his own mother would have had a hard time recognising him, he used to peer up into the box seats. Heart in his throat, he'd hope, dread, hope, dread—emotions tumbling from one to the other—that he might spy that dark, handsome head amongst the crowds.

He never did. And as time shifted forward, as Tommy himself shifted forward, he eventually ceased peeking around every corner or searching every smart carriage. His clever mind sought out other pastimes instead, all-encompassing endeavours of the fortune-making variety. These days, if he strolled through Vauxhall and his lordling by happenstance rode alongside, he might not notice at all. In fact, if one didn't know Tommy well, as his businesses expanded and his heart grew even stonier, one might assume he'd forgotten the striking youth altogether.

Tonight, a few feet below Tommy's head, that boy he'd once loved with every fibre of his being sipped Tommy's brandy in the company of his brothers. Exchanging pleasantries with one and disagreeing with the other. And he was a duke, no less. A blessed, bleeding bugger of a damned duke.

Tommy paced his small library, unsure whether to gulp down the goblet of pricey liqueur making his belly curdle or hurl it at the wall. His knees trembled, and his impeccably starched collar felt damp against his neck. He felt muddled, torn between his hatred for the duke and a horrid, sick yearning to see him up close. Fear whispered in his ear too; he was lightheaded with it. Though fearful of what? Ashington was no more likely to expose Thomas L'Esquire for what he used to be than Tommy would expose him. They would both be ruined.

"Mickey is on his way up with His Grace," announced Sidney from the doorway.

Tommy acknowledged this with a brisk nod, not trusting his voice.

"Do you want me to stay and look pretty? You aren't quite yourself tonight, Tommy. I can show 'im around if you want to put your feet up."

"No, Sidney. Thank you." He wiped away the moisture gathered on his upper lip. On shaky legs, he returned to the seat behind his desk and picked up his quill pen. "Go back downstairs. I'm…I'm quite all right. Tired, is all."

It was unusual to request a duke pay a call on a commoner. Invariably, Muhammed visited the mountain, not the other way around. And even when a duke *did* deign to climb two sets of stairs at the beckoning of an arrogant upstart, most arrogant upstarts would rise from their seat and proffer a humble bow.

The lack of any such ceremony might have accounted for the duke's grave expression as a visibly awed Mickey announced his arrival. Or perhaps he was always pale and unsmiling. Nonetheless, Tommy could not have clambered to his feet even if he wanted to.

"His Grace, the Duke of Ashington, sir," Mickey stammered and promptly scarpered.

Once upon a time, when he still believed in the magic of Covent Garden showmen, Tommy saw this man's silhouette in the shape of the clouds. Felt the trace of his fingertips in raindrops hurrying down a sheet of glass, heard his deep, needy sighs over the bustle of a crowded street.

As their eyes met, Tommy's grey and cold, the other's a warm, deep brown, his prepared speech suffocated in his throat.

"We're already acquainted," he said shortly. "Good evening, Your Grace."

Watching each stage of the duke's horrified comprehension would have been almost amusing if Tommy hadn't been equally overcome. Because, dammit, everything Tommy once found incomparable about his young raven's beauty still haunted him. The flawless skin stretched tight over high, noble cheekbones as pale as the winter storm raging outside his window. That blasted hair, of course, thick, sooty waves of it still curled over his forehead. Tommy remembered how they dampened and the tenderness with which he'd brushed them back. His red lips, full and sensual, now covered by a large hand as the dumbstruck duke staggered away from him. The fine black hairs dusting the back of that hand, how they'd tickled against Tommy's chin whenever he'd pressed soft kisses against each of the knuckles.

He remembered how that hand had grasped his wrist and tethered him to a bedpost.

"Tommy," managed the duke at last. "Oh, lord. Tommy."

"It's Thomas these days. Mr Thomas L'Esquire. You don't have the right to address me by my forename. Even though you're a duke. Wouldn't you agree, Your Grace?"

"Yes…I…Tomm— I thought you were…I thought you were…"

"Dead?" Tommy supplied. "Imprisoned? Assembling roads under a hot Australian sun, chained to another *whore?*"

Like a hurled egg, the hateful word splattered between them. The duke's skin turned even more ashen.

"Sorry to disappoint, Your Grace. But as you can see, I'm alive and well. And thriving."

"I'm not d-disappointed," stuttered the duke. "I'm… Good Lord. I'm thrilled obviously, that you are…here and…and well. And —" He swayed a little. "Do you mind awfully if I sit?"

As insubstantial as a house of cards, the duke fell into the spindly chair facing Tommy, his broad frame filling it. It gave an ominous creak. Churlishly, Tommy cared not if it sent the duke crashing to the floor. With a striped pocket square, the man rubbed at his eyes as if clearing his vision, maybe hoping the view might be altered if he did. Then he clutched the thing tightly in his fist.

"They said, people said, that this club is owned by a man who has come from abroad."

A rumour Tommy had set himself. "To my patrons, the stews *are* a foreign country."

"And yet it is owned by you." The duke shook his head in wonder. "You escaped."

A thin smile tugged at Tommy's lips. "Your powers of deduction do you credit, Your Grace. But it was less of an escape, more divine intervention."

"How...I mean...yes, that is what I mean. I mean how? I read in a newssheet that you had been arrested...names were listed. I...my cravat..."

Even as the duke stuttered and stumbled, that sonorous voice still gripped Tommy's craw. Deep, rich, and melodic, it was the sort of voice one craved to hear late in the evening, murmuring one's name from the adjacent pillow. Tommy gulped at his brandy, acid sloshing in his gullet.

"A friend saved me, someone to whom I am forever indebted." He swirled the drink around in his glass. "Someone not afraid to step up to defend one of his own. Your cravat, sadly, I cannot return to you."

Tommy was being deliberately cruel and yet couldn't restrain himself. "Have you ever seen a man pilloried, Your Grace? No? You really should if, perchance, one afternoon, you ever find yourself in Charing Cross and at a loose end. It's quite the spectacle. Quite the family day out. Even more thrilling if half the men are mere boys. It takes over seventy constables to escort seven defenceless sodomites to the pillory; did you know that? On account of the crowds, you see. They can turn horribly violent, often without warning. I can still rattle off all the names of those in chains, of course. James Cooke, James Amos — we knew him as 'Sally'.

Will Thompson, Dickie Duggan—Ma Duggan ran the place. Sidney Bolton…oh, and yes, a young trussed-up Tommy Squire."

"Please stop, Tommy." The duke's broken plea was barely a whisper. "I'm so sorry. I'm so, so sorry. Just, please. Stop."

Tommy gave a humourless laugh. "Stop? How funny, Your Grace. Because that's exactly what I begged to happen too. Except, on that occasion, they didn't listen, did they? Folks lob all sorts of rubbish at you, you know, when you're locked in there. Mud, potatoes, offal. To this day, I can't stomach a turnip. Not too fond of dead cats, either. Nor the scent of stale piss, not only the buckets of it showered at you, but your own, too, because one is trapped there for hours, you understand, and a man has to go eventu—"

"*Stop*," the duke shouted hoarsely. He banged a fist on the desk. "I said stop, dammit. Sir, I beg you."

Nine years or so had passed since Tommy Squire had shed a tear—of sorrow or elation. Except now, they stung hot and sharp at the back of his eyes. His throat closing, he stood abruptly, arms wrapped tight across his chest. Turning his back on his visitor, he stalked towards the window.

Silence spread between them, like spilt milk. The air in the small library settled around them, still and thick. Tommy fancied he could reach out and grasp it.

"What I…how I behaved that afternoon," began the duke. "It is unforgiveable. You must believe me when I tell you I have lived with my actions every hour of every single day since."

"Not as well as I," bit out Tommy.

"That is true. But also believe me when I tell you how gladly my…my soul sings now, finding you so recovered and prospering. What *I* did to you, what *they* did to you, a man would not wish on his greatest enemy, and yet…" He gulped audibly. "I allowed it to happen to my…to a person I once held more dearly in my heart than anyone else."

Tommy clenched his fists. If the duke began making excuses, he'd hit him. Nobility be damned.

But he didn't, the duke stayed quiet until Tommy felt sufficiently himself again to turn from the window. *A person I once held more dearly in my heart than anyone else.* How dare he stand in Tommy's office and say that. With effort, he schooled his features into a mask of cool indifference.

"Are you still of a mind to have a tour of the premises, Your Grace? Because I might cry off, if it's all the same to you. I could ring for Sidney to escort you, though it might be a little slower, as he has a limp, you see. A memento from his time in Newgate. Or, you can return to the gaming room and join Lord Francis for a few hands. Really, as the club's most esteemed and high-ranking member, the choice is yours. I am at your service, Your Grace."

For a snatched moment, their eyes met, one set hurt and bewildered, the other hardened into chips of granite. Tommy would die rather than look away first. But, God, how he shed blood on the inside.

"I would be grateful if you called for my carriage," the duke managed at last. "That would be for the best, I think."

Chapter Six

"*YOUNG MEN'S LOVE lies not truly in their hearts but in their eyes,*" the Honourable Beatrice Hazard declared as she took Benedict's arm. "At least, that's Will Shakespeare's learned opinion, anyhow. And his understanding of human desires has no equal."

Strolling through the gardens at Vauxhall, they deliberately dawdled a short way behind Francis and Isabella. As Benedict dully appreciated the plain simplicity of a broad avenue of trees, it struck him that he had never seen Tommy outside of a closed room. They'd certainly never strolled together, arm in arm.

A month had elapsed since Benedict and Tommy's worlds had collided. Naturally, Benedict had steered clear of Squire's, much to his brother's befuddlement. He'd not been very much of anywhere, in fact, except for his stables. Needless to say, the month had not been a happy one.

"Then my brother may have broken the mould," Benedict

responded. "Whilst he is undoubtedly enamoured of Isabella's outward beauty, I do believe his love for her is heartfelt and true."

"So do I," agreed Beatrice. "Sickening, isn't it?"

He laughed for perhaps the first time that week. "It pains them to be parted from each other for even a day. How will we ever find an undesirable to threaten her virtue and thereby tempt Lord Ludham to receive Francis's suit if she is forever in his company?"

"Perhaps your own presence, never far from your brother's shoulder, also shies them away, Your Grace. You put the fear of God into them."

"I do?" He glanced down at her in astonishment, his thick eyebrows huddled together.

"Yes! You are very forbidding, especially when you regard a person like that. Your eyes *scowl*."

"They do?" He twitched the muscles in his cheeks and wiggled his eyebrows up and down as if trying to rearrange them. Hopeless.

She laughed prettily. "You sound as if you are conjugating verbs, Your Grace. And…and appear to have developed an unfortunate tic. Yes, they do. You do."

"Huh." With difficulty, he refrained from frowning and encouraged his lips to curve up a little. Now, he probably looked like a simpleton. "Scowling is not my intent."

"Never mind." Beatrice gave his bicep a friendly little squeeze. "I would be thrilled if you persevered with the habit whilst strolling in my company. Being seen on the arm of one of the *ton*'s most eligible, dour dukes is a first-rate strategy for maintaining my unmarried status." She paused. "It also is excellent at maintaining yours."

"Hah!" Two laughs in one morning? Unheard of. "Then we must persist."

Smiling fondly, Benedict walked with her for a while in companionable silence before halting to admire a cheerful splash of early crocuses. Did Tommy ever pause to appreciate early crocuses? Did Tommy even like crocuses? Benedict had no idea, but the man crashed his thoughts at every damned turn. Ahead of them, Isabella's merry chatter cut through the crisp air.

"Francis is fretting about you," Beatrice ventured. "He says you work too hard and are not yourself."

"No," agreed Benedict cautiously. In the days following his unhappy skirmish with Tommy, he'd risen early to avoid sharing breakfast with his brother and then skulked in the second study for the remainder of the morning until it was time for his daily tour of the stables. In between those illustrious activities, he had brooded. "I have...I have suffered with melancholia of late."

"Ah." She nodded sadly. "Your usual equanimity is being drained by that old friend. I have, on occasion, been well acquainted with her myself." She gave his arm another tight squeeze. "I cannot imagine the strain a father's sudden death and taking on all his duties has on a person. Though worth very little, it is my opinion that you are coping admirably."

"Your opinion is one that I regard most highly, Beatrice."

Stooping, she plucked a weed from between two blooms. "You are most kind, Your Grace. But if I may be so bold, I am...I am also of the opinion that ensuring the smooth running of your affairs is not your only concern."

As Benedict stiffened, she added, "I have a sympathetic and discreet ear."

"You are most kind yourself, Beatrice."

At risk of losing sight of Francis and Isabella — heaven forbid someone spread rumours they were unchaperoned — they sauntered on in the general direction of their awaiting carriage. The breezy morning air carried the sharp tang of rain. Casting his gaze towards the lumpish grey sky, Benedict picked up the pace. Soon, they would be blessed by another dreary downpour.

"I recently had cause to spend time with a person I believed lost to me forever," he began suddenly. Even that simple sentence pained him; it wasn't something he had anticipated ever confiding in anyone. He pushed on. "A person, I am ashamed to say, I have treated very badly."

"Are you referring to Lord Lyndon? If so, let me assure you the only person who has wronged Lord Lyndon is himself. Since your father's passing, you have shown him nothing but compassion and generosity."

"No." Benedict shook his head. "Not Lyndon. Although I question myself over him daily too. Papa was of the strong opinion that one must be cruel to be kind. He believed keeping Lyndon poor would show him the error of his ways. But lately, I find myself questioning several of my own moralistic judgements and thus extend those questions to my dealings with Lyndon. And...I wonder if I come up short."

Beatrice pondered this as the path weaved around a copse. Few of Benedict's circle — and he included the menfolk — shared her thirst for knowledge, nor indeed, the wisdom she gained from it.

"I believe, Your Grace, that a man who thinks so deeply and questions himself so thoroughly ought, by his very nature, be more adept at guiding his morals along a wholesome route than a man arrogant enough to believe he is right simply because he is a man to whom others must defer."

"At risk of drearily repeating myself, you are very kind."

"Only to those who deserve it," she countered with a chuckle. "To most, I am a harridan spinster with a tongue too tart for her own good. And I shall make use of its acidity by being so audacious as to ask if what concerns you has anything to do with love."

Benedict made a strangled sound. What ailed him had *everything* to do with love. "Both your tongue and your perceptiveness should never be underestimated, Lady Beatrice."

The carriage was in sight; Francis and Isabella paused, ostensibly to admire the bare, clean branches of an elm but mostly to stretch out their fond farewell.

"I was in love, once," Benedict admitted, his heart inexplicably racing. "When I was very young."

Beatrice's fine eyebrows arched with curiosity.

"I imagine you find that hard to believe, do you not? Someone like me, with this *scowling* countenance?"

Examining him for a moment, she shook her fair head. "It's not so hard to imagine. I see how your eyes rest so fondly on your brother and Isabella. You are not without soul."

A soul which, at this exact moment, lay in tatters. His encounter with Tommy had awoken complex emotions dormant for many a year. He sucked in a breath. "Our love was unquenchable. Or so I believed."

A stark memory of Tommy's chest heaving against his own flooded his mind. Of him panting, laughing into Benedict's mouth. "We…we thought we'd invented the damned thing. I was so enamoured. I trusted our roots would be entwined forever."

"But it wasn't meant to be," Beatrice prompted.

He reached out to a low twig and snapped it off. Early crocuses be damned; hope, light, and spring were barely imaginable.

"It could never be," he corrected. "Though neither of us considered it. We were too young and foolish to ever look beyond the end of our noses. The future was another continent, as far as we were concerned."

"I'm surmising she was married," Beatrice responded in her usual blunt fashion. "Or betrothed to another."

And therein lay the problem. Tommy was neither. "If only it had been that simple."

"This is the same person you thought you had lost forever and whom you'd wronged, is it not?"

"Yes. And I have no excuses for my actions. I panicked, you see, and behaved abhorrently. I have never forgiven myself. And now this person hates me with a passion burning as brightly and fiercely as the flames of our lost love. And there is nought I can do about it. And…and yet, for my part, there is no hatred. I would like nothing more than to make amends in any way that person sees fit."

"And you cannot? There is no path back?"

Benedict shivered as the first few spots of rain pattered onto his shoulders. Thunder grumbled like the boom of a distant cannon. Did Tommy enjoy thunderstorms? Or did he flinch at every crack? Ahead, a groom held the carriage door open, ready to transport the duke to wherever he wished to travel next. If only he knew.

"I am of the opinion that person wishes I never darken their door again."

*

THE PEACEFUL DAILY routine of Benedict's stables did not have its usual restorative effect. Despite being firm favourites to win, two of his horses had failed to finish in the top three at Newmarket. One had pulled up a furlong short, the jockey declaring him lame. Watching the creature now as a groom walked him around the water pump, all four limbs seemed in perfect working order.

Benedict leaned against Nimbus's stable door, sneaking him extra carrot treats. Another thing he didn't know about Tommy. Did he ride? Did he wager? He owned a blackleg business—a thriving one if Joe Jonas, his stable master, was to be believed. Squire's stands lined all the racecourses these days. Perhaps Tommy frequently attended himself. Perhaps he and Benedict had already brushed shoulders.

He didn't think so. He would have felt it, a crackle between them like the frozen split second before a fork of lightning struck. He would have jerked around; his eyes would have landed on those harsh cheekbones framed by neatly cropped hair, an ordinary sandy blond until one touched it and discovered it was soft at silk. And that slightly cruel, thin-lipped mouth that had flitted so readily between kissing Benedict and being kissed by him. He'd have been drawn to those flashing eyes, too, unable to wrench his gaze away. The eyes of a feral cat. Were they blue or a devilish grey? Benedict never could tell.

Tommy could never loathe Benedict as much as he loathed

himself. The intervening years only served to highlight the unpalatable truth; he'd left an innocent boy he'd loved to his fate. So many promises had spilled from his mouth back then, in between the kisses. It made him heartsick remembering them and how he'd broken them all to save his own pitiful skin so he could become an imposter of a venerable duke, with eighteen racehorses, umpteen fawning staff, and homes littering every county. And Benedict had the nerve to censure Lyndon's callous behaviour? His brother might be a cad, but he wasn't a damned fraud.

Chapter Seven

NEEDING TO DISTANCE himself from endless internal gloom, Tommy called upon his friend, the earl. It provided the perfect distraction. Rossingley and his *mistress* were, as ever, charming company.

"Only minutes before you appeared, Tommy, I had mentioned to Catherine that I hadn't seen you in a while." The earl reached for a napkin, eyeing his visitor across the small table. "Fancy that. And now you're here, my darling, which makes me much happier."

"Yes." Tommy shifted, uncomfortably aware he was being scrutinised.

"But it is clear you are not."

"Ah...no."

Of course, Mrs Catherine de Villiers never had been, and never would be, Rossingley's *actual* mistress. Not that she lacked appeal. Very few wealthy and handsome widows did. Regardless, she was a useful and willing smokescreen, playing her part in public admirably and simply for the fun of it, as far as Tommy could tell.

She was also remarkably astute. "It's high time I left you gentlemen to your own devices and hunted down Mr Angel," Catherine declared, rising from the chaise. "I'm sure you have much news to catch up."

Tommy and Rossingley rose also. "He's waiting for you in the ballroom, my dear." Embracing her, Rossingley planted a chaste kiss on her cheek. "Limbering up," he added, wickedly. "Although, I found him to be already quite supple before breakfast."

She laughed, rather more heartily than a well-to-do lady ought. Tommy harboured a sneaking suspicion her origins might be as murky as his own. "You are as incorrigible as ever, my lord."

"And you are as divine as ever, my darling."

As the soft swish of her skirts faded away, the two men took to the armchairs by the fire.

"Ballroom, Lordy?" queried Tommy.

The earl beamed. "Yes. The lady has taken it upon herself to advance my beloved Kit's dancing skills. He and I share a bothersome tendency to both seek the lead." At this, his pale eyes gleamed. "You know, turn and turnabout. And one quickly finds oneself becoming distracted."

He poured them both fresh teas. "Under Catherine's tutelage, Kit has become rather adept. More importantly, after his lesson concludes, she takes her leave in a flurry of activity via the front door." There was a delicate pause. "With the glowing air of a woman who has been thoroughly exercised, allowing the *ton* to go back to gossiping about some other poor soul." He sipped daintily. "Everyone is a winner, as they say."

For a minute or so, Tommy supped his drink. *Tea* with cream. Served in a bone china teacup and stirred with a silver spoon in an earl's lavish drawing room as a guest of the earl. He'd come a long way and endured a torrid journey to reach this point, if only to discover his past had kept him company.

"A rather funny thing happened recently, Lordy."

Though Tommy's tone was light and even, Rossingley was damned difficult to fool. His silvery gaze fixed immediately on his companion, no doubt assimilating his haggard appearance and affected breeziness and leaping to all the right conclusions.

"I thought it might. You've been avoiding me."

"Yes. Possibly. I've been avoiding everyone, actually. You see, I...I... The devil of it is...I came across my...my lordling. Unexpectedly, after believing I never would. And I confess, considering how much time has elapsed, I found the encounter far more bruising than anticipated."

Tommy examined his nails, letting this new information sink in. After the duke's strained departure, he'd opened a fresh bottle of port and drunk himself into oblivion. When Sidney discovered him next morning, half-conscious and slumped over his desk, Tommy had cursed, cast up his accounts, then killed a second bottle as swiftly as he'd dispensed with the first.

Sickeningly, in the three weeks since, the sour stench of Ashington's betrayal over a decade earlier had been supplanted by a far rosier fragrance, though no less welcome. The bittersweet scent of fresh heartbreak had reacquainted itself all over again.

Bruising didn't even begin to cover it.

"Is his intention to make life difficult for you?" the earl asked sharply. "For a second time?"

"God, no." Tommy frowned. "I rather think not."

What duke alive wished to destroy their family's reputation in one foul stroke?

"We reached an unspoken impasse in that regard because I could rather throw him under the carriage wheels with me, couldn't I?"

"Mmm." Rossingley steepled his long, elegant fingers. "So, he's a man of substance with much to lose. That's something, at least." He tilted his head to one side. "How did you expect this unforeseen encounter to play out? You must have imagined it might happen one day?"

"I always believed I'd want to kill him."

Tommy's smart accent lapsed under stress, and it failed him now, betraying traces of his humble origins. "I'm not saying I'd have gone through with it, of course. I'm no murderer. But I must own to all sorts of unseemly dark fantasies. I also expected to be rather more...in control."

The earl's brow creased in concentration as his gaze left Tommy to survey the array of delicate candied fruits and jellies spread out before him. "Yet when you found yourself facing him once more?"

"I...I don't exactly know," Tommy admitted. "I still don't. It was such a shock, you see. I assumed he must no longer reside in London or even England. Have travelled abroad, perhaps. Or even...be dead."

He shuddered. Whatever his jumbled mess of feelings were

regarding the duke, none of them included a wish for that. He grimaced. "I wanted to shake him by his aristocratic neck until his teeth rattled. I'll say that much."

"*Shake* him, darling?" Rossingley paused as he selected a glazed gooseberry, giving it a neat lick with the pink tip of his tongue before popping it in his mouth. "Or do something else to him as equally and vigorously satisfying?"

Tommy groaned. Trust bloody Rossingley to spear the heart of the matter within seconds. Ever since the wretched duke with his damned raven hair and his oh-so-serious heart-shaped tease of a mouth had presented himself in Tommy's study, he'd frigged himself more times than he could count until he was shrivelled and sore and utterly despised himself. And blasted Rossingley, the only person he ever dared open his soul to, sensed it.

"Something else, damn you."

If angry, frustrated tears didn't drown him first, then a crimson flush threatened to swallow Tommy whole. He snatched at one of the sugared candies and tossed it into his mouth. A very poor substitute for alcohol. The temptation to continue pickling his bones in port wine was as strong as ever.

"Oh, Tommy." The earl heaved a sigh. "I know you've tried your damnedest to turn it to granite, but you always were a tart with a heart. And I always feared it might be your downfall."

Another candy went the way of the first. "That is singularly unhelpful, my friend. But yes, me and my bleeding soft heart."

Rossingley threw him an affectionate look. His own heart was softer than he let on too. "The walls separating love and hate are so very paper thin, aren't they?"

"Extraordinarily so," Tommy agreed tightly. "Even when

more than a decade splits the two."

Rossingley carefully picked out another fruit, this time a syrupy sliver of apricot, and hummed his appreciation. Tommy was yet to meet a sweet dessert the earl couldn't defeat.

"Your lordling," Rossingley ventured. "Is now a young man in his prime. Is he hale and hearty?"

That the earl didn't speculate upon the man's identity was commendable. And a relief. Whilst he'd a desperate need to unload, Tommy couldn't be sure his mouth would form the name.

"He's both healthy and wealthy. And remains a bachelor."

"Ah." They exchanged a glance requiring no words. "And now that you have this knowledge, Tommy, regarding this individual, may I be so bold as to enquire what you plan to do with it?"

"Certainly," said Tommy with a rueful smile. "I shall cast it to the back of my mind in the hope it withers and dies there."

"A lesser man than I would wish you heaps of luck with that, darling." After a final rummage through the jellies, the earl pushed the plate away. "But I think we can both agree" — he unwrapped the sweet as if it was priceless porcelain—"that in the grand scheme of excellent plans, you've conjured a truly abominable one. If I'm not mistaken, you've attempted the amnesia strategy for the past decade. And failed." Another sweet fancy disappeared down his gullet. "What on earth makes you think it will work now? Unless he's turned into a festering gout-ridden toad?"

If only. Eyes screwed closed proved no shield against unhelpful images of His Grace's handsome, yet utterly miserable, face popping into his head. Tommy groaned again.

"I assume that is a no," said the earl.

"Far from it, unfortunately."

"Hmm." Sitting back, Rossingley patted his whippet-thin belly contentedly. "To recap — you loathe him, you still lust after him, and you have purged more words about him in the last three minutes than you have about another mortal in the last ten years. Darling, I haven't seen you this animated since you rushed through your performance of Petruchio at the Theatre Royal. And that was only because Lady Horsham offered you a gold guinea to pleasure her during the interval."

Tommy reply was short, non-verbal, and vulgar.

"Precisely," agreed the earl, not missing a beat. "The delectable *Lord* Horsham, on the other hand…"

Chapter Eight

SOME MEN, OR so he'd been told, adored parties and balls. Benedict had a suspicion Francis was firmly among their number. He almost cracked a smile as his youngest brother, with a giggling debutante attached to each arm, galloped laps around Lady Butterworth's ballroom. Benedict could still take pleasure in it, despite having caught sight of himself in the glass opposite and mistaken himself for the personification of winter — and not the merry, frosty sort either, with ice crackling underfoot or Regent's Park Lake turned into a skating rink. Oh no. No hot chestnuts peeked out from between his glowing embers or, in fact, glowing embers. Benedict's reflection was a heavy charcoal cloud blanketing ponds of slush, a gust of foul weather with nowhere to go.

"May I suggest Lady Butterworth's twin upper balconies might be more to your liking, my dear Ashington," a cool voice murmured in his ear. "Over the years, I have always found them to be reliably comfortable, capacious, and, best of all, tucked well out of sight."

With a start, Benedict turned to find an amused Rossingley at his shoulder. He blushed furiously. Had his drifting mind left him staring at a young lady's decolletage? Was Rossingley making an improper joke? Goodness, he should force himself to venture out more and explore the company of other men. Just because Squire's was now out of bounds didn't mean Benedict couldn't find a club suited to him. He felt like a dry old stick in White's, already lumped in within the elders. He should give Boodle's another try.

Rossingley patted his arm. "Follow me."

Lady Butterworth's twin upper balconies weren't scandalous at all. Ever since a foxed reveller fell to his death three years earlier, few opened their top galleries for guests — leaving the dancers stiflingly hot. But Lady Butterworth was bucking the trend. Benedict soon found himself with other like-minded gentlemen, sipping at something stronger than tame fruit punch whilst enjoying an excellent view of the more strenuous activities below.

Fighting off the competition, Isabella had regained the adoring arms of his brother. Rossingley's chum, Mr Angel, waltzed most elegantly with Mrs Catherine de Villiers, a terribly exotic and, therefore, intimidating woman to whom Benedict had never dared speak.

"You must battle for the merry widow's attentions, Rossingley," a voice hooted from the adjacent balcony. Benedict recognised it as belonging to Bannister, one of the cheerful young bucks he'd been introduced to at Squire's. "He might not be as plump in the pocket as you," Bannister teased, "but he shows good leg on the dance floor. See? The lady is entranced!"

"My mistress," explained Rossingley in a mild tone, utterly unperturbed, "the handsome Mrs de Villiers, not Bannister, thank heavens. Though he's quite correct. They do look awfully good together, don't they?"

"Ah," responded Benedict, unsure whether one acknowledged a man's mistress or not. During his childhood, overlooking the existence of his father's had suited the entire family admirably.

As the couple trotted, light as air, across the dance floor, a half-smile played on the earl's lips. Though Benedict favoured Rossingley's company above that of the more boisterous members of the *ton*, the man had an uncanny gift for making him feel a little off balance. Shrugging it off, Benedict endeavoured to loosen the tension cramping his jaw, neck, and shoulders and, as they watched the couple float around the room, attempted to mimic the earl's easy, relaxed pose.

Presently, the waltz drew to a close, and the quartet fell silent, though no one had told Francis. He and Isabella were still very much in hold. Benedict sighed. Somebody—preferably Isabella's father—needed to put that boy out of his misery and let him pledge his troth. At the near edge of the dance floor, Mr Angel performed an extravagant bow before planting a flamboyant kiss on Mrs De Villiers gloved hand. Rossingley leaned forward at the exact moment Mr Angel's eyes looked up, searching him out.

Benedict experienced a peculiar sensation. Mrs De Villiers had wandered off, already snapped up by her next eager dance partner. And yet, as if frozen in time, Rossingley and Mr Angel continued to stare intently at each other, the latter's fierce dark gaze locked onto Rossingley's with an intensity that seemed to ignite the very air surrounding them. As for Rossingley, if Benedict didn't know better from his misty-eyed expression, he'd think the earl was swigging laudanum, not port.

"If you'll excuse me, Ashington, I may take a stroll around the gardens," announced Rossingley after an eternity. His lips curled into a small smile. "I've heard that Lady Butterworth's begonias are not to be missed. And I am of the opinion, after all that jigging around, Mr Angel might benefit from the fresher air too."

Though no horticulturalist, even Benedict knew begonias only flowered from mid-June. The January night was pitch black.

"Of c-course," stammered Benedict as parts of an awfully complicated puzzle — a puzzle he'd been trying to solve since his inexplicable boyhood crush on Rossingley — fell into place. "I...I must away too. I promised the Honourable Beatrice Hazard the dance before dinner."

*

RELUCTANT WOULD BE the best descriptor for Benedict's excursions across a dance floor. And though he was a member of that increasingly rare breed — an eligible duke — and a more than passable dancer, Benedict's small talk was notoriously painful. Several ladies were no doubt as grateful as he when Rossingley had dragged him away to safety.

The earl's overt display of affection for another man left Benedict nudging at the boundaries of his imagination. He wasn't totally daft; he knew men of his nature generally gave in to their urges when needs must. Indeed, he had once done so himself with

Tommy Squire. But that they dared live alongside one another — and in plain sight if one knew where to look — tilted the very fabric of his being off centre. Benedict could be no more discombobulated than if Rossingley had declared the world a triangular pyramid.

Partnering even-tempered, no-nonsense Beatrice was the perfect antidote, even if for the minuet, a dance not designed for a larger man. Nonetheless, with a bit of luck, she'd have him back on a sufficiently even keel to navigate dinner.

"Emerald-green taffeta is very fetching on you, Beatrice," he began as she dipped in a curtsy. He bowed in response. Indeed, it was the truth. The colour complemented her auburn hair and fair, freckled skin.

"Thank you, Your Grace. I chose it to clash with my mother's scarlet organza. She is refusing to speak to me this evening because of it, which is a veritable bonus."

Already, as Benedict took her small, gloved hand in his own, holding it lightly, he felt more at peace. "Francis and Isabella have had three dances in succession," he observed, catching sight of his brother's dark head closer to Isabella's than the minuet warranted. "I fear it is my duty to have strong words with them both. The gossipmongers at *The Morning Herald* will be sharpening their quills."

"Oh, you do not need to concern yourself," Beatrice answered gaily. "Trust me, they'll hardly warrant a mention in dispatches tomorrow."

They each took a dainty step towards the other, in perfect accord with the music. "A scandal brewing this evening will finally give them some other excitement to scribble about rather than rehashing Lord Gartside's old crimes. Lord Lyndon's thieving antics will seem positively childish by comparison and tittle-tattle about Francis and Isabella, nothing but crumbs for the birds."

Benedict and gossip weren't natural bedfellows, yet Beatrice's heightened colour piqued his interest. "Oh, yes?"

Irritatingly, they had to step away from each other and to the side, obliging Beatrice to execute a delicate turn.

"Most certainly," she responded when she became close enough once more. "Though the scandal is not a topic suitable for a naïve young lady." At this, she demurely lowered her eyelashes.

Benedict laughed, pretending to look this way and that. "Well, we're in luck, Beatrice, as none will overhear."

"It concerns a bawdy house," she mouthed as they drew even closer. Her own gaze darted theatrically from left to right too. He'd never seen her so missish; the performance was delightful. "A bawdy house that was raided," she added sotto voce. "A list of gentlemen who used to frequent the place has fallen into the hands of a person of nefarious means." She embellished her revelation with a little twirl and a raised eyebrow. "One of the gentlemen on the list is, supposedly, very high *ton* indeed."

Benedict pondered this tidbit of gossip during the next sequence of steps. Unsure what all the fuss was about, he wondered if his plodding brain had missed something. Raids on bawdy houses were hardly news, and Beatrice wasn't usually one to get caught up in such a trivial matter. Nor was it noteworthy that high society gentlemen made up the clientele. Indeed, plenty of chaps of his acquaintance — decent fellows, too — paraded their exploits as a badge of honour. Truth be told, rather than finding them discomforting, he experienced a pang of envy that they could brag about their carnal urges so openly.

The dance was reaching its conclusion. Beatrice stepped gracefully towards him once more and then to his left.

"Has this fellow caught the pox and spread it to his wife?" the duke queried, amusement creeping into his tone. "Or some-body else's wife? Is that it? Because — and before you say it — " He held up a finger as Beatrice made to interrupt. " — I'm failing to understand what is so enthralling. And yes, I do fully acknowledge the inequity of the situation, given that you are a woman with healthy and strong views, and yes, I fully agree the universe is so terribly tilted in the favour of men. Et cetera. Et cetera."

Beatrice's clever gaze flicked to either side of them as she waited to move in close. When she did so, it was far more intimate than the dance warranted. Her sweet breath skimmed his ear, and not for the first time, it sadly stirred absolutely nothing within Benedict except genuine warmth towards an exceptionally de-lightful human being.

"The furore," she murmured, her voice shaky with barely contained glee, "is that the bawdy house in question used to be one of the *other sorts* of bawdy houses. And the nobleman on the list was a frequent visitor."

Other sorts? Benedict must have looked puzzled.

"You know, one of those bawdy houses that dare not be named, the kind an innocent young lady like me certainly has no knowledge of. Indeed, the very mention of one within thirty yards of my ears would bring me into a fit of vapours."

Ah, she meant a *molly* house. That was very a different story altogether. Benedict blew out a breath. His immediate thought was, *There but for the will of God go I.* A bare minute was all that had separated him from an appalling fall from grace all those years ago. A bare minute in which he could have untied Tommy and... No, he couldn't dwell on it. Not here, not now, in the middle of a packed ballroom.

"Did you say there was a list?" he asked in a careless fashion, pushing thoughts of Tommy aside. And then another thought struck him. *Rossingley?* His heart did a flip, causing him to miss his step entirely. *Oh no*, he sincerely prayed, not Rossingley.

"My toes, Your Grace." Beatrice winced. "I'd prefer to return home with all ten intact."

"My most humble apologies," he muttered, "to all ten of them."

"They accept." Once more, they fell into step. "And yes, there is a list."

"What is to be done with it?"

As Benedict swept her lithe body around another pair of dancers, Beatrice executed an agile turn. They were very well-matched in so many ways. Which made it such a shame that...

"Rumours abound," she murmured, thrilled, "that the owner of the list will announce the gentleman's name in the coming weeks, perhaps at the Earl of Horton's end-of-season ball. Unless he pays a ransom."

"A ransom? How very cloak-and-dagger." Benedict shook his head. "This is starting to sound terribly far-fetched. The sort of mad caper Isabella and Francis might dream up during a sunny picnic. If it wasn't so indecent, of course," he added hastily.

The minuet drew to a gentle close, and Beatrice bobbed a

rather perfunctory curtsy.

Smiling fondly down at her as he returned a deep bow, Benedict tutted. "I'm surprised at you, my dear. Spreading idle tittle-tattle. Your mother would be dismayed."

"Only because she hasn't discovered it first." Beatrice took Benedict's proffered arm, and he led them from the dance floor. "But I daresay you're right. It won't amount to anything, and by the end of the week, us ladies will all go back to playing charades and embroidering kittens on cushions whilst the men pretend to have learned opinions regarding Canning's feud with the new king. Anyhow, the raid happened years ago. And Francis says this bawdy house—he mentioned it went by the name of the White Hart?—has long since burned down. So, who cares about something that happened all the way back in 1813?"

*

DINNER WAS PORK. Or beef. Or straw mattress stuffing. The claret boasted the consistency of thick sludge, and if Lady Butterworth (seated to his left) had the slightest awareness how nearly the Duke of Ashington almost cast up his accounts into her soup tureen, then she might have ceased torturing his soul with a voice like the scrape of metal on metal for one damned minute. The identity of the unfortunate bugger seated to his right was lost forever in the mists of time. Needless to say, Benedict strengthened his reputation as a dullard.

When he finally escaped, the bitter night air closed in around him like a strong hand, tightening his throat and making the skin on his cheeks tingle. Claret, rage, and raw panic were a heady mix; Benedict fair stumbled down Lady Butterworth's steps, saved only by a hideous stone bust of the late Lord Arthur Butterworth at the bottom.

A row of a carriages stretched out like a colourful serpent along the dimly lit street. His own fine landau was at the head, of course, what with him being a damned duke. As his liveried groom rushed to open the door, a deep primal sound rumbled from the duke's chest. He experienced a frightening, overwhelming urge to inflict damage on something, to punch through his carriage window, rip out a curtain or two. Kick the damned ugly bust.

Naturally, Benedict did none of those things. Instead, as the first few drops of rain chittered against the shiny carriage roofs, he adjusted his hat, graciously dismissed his groom, and began a brisk walk in the direction of Squire's.

Chapter Nine

RAIN LASHED DOWN against Tommy's windowpanes, fit to turn a dog. A fancy ball over at a rich dowager's place had swallowed half his patrons, and the inclement weather was doing the rest. Somewhere above him, water poured from the guttering, splashing into puddles collecting below before joining the ribbons flowing down the middle of the street.

Tommy didn't mind closing early for once. The club flourished. He'd taken on three new members of staff in the last month, and his profits had still risen by a fifth. Soon, he'd take Sidney's advice and introduce young Mickey to the rudiments of bookkeeping. Poking the small fire burning brightly in the grate, he loosened his cravat, then settled down to one more page of accounts before turning in for an early night. He'd felt depleted of late, his sleep plagued by remembrances of the past and the raw, unfiltered truth hiding amongst them that he tried his damnedest to ignore.

After his characteristic signal—more a series of thumps than a polite scratch—Sidney's broad, plain face appeared in the doorway. "One of the swanky gentlemen is at the front desk demanding to see you, Tommy. He's right pissed off about summat."

Juggling a column of figures in his head, Tommy barely looked up.

"I told him you weren't here," huffed Sidney. "But he's one you might want to see."

"There's none fitting that description. Tell him to arrange an appointment like everyone else." Tommy dipped his quill in a pot of red ink. "I'm a little tied up."

"Tied up ain't going to cut the mustard, I'm afraid, Tommy. You could have ship's riggin' pinning you to that chair in a figure eight, but he ain't budging. So, unless you want a duke kipping on the front steps, I'm going to...*oompf.*"

A man of lower social consequence would live to regret shoving Sidney aside. The fourteenth Duke of Ashington, however, his chest heaving and jaw clenched so hard it might snap, had run out of regrets to give. With a pounding in his own chest, Tommy rose from his desk.

"In retrospect, *tied up* was a poor choice of words," he managed. "Good evening, Your Grace. Such a pleasure, as always." He dug a nail into his palm. "Sidney? You may leave us."

The storm raging outside had nothing on the duke's pent-up fury. Hardly had the door clicked shut before he unleashed it.

"Damn you, Tommy," he roared. "May God damn you to hell!"

A spray of silvery raindrops flew from the sodden shoulders of his overcoat as Benedict thumped his fist hard on

Tommy's desk. Quills and foolscap leaped into the air. The inkpot tipped onto its side; a thin line of crimson ink slopped across the hidebound desk spattering to the floor below like a life oozing away.

"Damn you, Tommy!" the duke vented with no less fury. "How dare you? How dare you do this to me!"

Dark eyes ablaze, he planted both hands squarely on the desk, looming over Tommy. "Tell me what you want, and we'll settle it now. A thousand guineas? Two thousand? Do you have expensive tastes, Tommy? Is it a fine racehorse you're hankering after? A manor house in the country? Or will you not be content until you have prised this linen shirt from my back?"

It took all of Tommy's nerve not to take a step backwards. He half expected Sidney, who must have heard all the commotion, to come rushing back to his defence. And he would have done, if the furious gentleman hurling curses at him over the desk wasn't a bloody duke. As Sidney had no doubt swiftly concluded, Tommy could handle himself, and one crossed a wealthy duke at one's peril.

"Your Grace." Tommy hoped he sounded cooler than he felt. "I'm afraid I am at an utter loss to comprehend the nature of your problem. But clearly, it is pressing." He indicated to a drinks table near the fireplace. "Perhaps we could discuss it like gentlemen over a thimble of port. And you could dry off a little."

"Ballocks!" the duke snorted. "You know exactly what you're doing, you…you snivelling guttersnipe." Spittle flew from his lips. "I thought you were…were a… But I see that you're not. You're nothing but a wretched—you said the word yourself—a wretched money-grabbing *whore*!"

Tommy fumbled behind him for the small bell hidden amongst the fronds of a large potted plant. He kept a switchblade there, too, but he wasn't foolish enough to brandish that at a duke, no matter the provocation. But, by God, he was sorely tempted.

Grabbing the bell, Tommy lofted it between them. "This is louder than it looks when dropped from this height. They'd hear the thud and ringing all the way down in the kitchens." He gave it a little jangle. "So, any more of that and you'll be escorted from the premises, Your Grace. And none too politely. You might be a high-in-the-instep duke; you might be the bloody King of Spain for all I care. But no one, and I mean *no one*, barges into my garret uninvited and calls me a whore."

Tommy didn't know which part, if any, of that speech had resonated. Perhaps it was the repetition of *whore* (such a coarse, reductive term, even worse when dripping from a duke's lips, a man who'd never had to fight for a penny in his life). Or perhaps the duke had simply run out of steam. A whole heap of misery was stacked up under that anger. Now Tommy looked properly, it was there for all to see in the shadowy bags under the man's eyes, the creases bracketing his fine mouth, and the unhappy manner in which he rubbed at his chin as if waking disoriented from a ghastly dream. As if already shocked at his own vile utterances and an abject apology would hastily follow.

Whatever the trigger, as abruptly as it had begun, the duke's outburst bled away, his high colour paling with it, leaving his handsome features a sickly grey. His body swayed, and Tommy, his damned soft heart flickering to life, rushed around the desk to catch him.

"Have a seat, Your Grace. You…you are not yourself."

The duke staggered backwards, his behind thankfully landing in the grumbling, spindly chair. He made a desolate sound, caught somewhere between a sob and a groan.

"I fear I have not been myself, Tommy, since…since…ah, since you know when." Another sound, yes most definitely a sob, and he covered his face in his hands. "*The duke* this, *Your Grace* that. Hah! I'm nothing but a poor facsimile of a man, and that is God's own truth. And now, all of London is on the brink of discovering it. And it is everything I deserve."

His head fell back, his eyes closed. Raindrops—or were they tears?—sparkled on his thick, sooty lashes. "A poor facsimile?" In Tommy's biased opinion, his lordling was being a little hard on himself. Despite looking like lukewarm death, with his reddened nose and loud sniffling, he still cut a fine figure.

Tommy threw another log onto the fire and stoked it. He ran a shaky hand through his neat hair as he hovered over the still figure slumped in the chair. Then he moved to the drinks table, wavering between the port and the brandy. Why did he never know what to do with himself in the presence of this man? Should he call for some hot soup? Insist the duke took a restorative? Throw him out? Should he stand, sit, or stare up at the ceiling? Should he beat his chest and scream?

As if winter's icy breath gusted over him, a violent, bone-deep shiver wracked the duke's body, accompanied by a despairing moan. Tommy elected for brandy.

"Your Grace, let me ease you from your sopping overcoat. You shall catch your death, and I do not wish that on my conscience."

The duke prised open an eye. "Your conscience hangs heavy enough, I'll wager."

"My conscience is regretting its good manners and charity towards someone wholly undeserving. Nonetheless, remove yourself from your coat and drink this. Then tell me what this terrible thing is I've done so I can grovel at a duke's feet accordingly."

"Enough with the pretence, Tommy." The duke knocked back the brandy in one. "Just tell me what it is you want from me, and you shall have it. Anything to prevent my brothers' names and my father's memory dragged through the mire."

Tommy wrapped his arms tight about himself. "And I shall repeat, though it is falling on deaf ears, that I am in the dark about what it is I am purported to have done." Another shiver cascaded through the duke's body. "And for God's sake, stop being such a stubborn ass and take off that blasted wet greatcoat."

The duke laughed, a hollow, broken sound. "A stubborn ass? I should slap you with my glove for that."

"That would end badly for you," Tommy warned. "Duke or no."

The duke wore full evening dress under his heavy wool travelling coat, the pristine starched collar seemingly the only thing holding the man's head up. Whether his tailcoat was also damp, Tommy couldn't bring himself to enquire for fear of the answer and the man revealing even more of his well-shaped body. Tommy cursed under his breath as he poured the duke a second drink, trying to ignore the damp fabric stretched inconsiderately tight across the duke's thighs. Unhappily, he failed.

Bloody Rossingley was right. Tommy sprinkled a few muttered curses in his direction too. *Tart with a heart.* How was

Tommy supposed to pretend to himself, never mind anyone else, that he never wanted this man again? He might as well kid himself he could blow spots from bloody playing cards.

"There is a list," said the duke weakly, nursing the balloon of strong liqueur between his palms, "of gentlemen known to have frequented the White Hart. Of gentlemen on the premises on the night of the raid of 1813. Someone has obtained it and threatens to announce it at one of the biggest society balls."

Tommy's soft heart stalled. "And you…your name appears on it? You have been blackmailed?"

"Not yet." The duke threw him a watery smile. "But it is rumoured there is a gentleman of the high *ton* on the list. So, it is only a matter of time, is it not?"

The question and its inevitable, disastrous consequences for the duke and his good standing lingered between them. Of course, Ashington had put the blame squarely at Tommy's door. Who else would have known he was there? After all, it was only in recent times that Tommy himself had learned his precious raven's true identity. Molly houses didn't keep neat ledgers. Gentlemen with their predilections didn't exactly sign themselves in and leave calling cards.

Eventually, Tommy broke the silence.

"Revealing your name and exposing your nature would be of no benefit to me, Your Grace," he said softly. "How could it? When I have much to lose also? I speak the truth when I swear to you that I am not the one behind this."

The duke stared wanly at the fire, lost in the flickering flames. "I am…yes. I see that now. The youth I once knew would not behave in that way."

"And nor would the man," said Tommy. "Even if he was once a whore."

The duke contemplated his drink as if he'd like to drown in it. "He was never that to me. I… Yet again, I find myself seeking your forgiveness. I should not have used that word in anger."

"But perhaps neither of us should shy from the truth of it. If we had not been raided that day, if I had not been…trapped, no good would have come of our liaison. I would still have been a whore, and you would still have been…you."

"And I would have still lov…cared for you."

Tommy sneered, hating himself but unable to resist. "Like you cared for other pretty things you owned? Such as your race-horses and silk cravats? In time, I would have belonged to last season, too, when you grew tired of me."

"I cannot say." Shamed, the duke hung his head. "But that feckless youth was also raided that day." He rested a palm against his heart. "In here. He was robbed of his joy, and believe me when I tell you, Tommy, he has never regained it."

For a long moment, as each man contemplated the other, both lost in misery, Tommy wondered what the duke saw. A servant of sorts perhaps? One of the many faceless, nameless, inconsequential factotums orbiting his existence whose primary purpose was to oblige? Or did he still see the boy on his knees with his lips spread wide around his prick?

Tommy knew precisely what he was, what he'd become after that raid, even if his very existence puzzled the *ton*: A grifter who'd beaten the odds to drag himself up by his bootstraps from the armpit of the underworld. Someone who had debased himself for every sou in order that he might sit in this fine study in his fine costume, sipping his excellent brandy, kidding himself for a few minutes he was just like them.

He never would be, of course. His veneer of respectability was as brittle as the spindly legs holding up the duke's wooden chair.

"I accept you were not thinking straight," acknowledged Tommy at last. "You have suffered a shock."

"Yes, but you are too kind. If I weren't a damned peer, you would have rung that bell and summoned your man in a trice, and he would have slung me out. Deservedly so."

Raising himself from the chair looked painful now all traces of anger had gone. "I shall not intrude on your hospitality any longer. Forgive me for believing the worst of you."

Heavy and dark, his wet greatcoat blanketed Tommy's desk like a burial cloth. As Tommy handed it to him, the duke regarded it as if he'd never seen it in his life.

"It is a cruel night," he said as he shouldered it on. His body shrank under the weight of it. The kidskin gloves were next, as pale as the fingers they hid. Tears bled from his eyes.

"I have stared at the past every day, Tommy." The duke brushed at a teardrop before carrying on. "And every day, I have wished I could correct my dreadful mistake. To have carried you with me in my escape. To feel cherished once more, as I felt in your arms. Because, God knows, I have not felt it since."

His distress leached into Tommy's skin. It called to his very core, sapping every last bit of his strength not to weep himself and reach out for this man, to hold him, to comfort. How easy loving him again would be. But how easily his fragile, guarded heart broke.

"The past is a place to learn from, not to live, Your Grace," Tommy uttered with as much conviction as he could muster. "There is only the here and forwards."

"Thus now, more than ever, I wish I could go back."

As the door snicked softly closed, Tommy counted the heavy tread of footsteps as they receded down the corridor. Only when his house fell silent, except for the dripping of the gutters, did Tommy curl up in his armchair and allow grief to come.

Chapter Ten

THE PLAIN SHEET of good quality foolscap was buried amongst the rest of his morning missives, unsealed and neatly folded into four. It had been hand delivered, according to the duke's butler, by a boy paid thruppence for his efforts. If the lack of blots and errors were any indication, it was meticulously composed, the list of names in block letters, orderly and legible. As far as his trembling mind could recall, they were the same names Tommy had recited, a register of pilloried mollies, except with the addition of a handful more tacked onto the bottom. One of which, with the courtesy title bestowed on him by his father, stood out more boldly than the rest. *BENEDICT FITZSIMMONS, MARQUESS OF ROCKBOURNE*. Ever since reading it, a skittish ball of panic had taken root in his chest, ready to take over at the slightest provocation.

And now Benedict had to pretend, being a duke and

everything, that all was well.

He rolled his shoulders, letting out a slow breath as he steered his focus back to the present. He could have sorely done without this trip to Tattersall's and had nearly cried off. But the viewing was one he'd looked forward to, and he'd even persuaded Francis to accompany him. Benedict had his eye on a two-year-old gelding from good French stock, which he hoped might take his brother's mind off his lovesick woes. And if Benedict stayed another second inside his house, after his miserable encounter with Tommy, he might go insane.

The chilling discovery at breakfast had merely been the icing on the cake.

Deep in conversation with one of Tattersall's men, Francis ran a hand down the gelding's withers, while across the yard from him, Benedict had been cornered by Joe Jonas, his head groom. The man's commentary on yesterday's race was in full flow. And yet, Jonas's words hardly registered, streaming through Benedict and out the other side in a jumble of vowels and consonants as if his cranium were as insubstantial as gossamer. Ganymede had lost again, was the gist, and he'd finished outside the placing. In his defence, the field had been strong, and the duke's jockey off-colour. Feeling decidedly off-colour himself since prising open this morning's correspondence, Benedict empathised. Nodding every few seconds, he tipped his head on one side, his finger and thumb pinching his lower lip, the very image of a man paying close attention.

"Ashington!"

Like a clashing of cymbals, Benedict's name rang in his ears. He jerked around, heart thumping fit to burst, only to find

Rossingley leaning against a pillar and smiling warmly at him.

"Gadzooks, my friend. Sorry awfully for making you jump."

Benedict breathed a sigh of relief. "Rossingley, good morning to you." He mopped at the fine sheen of sweat gathered on his brow, dismissing Jonas with a grateful nod.

"Are you quite all right?" Rossingley enquired. "Is that excellent gelding proving too rich even for your purse?"

"Um…what?"

Something in Benedict's countenance bothered the earl sufficiently for him to prowl over and regard him properly. "I have been trying to garner your attention for a good minute or more, Ashington. You were knee-deep in the far-flung corners of your mind." Rossingley looked worriedly up into Benedict's face. "They can be lonely places."

The unexpected concern in the earl's extraordinary silvery gaze had Benedict making quite a performance of folding away his pocket square. He swallowed rapidly. "I'm…yes."

"Then let us not dally here," suggested the earl brightly. "No one will dare bid on that gelding at auction tomorrow, not once word of your interest gets around." He cast his gaze up at the clear, pale blue sky. "And, for once, the rain gods are smiling upon us. Join me in my curricle for a spin around the park. I came here looking for an animal suitable as a gift for my Mr Angel, but so far, nothing of interest has caught my eye." He gave a curious smile. "Except you, my dear."

Expertly guided by their master, Rossingley's handsome pair of greys led them into Hyde Park at a brisk trot. A gentle breeze frolicked through the trees, carrying with it an uneasy promise of more rain later. But, for now, the skies remained cloudless, and the cool air cleansed Benedict's mind somewhat. *My* Mr Angel. A peculiar turn of phrase, bolstering everything Benedict already suspected about the man. A man who had never shown him anything but kindness. And at that moment, Benedict was desperately in need of some.

"I fear I'm on the cusp of being blackmailed," he blurted as they entered a straight section of path devoid of other carriages. "For a scrape I found myself embroiled in over a decade ago. And I haven't the faintest idea how to proceed."

The curricle jolted over a pothole, sending his roiling belly up into his throat. If he'd read Rossingley wrongly, spilling to him would make matters tenfold worse, not better. Someone else would be in possession of his greatest secret. Tommy knew it, Benedict's unknown tormentor knew it, and now Benedict was about share his burden with a person he greatly admired but, when all was said and done, hardly knew.

"Are you...are you aware, Rossingley, of a fresh scandal brewing regarding a raid on a bawdy house known as the White Hart?" Eyes fixed directly ahead, Benedict felt himself withering inside but determined to get to the end. "Back in 1813. Do you know to which...which particular type of raid I'm referring?"

"Ah." Rossingley nodded. "Yes, I see. You're in the devil's own sort of scrape."

Nothing more needed to be said. It was all there in the simple questions Benedict already regretted having posed and Rossingley's tactful acknowledgement. He extracted his damp pocket square once more, not sure whether to use it to mop his face or catch his breakfast when it reappeared.

Rossingley didn't say anything straightaway. In fact, except for a tightening of his hands on the reins to slow the horses a fraction, one would be forgiven for thinking he'd already dismissed the matter from his mind. Benedict shot him a quick, sidelong glance. In haughty profile, the earl possessed a chiselled, chilling beauty, and Benedict concentrated on it, trying to keep his breathing under control as he awaited his response. If Rossingley denied further knowledge of either the raid or the current gossipmongering, Benedict would make his excuses then beg him to forget he ever mentioned it.

"I know more about the White Hart than you might imagine," Rossingley volunteered.

On the receiving end of the full scrutiny of that silvery gaze, Benedict tried not to squirm. Rossingley inclined his head a touch as if everything was suddenly very clear to him.

"I always wondered if you were of the same persuasion as myself." Rossingley paused a beat, flashing his small pointy teeth. "And now I know." With a click of his tongue, the horses picked up speed. "Good to have you on board, Your Grace. How may I be of assistance?"

As several of the knots in Benedict's chest untangled, he exhaled with relief. "God knows if you can. If anybody can. My family name and that of my brother, Francis, who wishes above everything else to marry Lady Isabella Knightley, will be in tatters when it gets out. And my poor mother, though she spends most of the year living in the dower house on the Ashington estate, should not have to hear from idle gossips of her son and heir's—"

"The beginning, I think, my dear Ashington," cut in Rossingley. "Though from the tremble of your hands, may I surmise that your name is on this godforsaken list rumoured to be blast across the *ton* any day now?"

"Yes," breathed Benedict, clutching his pocket square tight enough to wring all the dampness from it. "I received a copy of the list amongst my morning correspondence. My name is there, on a neat sheet of foolscap in stark block letters. Amongst the…ah employees of the establishment and one or two other chaps whose names are unfamiliar to me. Surely, it is only a matter of time before the blackmail follows."

"Do you know of any enemies? Anyone who wishes to see you or your family ruined? One of the mollies, for instance?"

"No!" Benedict's brow furrowed. "Um…there is one person on the list—one of the… employees, who—good God, this is hellishly awkward—with whom I shared…"

"Bodily fluids?" supplied Rossingley. "Don't be coy, Ashington. You're not the first duke to swive a pretty molly boy."

Swive? Back then, naïve Benedict hadn't even understood swiving another man was anatomically achievable. And now that he knew—for many a good year he had fantasised of little else—he was still no closer to having ever done it.

"And if the molly was willing and eager," continued a blasé Rossingley as if this was the most routine of conversations, "then it's nothing to be ashamed of, despite what our precious society and the English lawmakers wish us to believe about ourselves. Anyhow, back in 1813, you weren't much more than a boy yourself." He pulled on one rein, steering the curricle smoothly into a bend. "You were going to tell me you don't think this person is our culprit. For what it's worth, I happen to agree."

If he wasn't so preoccupied with trying to conceal the fierce brush of crimson cantering from his neck to the tips of his ears,

Benedict might have paused to wonder how Rossingley had drawn the same conclusion as himself regarding Tommy's sealed mouth.

"Y-yes," he stuttered. "I don't believe it is him."

"Good." Rossingley threw him another careful look. He jerked the reins, and the horses sped up again. "So, what we need to do henceforth is discover the identity of our potential black-mailer and teach him or her a lesson they won't forget."

He laid a hand on Benedict's arm. "A word of comfort, Ashington. People like them tend to underestimate men like us. They imagine your shame isolates you — it's a standard bullying tactic, is it not? But we are kindred spirits, and men like us stick together. Just because we are inverts doesn't mean we aren't still men, strong and capable and with fire in our bellies. Leave me to chew on things for a day or two, and I'll come up with the beginnings of a plan."

Chapter Eleven

"TOMMY, DARLING. FORGIVE me for barging in like this, un-invited."

"You're a spoiled aristocrat." Marking his place in the column of figures with his fingertip, Tommy added, blandly, "It's what you do."

"Precisely. I knew you'd understand. Alas, far too many don't." Rossingley flopped into the spindly seat facing Tommy's desk. Under his nimble frame, it made nary a squeak of protest. "But, more pertinently, I've discovered the identity of your lordling." He pulled a face. "Gadzooks, you don't do things by half, do you? *A duke*? Wasn't a common or garden baronet or a mere viscount, good enough for you? You had to tumble a damned duke?"

Tommy laid down his quill to properly regard his visitor, amused despite the seriousness of his growing predicament. "I assure you, Lordy, he wasn't very ducal at the time. He was gauche, clumsy, and spewed like a volcano the second I laid my hand on his prick."

And I loved him with every fibre of my being, regardless, he could have added, but Rossingley already knew that.

"And yet," murmured the earl softly as if reading his thoughts.

"Precisely." Tommy allowed himself a small smile. "I knew you'd understand. Alas, far too many wouldn't." He set aside the fat ledger. "My innocent lordling has grown into a beauty, has he not?"

"Albeit a petrified one, yes," agreed Rossingley. "Mind you, he's always been a timid chap. And someone out there is determined to ruin him." Adjusting his impeccable cuffs, he eyed the pot of barley sugar candies on the corner of Tommy's desk, reserved for the earl's consumption alone.

With a shake of his head, Tommy pushed the jar towards him. "I am already apprised of the situation. He came to see me in a state of great distress. How did you find out?"

"I chanced upon him trying to behave normally at Tattersall's."

Selecting a sweet, Rossingley untwisted the wrapper, then popped it in his mouth. "The man could barely piece a sentence together," he continued around the bulge in his cheek. "You know, I'd always fancied Ashington shared our *unnatural* tendencies. Since he was a boy, in fact. He used to trail around after me in the stables whenever his family came to stay. I'd build up a sweat brushing down my father's favourite mare and then strip to my undershirt and amuse myself by watching the poor boy becoming increasingly bewildered."

He crunched the sweet noisily. "Anyway, I digress. Seeing as he was so miserable, I invited him for a ride. Once I'd insinuated that we were both of a similar persuasion, he couldn't wait to offload his weighty burden from those broad, ducal shoulders. And may I just say how deliciously broad they are." He flapped his slim hand in front of his face, "Nothing beats a duke in danger to get the juices flowing, Tommy. Don't you find?"

Tommy sighed heavily. "You are irredeemable, you know that, don't you?"

"Gadzooks, yes." A second sugar barley disappeared the way of the first. "Kit encourages me daily."

A sense of unease plagued Tommy's mind, worst-case scenarios unfolding. "Have there been any new developments? Is he being blackmailed?"

Rossingley shook his head. "Calm yourself, dear. Not yet. He's shaken up, nothing else. So far, our unknown friend has merely signalled his or her malign intent by sending Ashington a list with his name on it." He gave an elegant shrug. "But I can't help thinking it's only a matter of time."

Tommy selected a crumpled scrap of paper sitting on the top of his pile of correspondence, holding it up by his finger and thumb. "You mean this list? My own copy arrived this morning."

The earl squinted at it. "I imagine so. What ghastly handwriting. Though at least we can narrow our search to illiterates with black ink stains on their cuffs." His shrewd gaze travelled back to Tommy. "Our perpetrator is demanding five hundred pounds from you but not from the wealthy duke." His brow wrinkled. "That's a little odd, is it not?"

Tommy nodded. "More than."

"And yet you don't appear as perturbed as His Grace, despite the blackmail."

"Mostly because I'm bloody livid," answered Tommy calmly. "That's why."

"Hmm." Rossingley pinched his lower lip in thought. "For yourself or for…?" The delicate question hovered between them.

"Both of us." Tommy glared at him. "His…His Grace has suffered enough for the natural instincts he was born with. He can no more help them than you or I. I would be furious on anyone's behalf."

"Do keep on telling yourself that, darling. I so enjoy a good yarn."

"I don't even know him anymore!" Tommy spluttered. "Why should I want to trouble myself for him? Why am I pacing the floor every minute of the day bloody *fretting* about him?"

"Because," explained Rossingley as if patiently elucidating to a small child, "a long time ago, that distressed handsome duke opened up a pocket of sunshine in your heart. And you in his. And even someone as boneheaded as you has noticed that in the intervening years, neither of you has stumbled across anyone else who has managed to do the same." A loud crunching followed this pronouncement. "When you know, you know. And now, your mate is in danger. Your body is sensing it and reacting accordingly, even if your head is taking a while to catch up."

Mate? Tommy wasn't a bloody sailor, nor a lone wolf. "Poppycock," he declared.

Placidly, Rossingley nodded. "There are cocks involved, Tommy, I'll grant you that." He rolled his sweet wrapper into a tight ball. "Are you going to sit here all day, wasting your breath and denying the undeniable, or go out and find this fiend determined to bring you both down?"

Rossingley was far too clever to ask questions he didn't already know the answers to. Tommy pushed his chair back, then stood and hefted on his greatcoat.

"His Grace's reticule might be overflowing with smelling salts at the idea of extortion, but if this fiend thinks Tommy Squire is going to lie back and quiver like a virgin bride on her wedding night whilst they destroy his business and reputation, they can damned well think again."

"Oh my." The earl flapped his hand again. "Even better than a duke in danger. Continue clenching your fists like that, darling, and I may succumb to a fit of the vapours myself. What do you plan to do?"

"Track them down, scare the living daylights out of them, and make them regret their mother had ever given them breath." He held up a finger as the earl began flapping again. "And do not, at this juncture, Lordy, invoke your juices again."

Tommy gathered up his ledger, snapped it shut, then locked it in the desk drawer. "Are you in the mood for a trip down memory lane, Lordy?"

He prayed Rossingley would answer in the affirmative. For all his fighting talk, revisiting his past life made Tommy queasy. Moral support from a devout and unaffected friend would make it all the more tolerable.

With a beatific smile, Rossingley palmed another barley sugar. "Gadzooks, darling. I thought you'd never ask."

*

"ISN'T THE WHITE Hart nothing but a sad pile of cinders, these days?" queried Rossingley as the carriage trundled through the less salubrious parts of town.

Tommy threw him a humourless smile. "Yes, it burned down in 1816."

In general, he avoided these parts of the stews like the pox; they stirred up too many traumatic memories. And too much heartache. Yet, thanks to his soft heart and a damned *duke in distress*, here he was again. "A lit candle became caught up in a tussle between a feisty young molly named Fox and a foxed madge who should have known better than to short-change him."

Tommy grimaced as he stared out of the window. Charred remains of three men had been unearthed from the rubble: a sixteen-year-old regimental drummer, a grocer with premises on New Road (who went by the name Miss Sweet Lips), and an ordained minister with whom Tommy had occasionally shared a bed. History did not remember them with kindness.

With Tommy's soft heart still oscillating between shedding tears for the three unfortunates and clenching in trepidation, the earl's ostentatious carriage drew to a halt on the corner of Vere Street. He forced himself to look at the land, now derelict, upon which the thriving White Hart once stood.

"We're here," Tommy said unnecessarily, working his tongue around his dry mouth. And then, because Lordy missed nothing, "How the devil does this pile of rubble still reduce me to a damp, shaky sack of fear?"

The earl peered up at their destination — the forlorn building adjacent—seemingly unoccupied and thereby drawing as little attention to its true purpose as possible. "I suggest you try to focus on remembering the good times," he murmured, finding Tommy's hand and giving it a squeeze. "Though I'm sure they were few and far between."

Images of the Duke of Ashington flooded Tommy's mind, but as he was then—a long-limbed, laughing raven-haired youth. That youth was deeply buried now if the severe duke's haunted, miserable demeanour on his last visit was anything to go by. He'd seemed uncertain and afraid. Alone. *A person I once held more dearly in my heart than anyone else.*

Tommy returned the squeeze. "Perhaps that's why, in my memory, they were all the sweeter."

"Perhaps," agreed Rossingley, turning his attention back to the window. "Or perhaps you and he were written in the stars."

"And then written to part dramatically and never the twain meet again," said Tommy drily. "Destiny is a vicious mistress, is she not?" He jerked his chin towards the door. "Shall we?"

Few people were about at this time of the morning, either toiling elsewhere, trying to scavenge enough blunt to put food on the table, or in their cots sleeping off the excesses of the night before. If the clacking wheels of the hoity-toity carriage hadn't roused them from their pits and set window drapes twitching, the earl's costume, a headache-inducing lavender, certainly would.

Though capable in a fight, Tommy's preferred tactic was to avoid them altogether. Given there were plenty to be had in these parts, and he'd been embroiled in enough to last several lifetimes, he'd had the foresight to bring burly Sidney along. Up above them on the driver's bench, Tommy heard him pointing out what was left of the ruined White Hart to the earl's groom.

Rossingley gave Tommy's hand another squeeze. "Are we using the element of surprise? Is our devious plan to creep up on them?"

Full of enthusiasm—and possibly one barley sugar too many—he'd chattered non-stop since they'd set off. No wonder his long-suffering valet usually demanded to sit up top with the groom. Nonetheless, Tommy had been grateful for the distraction.

"Hardly," he answered. "A crested coach and four rather trumpets one's arrival in these parts."

"Goodness gracious, darling. Are you telling me there are alternative modes of transport available?"

"And, believe it or not, less dazzling waistcoats too."

As Rossingley smoothed down his pristine coat, Tommy smothered a grin. His nerves were brittle twigs, ready to snap; bringing the earl along had been a good idea.

"Tell me, which part am I to play? Dick Turpin or Black Bess?"

"Neither, Lordy. We're searching for answers, that's all. And as I'm sure your horribly exclusive education taught you, the most straightforward way to obtain them is to ask nicely."

The earl tapped his lips. "Hmm. Very dull though. How about you begin, all affable and mannered, and then I march in looking tough and rough, demanding their money or their lives?"

Tommy shook his head at his ridiculous, dearest friend. "Lordy, you are dressed in a lavender coat and gold tasselled Hessians. And I am on a quest for neither money nor lives."

"Yes, but they don't know that, do they?"

The groom opened the carriage door, and Tommy alighted,

then busily adjusted his hat to disguise the tremor in his hands.

The earl fairly flew down the steps, nimbly skipping around a pile of horse dung. "Lay on, Macduff!"

"I said no fighting, Lordy! Your role is to stand behind me and look suitably grave. And allow me to do the talking. You have very little experience, I'd wager, in communicating with individuals not of your class."

"I assure you," contradicted the earl, "I discuss my diary with my valet and my first footman in great detail every day. I'm a very much down-to-earth sort of fellow."

Tommy sighed. "Yes, but not this earth. I meant speak with them as my equals and friends."

Rossingley's lip curled in disapproval, and Tommy saw a flash of the steel usually kept hidden behind the fey façade. The earl wrapped soothing fingers around Tommy's arm. "My dear," he said. "When you resided here, no one was your equal. And the bed bugs were better friends to you than this woman and her son."

*

THE SMELL IS what did for Tommy. A bilious collision of stale sweat and cheap scent wafted down the steep staircase as a skinny lad still awaiting his first whiskers led them into a dingy parlour. A familiar but no less unpleasant bouquet of fried onion and cabbage took over. Cold fear snaked along Tommy's spine. He gave an involuntary shudder.

"You don't have to do this," murmured the earl, his comforting palm resting at the small of Tommy's back. "I'm perfectly capable. You could wait in the carriage."

"I know. But I'm fine." Tommy swallowed. "We shall only be a few minutes."

As they waited for the mistress of the house, a raucous squeal sounded above their heads, followed by a heavy tread. Bed springs squeaked, and a door slammed. Light feet ran up a staircase. Familiar noises all of them, curdled into nothing, blending into the background like the ticking of a clock. Nonetheless, they plunged Tommy back in time. For an instant, he imagined himself up there amongst them, forced to his knees, on all fours, or pinned against a wall. Feeling like a passenger in his own body, he swallowed again, digging his nails into his palms. A few minutes might be all he could stand.

Ma Duggan hobbled into the parlour on the boy's arm, a desiccated ruin of her former self. Pickling herself in sufficient quantities of laudanum to fell an ox had left their indelible stains on her. As had the ravages of time. And still, Tommy had a dreadful feeling he might faint.

She eased into a sagging armchair, her breathless exhale echoing around the room.

"He's a pretty one, Tommy," she observed as if resuming a conversation broken off only minutes before, not ten years. She squinted up at the earl's incongruent costume. Rossingley coolly examined her back.

"You always did have a taste for the upper orders, mind. Ain't you learned anything?"

As the lad slipped out noiselessly, low murmurings—too hushed to make out the words—came from the hallway outside. Ma Duggan's ferret-like eyes drifted over to the door, then back to Tommy. She took her time looking him up and down.

"Always had ideas above your station too. You might fool the nobs in that fancy coat, Tommy. But I'll always know what you are. And how you got there on your knees, one cock at a time."

Such derision in so few words. With such capacity to wound.

"Tommy has always fended for himself. He gave up waiting for crumbs to fall from anyone else's table a long time ago."

Rossingley's words dripped like icicles. In a leisurely fashion, he examined his lowly surroundings with the dismissive air members of the aristocracy seemed to glean from their mother's breast milk. "It appears you have very few crumbs left to offer."

She lifted a shoulder with contempt. "A hog in a silk waistcoat is still a hog. And a whore is still a whore."

Like a storm rising from his belly, Tommy's hatred for this woman grappled with his fear. He counted to ten very slowly, fists itching to join the conversation. But fisticuffs wouldn't forward his cause. And though the noise outside the door had stopped, he wouldn't make the mistake of assuming the hallway was empty.

"Your accounts of the comings and goings at the Hart," he demanded. "Back in 1813, when it was raided. Were they burned in the fire?"

The woman's dead eyes closed in a slow blink. "Now, Tommy lad, why would you come sniffing all the way over here asking me about an old thing like that?"

"It's a simple query, that's all. A polite yes or no would suffice."

She tilted her head to one side. "What's in it for me?"

"Blunt. The exact amount depends on what information is on offer."

Money conversed in a broken, impoverished language; Tommy and Ma Duggan spoke it fluently. She moistened a cracked sore on her lower lip with her tongue while her busy brain weighed up the odds.

"They burned, all right. Along with everything except the clothes I was stood up in." She tapped her head twice. "But this in here wasn't so smoke-addled."

"And you've recently shared that information with someone else," Tommy stated.

"Mebbe I have," she countered with another shrug. "Visitors are the sort of thing that slips out the mind ever so easy-like." Making the universal sign of rubbing her knobbly forefinger against her thumb, she said sharply, "My memory needs to see the colour of your coin first."

"And it shall," interjected Rossingley. "You have my word."

The air was stifling in the cramped room as if the unhappy spirits of those less fortunate than Tommy loitered in its dim and dusty corners.

He reached for his purse and extracted five sovereigns. "A taste of what's on offer. Perhaps that might poke it."

In a blink, the coins disappeared into the folds of the woman's dress.

"A gentleman came calling, fishing about. Too much of a nob to be a runner. He pretended to be a madge."

"And?" Tommy prompted, his pulse quickening.

"And so we came to an agreement. All respectful-like. He gave me some dough, and I gave him what he wanted."

"Which was?"

"Not any of my young sodomites. Not even you flashing your arse would have tempted him."

Her poor joke landed flat. Tommy waited, and after a beat, she added, "He wanted a list of who was here the night of the raid."

Whilst Tommy digested this piece of information, Rossingley paced towards her, stopping a couple of feet away.

"Humour me, Mrs Duggan," he said, hands clasped behind his back. "And you shall be even more handsomely rewarded. Would you be a dear pet and run down all the names on that list?"

His long fingers tapped on his wallet.

"He was on it, of course." She cocked her head in Tommy's direction. "And his pal, Sidney. Don't know if he ever got out of Newgate. I'd be surprised after what they did to him. Bloody heathen he was anyhow. Good riddance, I say."

Tommy congratulated himself on leaving Sidney to guard the carriage. Otherwise, Ma Duggan might well have uttered her last words ever, and Tommy would be none closer to discovering the identity of their mystery blackmailer.

Rossingley smiled at her, baring his teeth. "Do go on, pet."

"Then there were the two Jimmy's. 'Sally' was what we called one of them so we could tell them part. Both dead now. One the pox, the other starved in the workhouse. Young Will Thompson—I think he's pushing up daisies too. And my own boy Dickie. He's still going strong. Thick as a barn door but strong."

"Very good." As Rossingley rustled the folds of his wallet, she was almost salivating. "And now the names of the paying customers, if you will?"

"One was a bloke called Edward—didn't ever know his other name, but he turned up like clockwork every Thursday. Mr Simms, the night watch over at the docks, old Mr Tennant, and some out-of-town merchant used to call himself Smith. Nice fella, not his real name of course. And Tommy's handsome young lordling. Fancy Fitzsimmons, we called him. The marquess of somewhere or other. He was too stupid—too led by his prick—to come up with summat false."

Too naïve, thought Tommy, with a pang. Too sheltered. Too much in love.

Concluding her work was done, Ma Duggan sat back and folded her arms. "I reckon that's the name this nob was after. He handed the blunt over as soon as he heard that one. Wasn't interested in the others at all." Again, she rubbed her yellowed finger and thumb together. "I'll have the rest of yours now, Tommy lad. Cough up."

"Have you come across this Fitzsimmons person since?" Rossingley stayed Tommy's arm, preventing him handing over the coins. "Any titled gent, perhaps, that goes by that name?"

"Titled gent?" she parroted, and her cackle of laughter turned into a coughing fit. "Oh, yes," she managed after catching her breath. "One comes here every afternoon. We have tea in a china cup and a slice of seed cake; we sit around talking politics for an hour."

Wiping her hand across her mouth, she threw him a scornful look. "'Course I bloody haven't. Not seen the likes of the Fitzsimmons boy since the raid. Not gone looking for him either. I don't go looking for trouble with nobs—lands you in all sorts of hot water. Clean forgot about him until this brother of his came calling."

"His…" Tommy faltered. Even Rossingley was taken aback. "How do you know your visitor was his brother?"

"There's an extra sovereign in it for you," Tommy quickly added.

Her shifty eyes turned towards the door again. "Listen. I said I don't go looking for trouble with nobs. Didn't say I wasn't nosy. Our Dickie went outside and chatted up the driver, like, while I was chatting up the nob. The brother wasn't half as good-looking as the lordling who used to tup you, Tommy. Proper carrot-top, this fella was. Liked the booze a bit too much, too, if you ask me."

Takes one to know one. Tommy and Rossingley traded glances. So, the duke's own brother was behind it. Lord Lyndon. Who needed enemies when one had family? Was a shortcut to his own ruination not enough for the cove, that he had to take his brothers, his hitherto good family name, and Tommy down with him?

"You'll be off, then," Ma Duggan remarked as Tommy handed over the extra coin. "Don't bother coming back any time soon, Tommy."

"Wild horses would have to drag me."

Having accomplished all they'd set out, he was eager to leave. Rossingley, however, seemed in no great hurry to say his farewells. With his lower lip pinched between finger and thumb, he was doing that glittery thing he did with those penetrating pale eyes, which meant his smart brain was whirring at thrice the speed of a normal person. Twice, his hooded gaze had flicked towards the door during their cosy chat with Ma Duggan.

"One further question," he said, not caring that they'd outstayed their welcome. "And I'll come straight to the point.

However did you suppose that you could blackmail Tommy and get away with it?"

"What?" Tommy and Ma Duggan stared at him, the older woman's astonishment as genuine as Tommy's. She gave a little harrumph.

"Blackmail Tommy? I'm not that daft."

Lips pursed, Rossingley eyed her thoughtfully. "No," he agreed. "I don't believe *you* are. Only someone as stupid as…say…a *barn door* would be so reckless."

Ma Duggan's gaze darted to the parlour door. A flash of genuine fear crossed her face. "I'm telling you. I wouldn't mess with Tommy. I've seen him take down madges twice his size that got too rough, with nothing but his vicious tongue and a switch-blade." Her tone, reeking of the truth, held a trace of urgency. "You tell him, Tommy. You're an evil little bugger. Can't say I like you, but I ain't got no truck with you."

"Lordy," Tommy urged. "I think our business here is done, don't you? We've achieved what we—"

"Hmm. I'm not yet convinced we have." Rossingley's clipped vowels rose above the sound of the other two. "What say you, Mrs Duggan?"

"I say you should get back in that fancy—"

Rossingley held up a silencing finger, cutting her off mid-sentence. "Let me tell you something, Mrs Duggan. A little bit about myself."

There was something about the aristocracy that set them apart, thought Tommy. When they spoke, they assumed everyone would shut up and listen. The annoying thing was everyone usually did.

"There are three things I love above all others in this world," Rossingley declared. Stepping closer towards her, he smiled, showing his pointy little teeth. Familiar with that disarming smile, Tommy braced for whatever hurricane came next.

"Shall I enlist them?" Like a sermon tossed down from a high pulpit, the earl's icy, cultured tones bounced around the walls of the tiny parlour.

"Do I have a choice?"

"Not really." Rossingley took another menacing step closer to Ma Duggan so that he loomed over her, almost as if he intended to rest his arm around her bony shoulders. "Now, where was I? Ah, yes. Three things."

"Get out," she hissed. "You've had what you came for. Now get out."

"The first, above all," he continued as if she hadn't spoken, "I love Mr Christopher Angel. Such a darling chap. And so terribly handsome. Some days, I have to pinch myself that he's all mine. Secondly —" His lip curled into the hint of another smile, even more unpleasant than the first, causing Ma Duggan to shrink back in the chair. " — and I can be forgiven for discussing this particular intimacy in my present surroundings — I absolutely adore the sounds Mr Angel makes mere seconds before he spills inside my mouth." He accompanied this shocking statement with a deep and obscene groan. "Divine. And thirdly…"

Oh Lord, Tommy dreaded to imagine the third item on the list. A misplaced bubble of laughter welled in his throat at the craziness of it all. Forget blackleg stands and gambling hells. He should focus on bottling whatever ran through the earl's extraordinary head to sell as a cure for nerves, fear, and melancholia.

"I recall that during the journey here, my lord," Tommy butted in, "which, frankly, seems months ago now, I requested you refrain from speaking."

"*Thirdly*—" the earl continued in a smooth and abnormally loud tone. "—and this is utterly unrelated to Mr Angel, you understand. *Thirdly*, I can't help having a peculiar penchant for the naked fear in a fellow's eyes as he realises a crazed aristocrat is about to slash through his dear old ma's jugular!"

In a flash, Rossingley lunged and wrapped his arm around Ma Duggan's scrawny neck. A switchblade appeared in his elegant hand, a horribly familiar switchblade generally found skulking behind a potted plant. He jammed it up against her throat. The woman let out a dry gasp of shock.

"I've taken the liberty of hurrying things along, Tommy," the earl explained, sounding as if he was apologising for rushing an afternoon pot of tea before it had properly stewed. "The company here isn't to my liking. And my dear Angel will be wondering where the devil I am if I don't reappear soon."

Good lord above. Blowing out an exasperated breath, Tommy shook his head. He stared at the blade hovering a hair's breadth from the woman's wildly beating pulse. "Which bit of 'stand behind me and stay silent' did you fail to grasp, Lordy?"

Rossingley beamed at him. "The entirety."

"I preferred you during your melancholic era."

With another grin, eliciting a short hiccupping squeal from Ma Duggan, Rossingley hitched the blade even closer, his arm winding tighter. "I daresay the lady of the house would agree with you, Tommy. If she could speak." He raised his voice again. "And she would be able to—she would be able to speak freely if I didn't have your lethal switchblade against her throat and a thirst to change the colour of this hideous carpet from green to red."

"You're bluffing," she wheezed, eyes bulging with terror. "You wouldn't dare."

The knife hitched higher, and as the flattened blade flashed, a thin trickle of blood oozed from the tip.

"Oops." Rossingley made a sound very much like a giggle. "Shall I do that again? Or maybe half an inch to the left this time?"

The door crashed wide. A white-faced Dickie Duggan charged through it, skidding to a halt at the sight of his mother in Rossingley's grip.

"Get your filthy hands off her!"

"If it's all the same to you, I shall remain as I am. We're having such a lovely cuddle, aren't we, Mrs Duggan?" Rossingley tutted. "Dear, oh dear, Dickie. Someone's been a naughty boy."

"Tommy," Dickie beseeched, his ashen features slack and wobbling. "Tell this madman to stop."

Tommy shook his head. He hadn't clapped eyes on Dickie for years, and suffice to say, the man's youthful good looks had gone the way of the original White Hart. Judging by his greyish complexion, he was no stranger to the laudanum bottle either. Tommy could have felled him with one blow, never mind a switchblade.

Wrapped around Dickie's mother like a lover, Rossingley grinned wolfishly. If Dickie resembled a grubby ageing cherub, the earl was the devil incarnate, packaged as a daydream.

"Listening at doors, sir, is a fruitful pastime," Rossingley drawled. "One I'm quite partial to myself. However, a word of warning. One will eventually overhear what one deserves." He twisted the knife a little harder, piercing the soft flesh in a fresh spot. Ma Duggan looked on the verge of a dead faint. "Now, if you would be so kind, sir, I'd like you to explain why on God's green earth you thought you might get away with blackmailing Tommy."

"I don't know what you're talking about. Let her go."

"I told you not to drag Tommy into this," Ma Duggan squawked. "I knew no good would come of sending that bloody note!"

Rossingley sighed, long and drawn out as though suddenly weary of the whole thing. His grip slackened a fraction. "Dickie, poppet," he said. "May I call you Dickie? Or are you a Richard?" He cocked his head. "No, I don't think you are. Another piece of advice, Dickie, and then I shall leave you at the mercy of maternal wrath. A mother's wisdom may not be what you *want* to hear, but is, more often than not, what a son needs to hear."

And with that, he pushed Ma Duggan and her idiot son aside and, towing Tommy in his wake, sauntered from the room.

Chapter Twelve

A WEEK DRAGGED by, and no blackmail request was forthcoming. An endless seven days passed, during which Benedict physically resembled the fourteenth Duke of Ashington and even managed to act in a manner befitting the fourteenth Duke of Ashington. In that regard, he was fortunate: his reputation for being a reserved, dreary sort of fellow set the expectations of others comfortingly low. As long as he laboured over his daily ducal affairs, sequestered in his second study, and showed an interest in his thoroughbreds, then he could probably declare a yearning desire to train as a hosier, open a shop on New Bond Street, and no one would pay heed.

When, following his recent day out at Tattersall's, Francis expressed an interest in cheering on Ganymede racing in the Ashington colours at Epsom, Benedict agreed to tag along. Anything to divert from the draining, frozen panic constricting his lungs.

The expedition turned out to be well worth the effort. Proving that some good could be unearthed during even the worst of times, Ganymede cantered home in first place, Ashington black silks billowing out at least four lengths ahead of the rest. And Francis's genial smile always made Benedict's world a little less cold.

He comforted himself with those twin small mercies as his victorious horse was washed and rubbed down before being brought to where Benedict loitered inside the winner's enclosure, awaiting the dreaded congratulations of all and sundry. As if he'd ridden the thing himself, as if his victory had nothing at all to do with having inherited more blunt than anyone else to throw at his damned hobby. He expressed as much to Francis after smiling at so many people his jaw ached.

"Oh, shush," admonished his brother. "Plenty of rich folks about here boast stables at least as fine as yours." He waved happily to a small group of well-wishers, nudging Benedict to do the same. "You are too modest regarding your accomplishments." He gave his brother a sidelong glance. "Too modest about most things, come to that."

"I have much to be modest about," Benedict muttered, and he busied himself with an invisible knot in Ganymede's sleek mane. If he involved himself in activity, then perhaps Ganymede's army of devotees might keep their distance. It wasn't that Benedict didn't *like* people; it was more a question of people not especially warming to him and him never knowing what to say to fill an awkward silence.

Francis did not share his problem, waving again, like a bloody daisy in the breeze, at another group. One of his chums beckoned him across. His brother really was awfully popular, blessed with Benedict's portion of merry disposition as well as his own. As they petted Ganymede, side by side, Benedict felt increasingly akin to a raincloud shadowing the sun. He jerked his head in the direction of Francis's friends.

"Go and join them," he said. "Have some fun. The next race starts in twenty minutes. Place a wager on that promising three-year-old roan for me. The clay soil is perfect for him."

Francis trotted off, his and his friends' raucous laughter becoming fainter the farther they wandered from the winner's enclosure. Blessedly alone, Benedict whispered soothing gibberish in his horse's ear. He pondered how long he could get away with seeming to be occupied before someone was brave enough to engage him in conversation.

Tranquil as autumn leaves, Ganymede nosed at a pile of hay. Only half an hour earlier, he'd eaten up the two-mile steeplechase faster than a blizzard descending. Hard to believe looking at him now. No longer blowing and his legs wrapped in cooling poultices, the horse was oblivious to his admirers gathered in the parade ring. Briefly, Benedict rested his cheek against the creature's damp shoulder, promised him he was his special pomegranate (amongst other similar nonsense), then listened to his heartbeat, now slowed to a placid *lub dub*.

"My accounts ledger tends to grumble when the favourite gallops to victory," said a voice. An ordinary voice, though its timbre had burned a hole in Benedict's mind and melted his soul for nigh on a decade. "Your Grace's recent run of losses has had my blacklegs cheering and me wondering if my man Sidney miscalculated the odds. But now, alas, normal service has resumed."

Oh lord. Lost in his own misery, Benedict hadn't heard Tommy approach, and now he was here and standing awfully close. Had he overheard Benedict reassure Ganymede that he was his sweetest iced apricot? His most treasured turtle dove? Benedict would die on the spot if he had.

"I'd begun to wonder if I'd lost my knack of selecting winners," Benedict blustered, trying to sound halfway jovial.

An inevitable hot flush crept around his collar, picking up speed as the recollection of his last encounter with Tommy reduced him to a limp crust. At the same time, he became aware of another heat, settling in a much lower portion of his body. He'd never seen Tommy out in the open, in broad daylight before. And without putting too fine a point on it, Benedict very much liked what he saw.

Tommy's lean, compact frame wore lighter colours well. The grey of his waistcoat, more of an unburnished silver, brought out his eyes. Sunshine, only averagely bright today, daubed the smooth skin of his face a rich clotted cream, leading Benedict to imagine how it might pinken under hot June skies. And how even paler bits of him might glow. Hidden by his coat, an unmentionable portion of Benedict's midriff gave a hopeful twitch.

Oh God, he really was very bad at being normal.

"I assure you, you haven't," answered Tommy. A little mysteriously, if Benedict was being honest. And if he were even more honest, he'd totally lost the thread of the conversation because, as Tommy adjusted his hat, a lick of fair hair obtusely sticking up as all the others lay sleek and flat, caught his eye and held it.

Darting his gaze over Tommy's shoulder, Benedict checked they were still alone and lowered his voice.

"Look, I…I really should apologise once more for intruding upon you in your rooms the other evening. I made a total and utter cake of myself. I spoke out of turn on a number of matters. I harped on about the past and my heart and…and some absolute ridiculous nonsense, and that's the truth of it. Rubbish that no man except his valet ever deserves to hear. And…and hurling those appalling accusations at you was absurd and unforgiveable. To even contemplate for a second that you would be behind—"

"I know who sent you the list, your Grace."

"You do?"

"I do." Tommy's watchful expression was grave.

"How…how did you find out? And more pertinently, why?"

"Because someone attempted to blackmail me in regard to the same matter."

Oh lord, this was worsening by the second. "They…what? Who?"

Tommy issued a long, drawn-out sigh. "Dickie Duggan, the son of the landlady who ran the White Hart. I received a list, too, a week after you. Except with the additional request for a sum of five hundred pounds in exchange for silence."

"But—" Benedict frowned, nonplussed. "His own name is on the list, isn't it?"

"It is," Tommy agreed. "Though he's pickled himself in such vast quantities of gin, watered down with laudanum, he probably didn't even notice. He was never the sharpest of creatures. But he was present the night of the raid, and he knows who else was there too."

"Oh." In a small way, Benedict was relieved. An opium-soaked degenerate was a manageable, if not unpredictable, foe.

"He became greedy," Tommy continued. "Not content with receiving a substantial sum from your putative blackmailer in exchange for your name, he erroneously believed he could make a few extra sous by blackmailing me too." He cleared his throat. "Following a…concise exchange of opinions, it's a moment of avarice he now deeply regrets."

Benedict scratched his head, feeling rather like an unsharp creature himself. "You said *my* blackmailer? Are you saying someone else is involved?"

"Yes, I'm afraid our blackmailers are not one and the same."

Still frowning, Benedict pinched the bridge of his nose. "I'm befogged. There are now two of them out there?"

"No," corrected Tommy, grimacing. "Not any longer. My own particular problem has been swiftly dispensed with."

"You have paid up?" Benedict's belly churned with alarm. He considered himself to have led a sheltered existence thus far, but even he knew blackmailers inevitably returned for second helpings.

Tommy shook his head. "Not at all, though a small amount of coin did exchange hands for information regarding the individual behind all this damned chicanery. Simply put, the involvement of my former employer and her son was not too difficult to guess. Who else could it have been? So Rossingley and I paid them a visit."

"*Rossingley?*" Benedict felt more at sixes and sevens by the minute. "What…what the devil's he got to do with it?"

"Peripherally?" said Tommy. "Everything." He paused before adding in a rather irritating, enigmatic fashion, "And yet nothing."

He threw Benedict the merest glimpse of a smile, and despite his topsy-turvy head, Benedict's heart lurched. "Though I advise you keep the earl away from your pointy silverware, Your Grace. For an idle pleasure-seeker, he possesses a frightening talent with a switchblade."

Registering Benedict's horrified expression, Tommy qualified. "The earl didn't slice the swine's mother's neck, per se, but simply *worried* it a little. Sufficient for Ma Duggan and her son not to be bothersome in the future."

"Oh." Now Benedict was even more perplexed. He barked a laugh, sounding a tad hysterical even to his own ears. "Perhaps I should ask him to perform the same service with my persecutor."

"Mm." Tommy's mouth pressed in a thin line again. Benedict had been fixating on that mouth, the lips neither too plump nor too thin but ever so shapely, once the golden lick of hair was safely back under Tommy's hat.

"When I reveal your persecutor's identity, you may not wish for that, Your Grace."

"I wish the bastard was food for the worms," cried Benedict. "And, I beg you, don't stand on ceremony with this *Your Grace* business. I can't abide it. I'm not worthy, especially as far as you're concerned. Ashington or…or Benedict when we are alone is perfectly adequate."

Colour suffused his cheeks once more. *When we're alone?* He might as well have laid down his heart's deepest desires and delivered them to Tommy in the form of a list himself.

"Your tormentor is Lord Lyndon Fitzsimmons," Tommy announced bluntly. "Your brother."

A wave of horror swept through Benedict. "L-Lyndon?"

"Yes."

Time stood still as Benedict stared at Tommy with dismay. He swayed against Ganymede, clutching at the horse's bridle as if he might tumble to the ground otherwise. The enclosure suddenly felt suffocating, as if all the air had been sucked out of it. "Are you sure?"

Tommy gave a bleak nod. "I'm afraid I am."

Of course, he was sure. One didn't toss around vicious accusations against a duke's twin brother without a modicum of truth stacked up behind them. Sagging like a banked fish, Benedict clawed a deep breath. "Oh, lord."

"Your Gr — Ashington," began Tommy. "People will think you are ill. Turn towards Ganymede as though we are discussing his form." Tommy stroked a hand along the horse's back as if admiring his fine lines. "In fact, let me quiz you about him. You are distressed. People will notice. Tongues will wag."

"I..." Burying his forehead against Ganymede's hot shoulder, Benedict breathed in his dark, rooty scent. That Lyndon, his own dear, tormented brother, would attack him this way. "Does it bring you pleasure telling me this, Tommy? Is that why you have come? To watch me break?"

Benedict hung on to the bridle with all his might. What he would give right now to gallop away. To hoist himself atop Ganymede, grab the reins, and hurtle off, never to return. Bloody Lyndon. Bloody, bloody, *bloody* Lyndon.

"Absolutely not. If he wasn't your kin, I would put a switchblade to his throat myself." Tommy's cool tones sliced through his misery. "Now, please, people are watching."

A tearing, guttural sound issued from Benedict's throat. "Your pity is worse than your spite. So what if I am watched as I crumble? Why wait for Lyndon to choose a time? Why not make a spectacle of myself here and now and be done with it?"

As Benedict's voice rose, Ganymede pawed restlessly at the ground.

"Because…because I will not allow it, damn you," Tommy hissed. "That is why."

Sensing his master's distress, the horse shifted again and then, with a fretful whinny, tossed his head back. Tommy's steadying hand shot out at the same time as Benedict's, and for a fleeting instant, their fingers came together.

"My apologies, Your Grace." As if burned, Tommy's hand snatched away. His heated gaze landed anywhere but on Benedict's. "I should have broken this news in a less public arena. I was not thinking."

Benedict drew in a deep, silent breath before letting it out slowly. And then another. "The sooner I discovered the truth, the better. Let us talk of normal things — horseflesh, anything — until I am more recovered from this shock."

With his arms wrapped around himself, hands safely tucked away, Tommy retreated a step. "Rossingley tells me you ride even better than he," he began awkwardly. "I confess, I find it hard to believe. I've accompanied him many a time on horseback. With that great black stallion of his between his legs, the man gallops like the wind."

"Uh. Yes." Once more, Benedict leaned into his horse for support. Coming so soon after the searing warmth of Tommy's hand over his and the stunning blow of his brother's perfidy, a visual of Rossingley's spread legs, breeches pulled tight over his slender thighs, proved a step too far. Frankly, Benedict owed himself congratulations on still being vertical. His own skin, he was sure, radiated even hotter than that of his damp horse.

A group of ladies strolled close by, and he was aware of Tommy doffing his hat in polite acknowledgment. Their bubbly, messy chatter pierced Benedict's light-headedness, bringing him back to the present.

"I was observing that Rossingley is a superb horseman," prompted Tommy. "One of the finest. But I have learned that you best even him."

The ladies were near enough to overhear, and Tommy's eyes urged Benedict to formulate a sensible rejoinder. He racked his brains.

"I raced Nimbus to victory in both the Derby Stakes and the 2000 Guineas in the same year," he eventually croaked. "Rossingley came second by a nose on each occasion."

"So, it is true." Tommy's delectable mouth flashed the briefest of taut smiles. "I expected as much as the earl is not one for false modesty. You do not race any longer?"

"I have too many demands on my time." *None of them pleasant.*

"But you were a famous winner," Tommy persevered. The ladies moved away, their shrill chatter fading into the distance. "You also had successes in the St Leger."

"Multiple times over. I..." Inhaling deeply, feeling a little more like himself again, Benedict dared turn back towards Tommy, giving him a sheepish look. "Perhaps the time was nigh to give others a chance at glory. And Nimbus was approaching his ninth year, old for a racehorse. You swear it is true? That Lyndon is behind all this?"

"As true as I'm standing here, Your Grace."

Enjoying the fuss being made of him, Ganymede nosed at Tommy's chest, and he stretched out a cautious hand, letting the horse nuzzle.

"He is often skittish with strangers," said Benedict, picking out the only coherent thought jostling his head. "He must have taken a liking to you."

Tommy's skin pinked at the compliment; the colour everything Benedict hoped it would be. Ganymede had discerning taste.

"I was much younger when I rode him to all those wins." Benedict congratulated himself on formulating such a lucid statement. "And freer."

"Yes." Now it was Tommy who appeared to be struggling to speak. "We have both grown older since."

In silent conversation, the two men regarded each other as they contemplated the past. A conversation neither dared speak out loud. *But if not now, when?* Benedict had so much to say to this man. All the things he'd wanted to tell Tommy all those years ago had never left his mind. Even now, amid all his other woes, they spun in his head like an incantation. Another opportunity might never present itself. Thanks to Lyndon, Benedict would soon be living an ignoble existence on a draughty estate far, far from London. For all eternity. Why waste this precious moment discussing a damned horse?

Resolutely, he moistened his dry lips. "Nimbus and I both enjoyed the heady glory of...of our youth." Gathering courage, he bravely plunged on. "And our youth was truly glorious, once, was it not, Mr L'Esquire?"

"Please…I…yes."

Tommy rushed his gaze away and up towards the sky, desperately searching it, as if seeking out and counting every single one of the thin, wispy clouds. In the natural daylight, his feral eyes shone a deep blue, like wildflowers. Back in the simple, dim bedchamber of their past, Benedict fancied they had taken more of a duller, slate-grey tinge. And yet still, he'd been captivated.

Behind them, a groom shouted lustily to another, and an iron gate clanged. Tension crackled in the air, and when Tommy levelled with Benedict again, his voice was soft and low, almost a whisper.

"I have requested before, Your Grace, that you refrain from speaking to me this way. It is too…too much."

"And I have requested that you do not refer to me as Your Grace." Benedict fondled Ganymede's ears. "But it is fair enough. We shall limit our discussion to a dear creature, my dearest *male companion*, whom, more than a decade ago, I loved so very greatly. Above all others."

"Loved?" The word appeared to catch Tommy off guard.

"Yes."

Loved. As if what they had could be consecrated to the past, when it accompanied Benedict in all his endeavours still. When it lived forever in his heart. "I have never loved like it since. Would you…do you care to hear about it?"

"I…I yes, if I must. Though I fear that this current excellent winning horse of yours is the only thing holding both of us up."

An older man and a woman sauntered by, pausing to

admire his champion. Benedict dragged his gaze away from Tommy and back to Ganymede.

He began softly. "I was but a stripling myself, of course. Very young and foolish, I admit, but I knew my own heart. And my love for such a fine creature. So fine in every way. I wrote poetry for him. *The earth sings when I touch him. When my body covers his, I soar.* Did I ever tell of that, Tommy?"

"Don't...don't...you cannot..." Tommy's lips parted, but nothing came out. Abruptly, he turned to face Ganymede.

Another strolling couple joined the first. One of the ladies pointed to Ganymede's wrapped legs, posing an enquiring question to the other. Clearing his throat, Tommy tried once more.

"This...this fine creature you loved. Was he fair? Or was he dark, like Rossingley's beloved Twilight?"

"He was fair." A lock of Benedict's hair fell across his forehead. "Twilight is a fine and bold beast, to be sure, but my love was even more beautiful than that. He was the colour of fresh hay, light of limb, and golden-hued. And when I stroked him, the fiery sun of a late August afternoon burned under my fingertips."

A light sheen of moisture covered Tommy's brow. "You have not had other c-creatures so fine since?"

"Not even close. Every other is a mere beast by comparison. When my first love spoke, he called me home."

The garrulous groom behind them came closer, rattling a metal bucket. The sharp clinking snapped them both out of it.

Tommy took a pace back, checking his fob watch, fussing with his hat. "Please excuse me, Your—Ashington. But I must away. The next race is due presently."

Chapter Thirteen

DAYS LATER, TOMMY still reeled from the duke's — Ashington's — forthrightness. Like lumps of steak swallowed before chewing, his quixotic (did that word even fit?) avowals lodged in Tommy's chest, refusing to budge. Starry-eyed declarations when one was but a mere pup were one thing, but now? The man tested the very fabric of Tommy's existence. Never mind the paper-thin wall between love and hate, Tommy was no longer sure it had ever been built.

Fortunately, he could always rely on Sidney to drag him away from lofty notions of love. His friend lumbered up to the mezzanine above the gaming room, where Tommy leaned his elbows on the railing, looking down on his clientele. Though reluctant to admit it, he half hoped the Duke of Ashington might put in an appearance, which wasn't entirely a proper emotion pertaining to a man he'd ostensibly hated these past ten or so years. Lord

Francis and his friends were in their usual corner; Lord Lyndon hadn't been seen for a while.

"We've trouble brewing," Sidney announced, "with the horses coming out of the Duke of Ashington's stables."

"Yes?" Tommy didn't relish a conversation in which the duke's name cropped up. It interfered with his weak plan to push the man from his mind altogether.

"There's summat fishy about his recent run of poor form." Producing a familiar thick ledger, for the next couple of minutes Sidney befuddled Tommy with columns of figures, which, he summarised, didn't quite add up.

"You think someone is nobbling the duke's horses?" Tommy enquired, coming straight to the point.

When it came to calculating the likelihood of racegoers wagering on a particular race outcome then stacking the odds in favour of Squire's blacklegs, there was no better mathematician in the trade than Sidney. A man of few words and even fewer social graces, when he wasn't herding foxed noblemen in and out of Tommy's premises, he could be found poring over the form books. Where Tommy saw his accounts and rows of numbers as a necessary evil to be endured, Sidney viewed them as the poetry of logic.

Sidney shrugged. "Or Ashington's behind it himself, to fool the punters. Saving for a day when a horse has a lighter weight to carry and the money is down." Pursing his lips, he tapped his quill against his jottings. "Can't see it meself. The man's rolling in gold."

"Quite."

A door opened below, and Tommy quashed the flutter of

anticipation behind his ribcage when Mickey led a portly older gentleman over to his waiting friends. "But you think it's more than simply a run of bad luck."

"My gut tells me it's looking that way."

Tommy sighed. Sidney's entrails tended to be a reliable barometer. "Could his trainer be behind it? Making coin on the side?"

Head grooms had a dozen tricks to prevent a horse from winning. Fitting its shoes too tight, for instance. Giving it a belly-filling bucket of water five minutes before the starting pistol. Running it on firm ground when it needed soft, on a left-hand track when it preferred the right.

"Nah." Sidney shook his big head. "Joe Jonas has been at Ashington's since he was a nipper. His dad ran the stables before him. No one who's worked there ever has a bad word to say about either. Nor about the duke; he's a fair employer by all accounts."

Tommy cast his mind back to Ganymede's confident romp to victory in the steeplechase the week before. Thanks to his heart-stopping tête-à-tête afterwards, he'd had the opportunity to study the creature up close. The thoroughbred was perfection, from every angle. As was his blasted owner. Of course, Ashington was a fair employer; yet another thing making him impossible to dislike. In addition to the small fact that twice now he had confessed to Tommy how much he'd loved him. And how he'd never loved another since, a declaration bothering Tommy much more than it should. Mostly because it held a looking glass up to his own wretched heart.

Studying the punts below (all much plainer than the duke) amusing themselves in the gaming room, Tommy steered his thoughts back to the issue at hand. "It's not every race though, is it? Is there a pattern?"

"Not one I can see." Sidney grimaced, showing the gap where a front tooth was missing, another consequence of his incarceration in Newgate. "So, I reckon no. But if you want my advice, Squire's should suspend giving odds on races the duke's got favourites running in until it's settled down."

"Mmm." A strategy guaranteed to get tongues twitching, though it served to protect Tommy's assets. "Do you know anyone in his employ at the stables? Excepting Jonas?"

Sidney threw him a knowing look. "Fancy sniffing around, do you?"

"Perhaps," Tommy admitted.

"Mebbe I'll have a chat with one of the lads."

The second time the door below opened, the flutters simmering behind Tommy's rib cage took flight. Led by Mickey again, the duke himself entered, a slight hesitation in his step. As his midnight eyes anxiously skirted the tables until they settled on Francis, Sidney let out a low whistle.

"Very tasty. He's like a nice knob of Stilton, Tommy." He gave his boss a nudge. "He gets better with age."

He returned Tommy's incredulous look with a smug smile. "What? Yer didn't think you'd get away with it, did yer?"

"I'd say I don't know to whom you're referring, you blasted oaf," Tommy growled. Wearily, he shook his head. "But we both know I'd be lying." His own lips curved into a smile as the duke ran a hand through his thick dark locks, pushing a clump away from his forehead. "And I happen to agree with you."

Half of him willed the duke to tilt his gaze skywards; the

remainder was happy to bask in the shade all evening, drinking him in. Ashington commanded notice despite himself—the curse of a dukedom—even if his dull but perfectly tailored attire seemed chosen to meld seamlessly with the shadows. And though he shrank away from attention, the play of flickering lamplight only served to accentuate his brooding dark looks.

"When did you realise who he was?" Tommy tracked the duke as his brother's chums leaped to their feet to greet him. Knowing Sidney, he had a feeling he already knew the answer.

"As soon as he stepped through the door the first time. Even with all his finery. Your lordling wasn't the sort of madge you forget that easily."

Ever, thought Tommy glumly.

"Yer going to go down and say 'allo, then? Or are you going to just stare at 'im all night with your mouth lolling open? Yer like a moonstruck country lass after one sniff of the fruit punch."

"If I wanted your smart commentary, Sidney, I'd ask you for it."

His friend snorted. "Well, somebody's got to put you straight. And if I've learned anything from all those years servicing men in the upstairs room at the Hart, it's that you can't suck a prick when yer gob's twenty foot away from it."

*

MUCH TO TOMMY'S chagrin, Sidney shadowed him into the gaming room, most likely to prevent a swerve into his study at the last moment. Tommy didn't make for the duke's party immediately, pausing to exchange pleasantries with Mr Bannister and then agreeing with the Earl of Horton and a chum on the predicted state of the turf at Newmarket's coming Saturday meet. Invariably, however, his glance returned to Ashington, to the errant lock of hair falling over his forehead and catching the candlelight, to his long legs comfortably stretched out before him, to the large square hand resting on a thigh, to the heavy gold signet ring circling his smallest finger.

"Over you go, then," murmured Sidney in Tommy's ear. "Yer dribbling on the carpet."

"Sidney?" Tommy nodded a greeting to another regular. "If that cluster of putrid cankers spreading along your prick don't kill you first, I shall do it myself. Except even more slowly. Consider this a warning."

With Sidney's rumbling laugh ringing in his ears, Tommy made his way towards the duke, feeling like a damned debutante skirting the fringes of her first ball.

"Your Grace," he said, with a slight bow. "Thank you for joining us this evening."

Two glasses of brandy had brought an attractive flush to Ashington's cheeks. "Mr L'Esquire. How do you do."

At the duke's obvious pleasure, Tommy experienced a sweet kick, low in his belly. Not too obvious, he hoped. Fortunately, Ashington was angled away from Lord Francis and his pals, now happily arguing over whether to open a game of loo or play another hand of baccarat.

"You have stayed away," Tommy stated. Though his intonation suggested he was clarifying, he could swear on a heaped stack of bibles and every mother's grave north of the Thames that this absolutely was the case.

"I...I, yes. I have been reluctant to intrude on your

establishment lest it inconvenience you," the duke admitted. "As a-a peer of high rank, I recognise it would be difficult for you to turn me away. I would dislike placing you in that awkward position."

He brushed his hair from his high, pale forehead. An image tumbled through Tommy's mind of his own hand sweeping it away, of placing his lips against the little crease where Ashington's brows frequently pinched into a worried frown.

"It is no inconvenience," he managed, guiding his thoughts back to where they needed to be. "I am rarely in the gaming rooms myself."

"Oh."

A pause stretched between them. Why did every conversation Tommy exchanged with this man feel like the push and pull of a dance? One which both were reluctant to lead? And why did he persist with this stiff, cold politesse when so many more pertinent questions filled his mind? Such as, when had the duke become so cautious? So scared of his own shadow? And why? And how awful timidity must feel, thrust into in such an august position.

"Your Grace," Tommy began in a low voice, determined to confront the chasm yet again opening up between them. "You and I. I think it best that—"

Raised voices and a commotion at the door claimed his attention. Ashington jerked around at the fuss, then swore. From the stiffening of the man's shoulders and the tightening of his fingers around his brandy balloon, Tommy didn't need to turn to know who the newcomer must be. He didn't need to hear the imperious, if not a little slurred, dismissal of Tommy's footman, nor the raucous greeting of a fellow nob. Nor the shattering of crystal as his latest unruly guest staggered against a table.

"Clumsy fool," Lord Lyndon Fitzsimmons barked at a cowering Mickey. He cast his bleary gaze around the room until landing on his twin brother.

"Oh, God." The duke cringed. "He's…what if he…"

"My thoughts exactly," Tommy murmured. "Though in this foxed state, I doubt anybody would believe a word of it."

"That is small consolation, sir. Since your warning, I have dreaded this encounter. I have barely left my house. And now I'm petrified." The duke bit his lip, shaking his head ashamedly. "I am a coward of the poorest rank, am I not?"

"Some might say wise."

Another glass splintered on the floor, deliberately this time, it seemed.

"Your brother is a man of few morals, and, I fear, even fewer social graces."

"Whoopsie!" Lyndon trilled, pleased with himself. Young Mickey had fled, so he clicked his fingers at Sidney, skulking by the window and looking murderous. "Hey, you! Man! Job for you. Over here."

"Please excuse me a moment, Your Grace. I may have to intervene." Tommy gritted his teeth. "Sidney does not care to be summoned like a street urchin, and he's rather handy with his fists. A year in Newgate will do that to a man."

Never pick a fight with a Rom, a redhead, or an Irish was Tommy's motto. And growing up with a father boasting the blood of all three, it had served him well. Pale-skinned, black-eyed, and hot-minded, Sidney swore blue he'd never started a brawl, yet invariably managed to be the last man standing. And despite being drunk as a wheelbarrow, Lord Lyndon Fitzsimmons had the same half-crazed look in his eyes that Tommy recognised far too well. A look only matched by the one in Sidney's, goading, tempting some-one—anyone—to give him the smallest excuse for fisticuffs.

"Lyndon." Ever the peacemaker, Lord Francis weaved through the tables towards his brother. "Jolly nice to see you."

Perhaps, like Tommy, Francis had spotted Sidney flexing his meaty fingers. More likely, he'd recognised Lord Lyndon was spoiling for a fight and had picked the wrong opponent. "Do join us over here, nearer to the fire. Have a seat, take the weight off your feet. Thrash us at loo."

"No." Lord Lyndon folded his arms. "I'm going to stay here and supervise this brute as he picks up every last shard of shat-tered glass."

"Good evening to you, my lord." Smoothly, Tommy slid be-tween Sidney and the drunk peer. The duke stood a more cautious pace behind him. "May I lead you to Lord Francis's table?"

"No," Lord Lyndon repeated like a spoiled, petulant child. "I'm perfectly fine here." Turning his attention to the duke, he performed a mocking bow, nearly toppling in the process. "Your Grace. It's…been a while."

"Lyndon," managed Ashington hoarsely, then stiffened as Lyndon lay his hand on his arm.

Tommy had an insane urge to swat it away. Side by side, their similarity to each other was unmistakeable. Except, as with roast chicken carved and split into two, one portion contained the breast and thigh meat, the other the scrawny wings and parson's nose.

"How funny, Your Grace," Lord Lyndon continued, his snide tone implying nothing of the sort. "I was only chinwagging about you the other day. With some new acquaintances, south of the river." He leaned closer. "Not *quality*, of course." Jerking his chin towards Sidney, he added, "More like this chap. The sort of folks who hold dinner knives like quills."

He flicked an imaginary mote of dust from the duke's pristine topcoat before stroking along the sleeve. "You of all people, Your Grace, should know how it is when one ventures south of the river. A grim hike but *very* entertaining and informative, nonetheless."

Tommy's stomach clenched. There was something quite odious about Lord Lyndon's manner. How he toyed with his brother, like a bored tomcat batting around a half-dead sparrow. His proprietorial hold on his twin's arm jarred even more. Tommy hadn't ever especially warmed to the man. Now he vehemently despised him.

Caught between his two older brothers, Lord Francis's features held a half-amused, half-puzzled expression. Thankfully, Sidney had taken a step back, but not so far that he couldn't plant the sneering lord a facer or two. By God, Tommy was sorely tempted to do it himself. He didn't dare look at the duke, though he sensed his breath quicken.

"May I offer you some refreshment, my lord?" Tommy persisted. "Perhaps a strong coffee might be to your taste?"

"Hmm." Lord Lyndon studied the assembled group, pretending to contemplate. "No, thank you. Though it's a rum thing, *taste*, isn't it? For instance, how we all differ in our tastes. And our need to assuage it from time to time. Our *bodily* need for refreshment. Isn't that right, Your Grace?"

"I'm afraid I don't follow," answered the duke stiffly. "However, Mr L'Esquire has suggested you—"

"I, for example, Your Grace, am one of the many gentlemen whose preferred *taste*, when the urge is upon them, is to seek horizontal *refreshment* by indulging in a stroll down Petticoat Lane. Whilst others, sadly, can only quench their quite peculiar thirsts with nothing more than—"

With one sharp glance from Tommy, it was all over. Before Lord Lyndon could fathom which way was up, Sidney had grabbed him by the scruff of the neck, bungled him through the salon door, and dragged him kicking and screaming along the narrow corridor.

It happened so swiftly Tommy wagered the man disappeared from the gaming room before most of the patrons even registered the scuffle at all. Lord Lyndon wasn't the first to be ejected for bawdiness, and he wouldn't be the last. But he was the first Tommy had wanted to spear with a rusty switchblade.

Tommy, the duke, and Francis hurried after to find Sidney dangling Lord Lyndon over a short flight of stone steps at the rear of the property. Much like he was about to empty a chamber pot full of piss down them.

"Hey! Get your filthy mitts off me! At once! I demand it!"

Tommy peered down at him coldly. "Sidney will keep a hold on your collar until he's tossed you into the street. This is my club, whereby we obey my rules. My *lord*," he tagged on mockingly.

At Tommy's nod, Sidney firmly encouraged the man, yelling blue murder, down Squire's back steps.

"You bleeding thug!" Lord Lyndon's arse smacked every stone. "Ow! I box, I'll have you know!"

"I daresay you do." Sidney brushed his hands together before straightening his neckcloth. "Love a bit of boxing myself, so I do. Gentlemen's boxing clubs are wonderful at keeping a man trim and teaching him how to win a fair fight."

Lord Lyndon pulled himself up from the kerb, making a sly grab for Sidney's ankle. He received a smart kick in the face for his efforts.

Blithely, Sidney carried on. "But I learned to fight in the back privy at Newgate, not at one of yer fancy clubs. And the back privy at Newgate teaches a man how to wrestle like a pig." He tidied his waistcoat. "And pigs like to fight dirty. So yer pretty boxing fists will be no help whatsoever 'ere. My *lord*."

A great deal more dishevelled than when he first arrived, Lord Lyndon stared dazedly up from where he sat, his fine breeches covered in street filth.

"Oh, and if anyone happens to enquire, my lord," Tommy informed him before turning to leave, "His Grace, Lord Francis Fitzsimmons and, indeed, several other gentlemen of the *ton* will bear witness to the fact that you were already half sprung when you arrived this evening. And a tad bad-tempered, to boot. It is not a huge stretch of the imagination to believe that you tripped and fell against a newel post on your way out."

He turned back to where Sidney rubbed his knuckles, the duke and Lord Francis both staring at Lord Lyndon with gaping mouths. "What say you, Lord Francis?"

An agog Lord Francis eyed Sidney as if afraid he'd be next. "I'd...I'd say it's a damned awkward place to have a newel post, sir. Anybody could have barged into it."

"Quite. I couldn't have phrased things better, myself, my lord."

Tommy turned back to address a now staggering Lord Lyndon. "I'd also go so far as to suggest you nurse that shiner at home for a couple of weeks, Lord Fitzsimmons. We wouldn't want any contradictory stories spreading, now, would we?"

*

IN AWKWARD SILENCE, the group of men retraced their steps back to Squire's entry hall, whereupon Sidney melted away.

"Francis?" The duke sounded quite calm considering his hands were visibly shaking. "Why don't you return to your friends? Smooth the waters somewhat. Help yourself to another drink. I'll just...I'll just have a quick word with Mr L'Esquire, if I may."

Wordlessly, Tommy led him up the stairs. After closing the study door behind them, he turned the key in the lock, then marched straight to the drinks cabinet.

"Your quick thinking prevented a disaster, Tommy. I can't thank you enough."

"It has bought you a little time whilst his shiner goes down and his pride is restored. Nothing more."

The duke's hand was already outstretched. Both men knocked back a tot of brandy, and then Tommy took the duke's glass and refilled it. The oil lamps in the study had long run dry, so he lit a couple of candles, lending the room a dark, secretive air. The little moonlight not hidden behind clouds landed on the duke's pinched, white face.

"Lord Lyndon is clearly unaware that we have unearthed the identity of your list sender," Tommy said. "I suggest we keep it that way for as long as possible. We cannot best him until we discover precisely what it is that he wants and how to dispense with it."

Ashington swallowed, wiping the back of his hand against moist lips. "We?"

Tommy busied himself with the decanter. "Regardless of…of what has passed between us, I am a part of this."

A man less distraught than the duke would counter that Tommy's involvement had reached an end.

"Be that as it may, but I am at a loss to understand why you would offer your assistance further." Running his hands through his hair, the duke paced towards the window to look out over the street. "After everything I've done to you?"

Tommy regarded the duke, his strong frame hunched in on itself, his white knuckles fisted against the glass. He heard the abject fear in his voice, the bewilderment. The pain and the hopelessness. Damn the man for needing Tommy. Damn him for how Tommy had loved him. And how he should still hate him now for abandoning Tommy to his fate. The bald facts grated against one another like an out-of-tune violin.

Damn Tommy's own damned bleeding heart.

"That night at the Hart claimed enough innocent lives," he said at last. "God knows it is not deserving of another."

Tommy's head hesitated to reveal more; his blasted heart and tongue paid no attention. "Because you were young. And because I, too, have known terror. And I would not wish that desperate, bleak helplessness on anyone. Neither a duke nor a pauper nor my worst enemy." A choke rose in his throat. "And you...you are far from that."

"Youth is a pitiful excuse," the duke spat. "I will not hear it. It was the behaviour of a coward."

"No. It was the behaviour of a boy. A boy who, in the heat of the moment, saw his entire world crumbling." Tommy laughed harshly. "And he'd have not been wrong. A natural human instinct for self-preservation took over your conscious thought. You did not wish to be captured or die."

Wretchedly, the duke clawed at his hair. "Oh, Tommy," he answered barely above a whisper. "Would you believe me if I told you I have died a thousand times since?"

"Only a thousand?" Tommy's voice was brittle. "I wished you dead more often than that."

"You do not still?" The duke twisted from the window in surprise.

"I...no." Wearily, Tommy shook his head. "I grew into a man. I discovered that hatred is a heavy burden." *Especially when counterbalanced against love.* He permitted himself the smallest of smiles. "I channelled that fire into survival. Frankly, I did not have time for it."

The duke blew out a long breath. "Your capacity for forgiveness does you credit, sir."

Covering the floor of the small study in three long strides, he returned his empty goblet to Tommy. Uncertainly, they faced each other. Cheeks pasted with high colour, the duke was sadder, older, and wiser than the boy Tommy had once loved. But the boy was still there; a glimmer of him stared back at Tommy now, out of two dark eyes, bright with unshed tears. More than a glimmer.

"You don't hate me," the duke stated thickly. "Not any-more"

Tommy's tongue dried. He couldn't recall his heart ever pounding so fast. Very slowly, he shook his head. "No. I do not. But, by God, it is not for lack of trying."

The duke's cologne filled Tommy's senses—bergamot, woodsmoke, musk, the scent of a narrow bed in a tiny garret. He inhaled again, to be quite sure. He counted the lashes framing those oh-so-dark eyes, now hazy and restless. A small scar, only visible this close, marred the smooth bridge of the duke's nose.

And then a warm tongue pressed into Tommy's mouth. Tommy wasn't certain if he'd reached up or the duke had tipped his head down. But it mattered for naught because he knew that when he kissed this man back, when he melded his mouth to the other's, his mind would never hold a rational thought again.

The duke's shy reserve did not extend to his tongue. Tommy leaned into the heated urgency of the thing, into the wall of solid man kissing him as if the world would stop turning if he didn't. The duke groaned, a rumbling from deep in his belly, like a roll of thunder chasing a lightning bolt.

"You should be biting me, not kissing me after all I've done, Tommy."

"You mean like this?" On a husky laugh, Tommy nipped at his lower lip, pulling on the plump meat of it before deepening the kiss. Another needy sound escaped the duke's throat.

"How sweet you taste, as sweet as I remembered." The duke's breath hit Tommy's cheek in hot, shallow gusts. "Your lips…" In disbelief, he swiped a finger against his own wet ones. "They are like sugar. Nightly, I have dreamed of them."

Tommy shook his head. Perhaps his poetic raven was not so very changed after all. "I see you are still a foolish romantic."

"Yes!" The duke laughed hoarsely, sounding incredulous. "I do believe I am. Now the seal of the last decade has been broken, I'm only getting into my stride."

He plundered Tommy's mouth once more as if, in the space of a few minutes, he would make up the lost time. His arms came up, crushing Tommy against him, and for the sweetest of moments and on weakened knees, Tommy surrendered to it. To all of it.

"Lord Francis will be wondering what has become of you," he panted as Benedict finally put him down. "He'll be imagining you've followed your other brother down the back steps." Somewhere along the way, the duke's damp hair had separated from its neat part and now stuck up in delightful black clumps like ruffled feathers. "Or I've slain you with a blunt cudgel."

The duke's reply was a gentle smile. "You've slain me, it's true," he whispered. A fingertip stroked across Tommy's lips. "But with this deadly weapon."

He pressed a tender kiss against Tommy's temple. His hand cupped Tommy's face, and like an unloved damned alley cat, Tommy rubbed his cheek against the warm palm. His poor guarded heart had never stood a chance.

Long after the man bid him farewell and long after his footsteps disappeared down the corridor, the taste of the duke's kisses still lingered on Tommy's tongue. He still fancied they were there with him when he awoke the next day.

Chapter Fourteen

BENEDICT'S HEAD REELED the following morning. He'd hardly slept, the night broken into unrefreshing chunks of oblivion, interrupted by swirling, bolt-upright snatches of wakefulness. The disorienting sort of waking, whereupon one couldn't be sure what century one had woken in, never mind what time of night.

And then, after a few seconds, the horrors all came flooding back: Lyndon's slurred, artful insinuations, Tommy brutally cutting them off, Sidney's heavy boots and bold callused knuckles. A bloodied eyebrow and harsh stone steps. Francis's fascinated dismay and how Benedict wished his brother had witnessed none of it. Tommy again, his blanched features bristling with white-hot anger. His voice and its preternatural calm in the face of such abrupt violence. Tommy's wildflower eyes and how they softened when they looked upon Benedict. His sweet mouth. Oh God,

Tommy's lush, sweet mouth. If only that had been the cause of his wakefulness.

"What the dickens went on last night, Benedict?" demanded Francis, disturbing the much-needed peace of the breakfast room. "Mr L'Esquire seems a jolly nice chap and all that. And he runs a very fine establishment. But he can't have his…his henchman throwing punches at Lyndon simply because he's excessively trifled." He gave a humourless laugh. "He'd be black and blue by the end of the week if we allowed that. One minute, Lyndon's harmlessly bragging about his trips down Petticoat Lane, the next, he's flat out on the floor!"

Sipping his coffee, Benedict pretended to absorb his brother's righteous indignation. In truth, it washed through him. Because in the cold light of day, he recognised his nocturnal tossing and turning for what it was: Dread, coiled in his belly like a living thing, chewing his insides apart, engulfing him from the inside out. Cloaking him in a fog of fear that threatened to unman him every time he opened his mouth to speak.

Have any young colts caught your eye recently?

Lyndon knew. Somehow, his twin knew what he was; the bastard had always known. Even as a child, his brother had been a sly bugger, creeping around, listening at doors, earwigging conversations. Perhaps he'd followed Benedict one time he'd slipped off to Vere Street, or watched him fluster around men like Rossingley, or noted the paucity of his unenthusiastic dalliances with the fairer sex and put two and two together.

"I mean," continued Francis, waving a hunk of sausage around on the end of his fork. "There have been plenty of occasions when I'd have liked to plant Lyndon a few facers myself, but one can't go around… Goodness me! What on earth is the matter, Benedict? Your hand is shaking. Your cup hasn't stopped rattling against the saucer since I sat down, and now you're spilling coffee across the cloth. Are you quite all right?"

Hurriedly, Benedict put his cup down and grasped his napkin instead, tightening his fist around it until his knuckles shone. "No, I'm not. Not really. It's a pity Mr L'Esquire's man didn't give Lyndon much more than a fat shiner." Hot bile rose in his throat. "I'd say our brother should have had his neck wrung, but it would be too good for him."

"Steady on, old chap," answered Francis. "He was a tad bosky, that's all. We've all overcooked things once or twice, even you."

Benedict couldn't recall when, but he let it pass and jabbed with the napkin at the spilled coffee. Francis helped himself to another sausage. The rich, savoury scent wafted across the table, making Benedict nauseous.

Taking advantage of the lull in conversation, the first footman approached the duke to offer up a silver salver. Yet another bloody missive, a piece of foolscap folded over once, with *His Grace, Duke of Ashington*, handwritten in blood-red ink. Sweat broke out on the back of Benedict's neck as, gingerly, he accepted it.

"A love note from a secret admirer?" teased Francis.

If only. Barely breathing and trying to stay his fingers from trembling, Benedict shook it out. Then swallowed drily as last night's kisses came flooding back.

"Um…hardly." He moistened his lips. "It's from…ah…Mr L'Esquire. He's requesting an appointment with me at eleven. Says it's urgent."

"Good," answered Francis briskly. "His ears must have been burning. He needs to know he can't set his attack dog on folks willy-nilly, Benedict. And most certainly not on an Ashington! You might want to give that upstart a gentle reminder that Lyndon, for all his—let's just call them *peculiarities*—is the twin brother of a damned duke and, as such, should be granted a little respect." He stabbed at the sausage as if it needed killing first. "I'd be very happy to speak to him myself."

"I...ah...I'd very much rather you didn't."

Most days, Benedict admired and approved his brother's unwavering sense of justice and his pride in upholding the good Ashington name. But not today.

"Yes, yes. But listen, Benedict. I know you prefer to shy away from pointing out to folks what's what, and for a man in your esteemed position, that's highly commendable. But sometimes, one needs to assert one's authority before a situation gets out of hand. And you can rest assured, I'm perfectly capable of doing it in your stead if that's what's troubling—"

"Tom—Mr L'Esquire removed Lyndon from the gaming room in order to protect our good Ashington name. Not to dishonour it." Benedict's belly lurched as if someone had stabbed a knife through his entrails. "To protect me."

Francis responded with a half laugh. "Hate to disagree, old chap, but I rather think he didn't. Or were you also dipping rather too deep last night and missed the part where his man took a swipe at Lyndon and almost knocked his block off? And what do you mean by *protecting you*? What on God's green earth do you need protecting from?"

Under the table, Benedict's knee joined his hands in their

shaky dance. He swallowed the cooling remains of his coffee, feeling sick as a dog and aware of Francis's perplexed expression, bordering on alarm. Pulling air into his lungs, Benedict mopped his brow. What was it Rossingley had said? *They imagine your shame isolates you. A standard bullying tactic.*

"Johnson?" He addressed the footman standing at the door. "Would you be kind enough to leave us a moment, please."

Benedict could count on the fingers of one hand the number of times an Ashington had cleared a room of staff. Once, when his mother and father had a blazing row over a damned ugly painting of a spaniel (why that almost spiralled into the Second War of Jenkins' Ear, Benedict was still none the wiser eight years later). And, secondly, when Lyndon, in a fit of pique, lobbed a steak knife across the room, sending it whistling past their father's head by less than six inches to spear the wall behind him. To this day, the flock wallpaper and Lyndon's arse still bore deep scars.

Benedict stared down into his empty cup, searching for inspiration amongst the dregs until the door closed firmly behind Johnson. None was forthcoming.

"I'm afraid to inform you, Francis, that our brother has recently learned some truths about me. He's prepared to use them for personal gain and, in so doing, may downright ruin my reputation. And, by proxy, your chances of persuading Lord Ludham to allow you to marry his daughter."

He dared a glance up at Francis, whose boyish features bore a baffled expression that under any other circumstance would be amusing.

Benedict plunged on. "I can only assume this is an act of retaliation by Lyndon against our deceased father and his final wishes, which I follow out of a sense of duty and, broadly speaking, can see very little alternative to."

Again, he wiped his damp forehead, feeling utterly spent and dreading Francis's inevitable questions. Perhaps he wouldn't pose any. Stranger things had happened. Tommy kissing Benedict back, for instance.

Yet Francis did respond, of course, though his tone was much softer than the one he'd used to berate Tommy.

"Whatever Lyndon thinks he knows, he must be very much mistaken, Benedict. On every occasion, you behave impeccably. You put the rest of us to shame and have done so for the entirety of my existence. Whatever *ton* prattling Lyndon believes he has dug up, I would not believe a single word of it. Nor, I'd wager, would anyone else."

Benedict could weep. "I'm afraid, my dear Francis, you have me raised on a pedestal supported by feet of clay."

"Poppycock." Francis laid down his cutlery and leaned back in his chair. He folded his arms. "What is this thing, then? Tell me, that I may judge for myself."

They imagine your shame isolates you. A standard bullying tactic.

"If Lyndon had been allowed to complete his sentence yesterday evening, then…then he would have intimated, none too subtly, that…that I do not, and have never, frequented Petticoat Lane."

Even in the depths of his misery, Benedict squirmed at the stupid, coy euphemism. "He has discovered that I…I have, on occasion, preferred to seek…um…carnal refreshments elsewhere."

"You…you…" Francis's brow creased, and he screwed up his nose as if trying hard to make sense of things and failing.

Benedict could have added that nowadays he sought his pleasure not at all, not since that fateful night, but he really preferred not to allude to his prevarications more times than absolutely necessary. Once was enough, and the damage was done.

As comprehension slotted into place on his dear brother's face, Francis's confidence a few seconds earlier vanished like a candle snuffed out.

"Oh Lord," Francis eventually uttered. And again a few seconds later, more quietly, "Oh Lord." And then, compounding the issue and demonstrating that his mind wasn't half as nonthreatening as he led everyone to believe, he cried, "How the blazes did Mr L'Esquire find out?"

"I…I'd rather not say." Benedict blew out a long breath. "But he demonstrated last night that he has no interest in sharing his knowledge."

Francis made a begrudging noise. "We should count our small blessings, shouldn't we?"

"Yes."

Strangely, the shocking news didn't diminish Francis's appetite. Cogitating on it, he polished off another sausage, then mopped up the juice with two fried eggs. Benedict's stomach performed a few more miserable somersaults.

"Personally speaking, Benedict," Francis finally pronounced through an eggy mouthful. "I cannot possibly imagine anything remotely beguiling about ferreting about with another gentleman's block and tackle. Especially when, as a bloody duke, you have literally 99 percent of England's fairer sex at your disposal."

He gave a slight shudder. "Be that as it may, what I suppose I'm trying to say is that whatever you choose to do in the privacy of your own bedchamber with other likeminded gentlemen is not the business of blasted Lyndon. Nor of the lawmakers, Lord Ludham, or anyone else in the *ton*, for that matter."

A prickly heat stung at the back of Benedict's eyes. He blinked a few times. "Thank you," he managed.

"Don't worry about thanking me. I haven't done anything. *Yet*." Francis poured himself another coffee and stirred in a generous helping of sugar. "What we really need to be focusing on is this. Now our dear Lyndon is determined to spite you and, more importantly as far as I'm concerned, create yet another bloody spurious reason as to why Lord Ludham refuses to let me marry Isabella, what are we going to do about it?"

We. Twice, in the space of a day and a night. Maybe Benedict wasn't as isolated as he'd always believed.

Francis pushed his plate away, wiped his mouth, and then refolded his arms with a defiant look. A tiny weight lifted from the duke's shoulders at the same time as Benedict's love for his kind, generous brother overflowed, sufficient to fill a ballroom. And, if he hadn't inexplicably burst into tears, he might have told him so.

*

BENEDICT GREETED TOMMY in the library. Francis insisted on tagging along, and they entered together to find their visitor standing at the tall shelves with a book open, leafing through the pages. In a light grey tailcoat paired with a cornflower silk cravat, Tommy was one of the most welcome and prettiest sights Benedict could recall. Devastatingly at ease, one would never have guessed he hadn't been born into the gentrified classes. And if he was surprised or disappointed to see Francis bounding in after Benedict, he was careful not to show it.

"What a pleasure it is to see you again so soon, Mr L'Esquire," said Benedict, feeling as lumpish and socially inadequate as ever. "Johnson is bringing tea."

"I'm sure we'd all prefer a much stiffer drink," added Francis disarmingly. "Except boring Benedict here insists on keeping a clear head."

"It's barely past breakfast!"

"Yes, but the most extraordinary one of my life!"

Benedict attempted to glare at him, challenging when less than an hour earlier the man had lent him his pocket square to dab at his eyes. He turned back to Tommy instead.

"Lord Francis is aware of Lyndon's underhand dealings," he explained, not seeing much point in dragging it out. It wasn't as if things could become any more humiliating. "And the…ah…information he is holding over me."

"Like a veritable sword of Damocles," Francis supplemented. "And he's dangling it by a single hair!"

Regarding Francis properly, Tommy seemed bemused. "*All* of the information, Your Grace?" he enquired in a pleasant tone.

"He is abreast of my uh…proclivities, yes." Benedict felt himself turning the colour of a beetroot; he was relieved the library was devoid of a mirror.

"I say!" chortled Francis. "*Abreast* is a rather interesting choice of words, don't you think, Benedict? Seeing as, you know, us fellas don't exactly have —"

"Ah, good. Here's the tea tray," butted in Benedict as Johnson reappeared. "Do take a seat, Mr L'Esquire. And Francis, don't feel obliged to stay." This last bit he added with a pointed expression, which Francis overlooked.

"You are probably wondering, Your Grace, why I'm here so soon after last night's contretemps." Tommy made himself comfortable on the chaise before helping himself to the milk jug. "It's with more unpleasant news, I'm afraid."

Oh God. "I'm not sure I can stomach any more."

A fresh surge of ice-cold fear coursed through Benedict, only tempered by a prickling disappointment on registering that Tommy hadn't come calling for something else.

"It seems Lord Lyndon is planning a two-pronged attack," Tommy continued. "You may recall when we spoke at Epsom that we touched upon your stable's recent poor form at Newmarket? The blacklegs registered unexpected heavy losses, which my man Sidney brought to my attention."

"He has many talents," observed Francis, not entirely without malice.

"He does indeed," agreed Tommy coolly. "One would do well not to cross him." He took a sip of tea. "Fortunately, he is on our side."

"What has my stable's poor form got to do with Lyndon?" This time, Benedict did manage to glare at Francis. "He has never shown the slightest interest in horseflesh."

"He does, however, have an interest in blunt, if I'm not mistaken?" Tommy smiled gently, his expression soft.

With a smile like that, if he'd informed Benedict that Lyndon had blown his beloved stable sky-high with gunpowder, he'd have accepted the news with equanimity.

"And Lord Lyndon is short of it," Tommy added.

"Not as short as he should be," commented Francis. "We were only discussing this recently, weren't we, Benedict? He seems to have a limitless supply of ready funds he's drawing from somewhere. Though...oh..."

He screwed his nose up again in that way he had. Isabella must have once informed him it was endearing. "Goodness, he's...he's nobbling our horses, isn't he?"

"He *was*," Tommy corrected in a careful manner, affording Francis even more attention than previously, and no wonder. Francis had jumped to the meat of the matter much quicker than Benedict. Perhaps because Francis was focusing his entire attention on the words spilling from Tommy's mouth and not the mouth itself.

"You have a new stable boy, Your Grace," Tommy continued after another sip, "who is perfectly competent, except also a bit of a rogue. He was employed by Lord Gartside, until Gartside's hasty departure from the *ton*, and picked up a few bad habits. One of which is accepting coin from people with vested interests in wishing a particular horse to run poorly. To ensure it happens."

Benedict groaned with despair. "You're going to inform me that Lyndon has been paying him for his talent."

"Yes." Tommy inclined his head. "I'm afraid so. With hindsight, it makes perfect sense. Your brother has enjoyed a surprisingly good run of wins at my blackleg stands recently — he's been betting heavily on the second favourite in every race in which a horse running in Ashington colours was the losing favourite."

"That's why he's so flush in the pocket," exclaimed Francis. "Bravo for working it out, sir!" He paused, worrying his lip before regarding Tommy suspiciously. "How on earth did you?"

Tommy gave an elegant shrug. "It was all Sidney's work. Gartside had pulled that trick on more than one occasion, and Sidney put two and two together when he strolled down to your stables to speak to Joe Jonas and spotted the lad."

Francis raised a sceptical eyebrow. "What, and the boy kindly sketched a diagram while explaining his underhand methods over a pot of tea?"

"Sidney's approach yields results, my lord." A note of warning crept into Tommy's voice. "I suggest you don't pry too carefully."

"It matters not how he came upon it," stated Benedict, coming to Tommy's defence. "That stable hand shall have his marching orders within the hour."

"More like hobbling orders now Sidney's had at him, I'd wager," muttered Francis.

"Quite," agreed Tommy.

Benedict had seen the boy a few times, a chubby lad, expertly rubbing down Cleopatra. He reminded himself to ensure Jonas spread the word to other stable masters in the *ton* that he was not to be trusted. "Is he poisoning them? Will my stock have lasting damage?"

"No, thankfully. He was adding a shovelful of dirty sand to their feed. Enough to upset them for a day or so but insufficient to cause any lengthy, detectable harm. He had a feeling Jonas was watching him and becoming suspicious, so he stopped."

"If he's stopped, then why did Pericles pull up short in the four o'clock at Ascot yesterday?" demanded Francis. "Tuffy Bannister lost five pounds! He bent my ear about it for over an hour last night after all the hoo-ha died down."

Tommy smiled again, and despite the fresh horror of his revelations, a small corner of Benedict's mind thrilled with the devastating effect it had on him. "Your charming brother has changed tack of late by cutting out the go-between. Now, he's simply paying your jockeys direct to throw the race."

"Then we must jolly well call him out!" Francis leaped up as if about to lead the charge. "Race fixing is criminal behaviour!"

Benedict's skin heated as he and Tommy exchanged a look.

Tommy cleared his throat. "It's a delicate situation, my lord. You see, Lord Lyndon could make similar accusations about His Grace's…non-horse-race-related activities."

"Ah, yes." Francis's skin turned a similar shade to Benedict's. "That's a good point and very well made, sir. So, we are at an impasse."

He pursed his lips as a thought struck him. "Why are you being so damned helpful, Mr L'Esquire? And not once, but twice in the space of twenty-four hours? Not that His Grace and I don't appreciate it. But what's in it for you, apart from ensuring your blacklegs aren't robbed?"

"Can't a man be a helpful citizen, Francis?" asked Benedict lightly. "Without attracting suspicion?"

"Not according to Beatrice Hazard, no." Francis fixed his narrowed gaze on Tommy. And then swung it back to Benedict, who was examining the carpet. And then back to Tommy, who was examining a cushion.

"Ah," he said after an eternity.

Bravely, Benedict met his eye, looking as guilty as if he'd just strangled a litter of kittens.

"Um…right, ho." Francis gave an awkward cough. "So, the jockeys. And Lyndon. What's to be done?"

Chapter Fifteen

NOBODY REVELLED IN a full-bodied scandal as much as the collective *ton*, but they'd have to hoist their skirts and tailcoats over Tommy Squire's dead body before the Duke of Ashington would be the subject of it. And when Tommy Squire made up his mind to do something, then, as a string of blackleg stands and gaming hells could attest, it was already done.

Cyprians, mollies, macaronis, catamites—call them what you will—there were as many bashful euphemisms for men such as Tommy and the duke as there were pretty boys flashing their come-hither pouts in the back streets of St Paul's every Sunday afternoon. And, though everyone turned a blind eye, plenty swanning around the court of King George, too, flagrantly sashaying amongst the highest of society, safe in the knowledge they held the King's favour.

But a plethora of quiet and unassuming *bachelors* also

walked amongst everyday folk. The comfortable Albany resi-
dences, for instance, were home to plenty of unremarkable souls,
inconspicuously going about their business much like every other
man whilst occasionally making the most of discreet opportuni-
ties whenever they presented.

As far as Tommy was concerned, if the fourteenth Duke of
Ashington wished to live his existence passing as a man such as
that, then it was entirely his affair. Having experienced the sharp
end of the law himself — thanks to his own appetites — Tommy
was of the same mind. Not every man could be Rossingley, slippery enough to straddle both worlds. Tommy lacked the wealthy
earl's good standing, for a start, whilst the duke lacked the courage. Though the more time he spent with the duke, the more
Tommy wondered whether it was simply that the man had never
learned the skills to protect himself.

At least Ashington could rely on Tommy and Rossingley
fighting in his corner. Lord Francis, too, as it happened. His robust
support came as huge surprise. Between the three of them,
Tommy felt confident they should be able to nip Lord Lyndon's
plans in the bud before Sidney and an axe were called for.

A couple of days passed before they assembled in the duke's
well-proportioned drawing room — the duke, Tommy, Lord Francis, and Rossingley. Rossingley had brought Mr Angel along, too,
and he sat quietly, his handsome face impenetrable.

Rossingley cut straight to pouring brandy, an excellent vin-
tage at that. As he accepted a snifter, Tommy noted the deep circles cupping Ashington's dark eyes. The duke's countenance was
austere at the best of times. This evening, dressed in his usual
sombre attire and sharing a chintz settee with flamboyant

Rossingley, he was positively Spartan. The low lamplight did the rest, stealing all the remnants of colour from his features.

True to form, Rossingley took centre stage. "The Rossingley's and Ashington's have been friends and neighbours for nigh on three hundred years," he began. "Ever since the seventh Earl of Rossingley dug up a patch of dandelions, brewed them with burdock and nettle, and fed the concoction to his chum, the eighth duke, to cure his gout. Which it did, within minutes. Doubled his sexual appetite too. Legend has it he took on three mistresses the following month."

Tommy would wager his gambling hells that Rossingley was talking nonsense, but it brought the tension in Ashington's shoulders down a notch.

"Thus, when somebody mounts an unjustified personal attack on my fellow peer and old friend, it is an affront to me and mine." His pale gaze briefly flicked in Angel's direction, who nodded almost imperceptibly. "Even if the perpetrator himself is a close relative of my good and blameless friend, Ashington."

"Hear, hear," cried Lord Francis, beaming. "United we stand, bothersome brother be damned."

Why the man sometimes played the role of buffoon was anyone's guess. Underneath, Tommy thought he was sharp as a pin.

"The vital question," continued Rossingley, "is when and where will the hammer fall? Will Lord Lyndon attempt an exposé in one of the gossip columns? Or will he crave a more public shaming? For instance, at one of the clubs? Or, as the rumour-mongers are hinting, will he bide his time until a grand soirée? Such as the Horton ball, marking the end of the season?"

Tommy only half-listened to Rossingley's speculation; his

attention drawn by Mr Angel idly rolling a thrupenny bit across the knuckles of his right fist. He'd seen him perform this nimble sleight of hand before, other little supper party tricks too. His favourite involved claret glasses and vanishing farthings. Tommy would try his utmost never to let his eyes stray from the coins, but somehow, the blasted things would wink up at him one second and be gone the next.

The man could have his own stage show, he mused, as Rossingley nattered on. He could wow the *ton* with all kinds of outlandish tricks. His skills were wasted on a handful of foxed chaps at dinner. The ladies would be enthrall—

With a burst of clarity, Tommy cut Rossingley off. "I believe Lord Lyndon will make a performance of it," he declared. "Most definitely. The bigger his audience, the better. Especially now he's received a dressing down in public himself."

Having captured everyone's notice, Tommy became surer of himself. "Tit for tat. I wager he'll wait until the Horton's ball, the last hurrah of the season. Everyone who's anyone will be there— it follows on after Ladies Day at Ascot."

"His bruising will have healed by then," Rossingley pointed out, nodding.

"And, correct me if I'm wrong," Tommy continued, "not having ever been on the invitation list, but I believe it's the biggest event of the society calendar? From what I've witnessed, Lord Lyndon has a flair for the dramatic, does he not?"

"Quite possibly," the duke agreed miserably. "He most certainly never does anything by halves."

Francis frowned. "That's all very well, but bar kidnapping him and preventing him from attending any more social events this year, we can't stop him."

"No," Rossingley agreed. "So, we must think cleverly."

The duke held up his hands. "Not my forte, I'm afraid."

Tommy didn't think it possible for him look any more despondent, but somehow, he managed it.

"I've told you before that you're too hard on yourself," admonished Francis, adding a smile. "In everything."

As the room fell silent, except for the sound of minds at work, Mr Angel resumed his idle coin flipping. Watching him made Tommy feel decidedly unclever, too, especially as he'd missed the moment the farthing magically switched to a ha'penny. He could only conclude it must have happened when Francis finished speaking; Angel reached for his glass, then seemed to change his mind, and Tommy had been fleetingly distracted.

And suddenly again, just like that, he could see a way through.

"Let us allow him to make his big announcement." The plan unspooled in his mind. "Let him attempt to disgrace the duke. And then, we must ensure no one believes a word of what they are hearing."

"How the devil do you propose we do that, Mr L'Esquire?" mocked Francis pleasantly. "Are we going to cover their ears with mufflers? Wave a wand and cry *abracadabra*?"

"I don't know yet." Tommy felt slightly foolish. "But somehow, we need the *ton* to find the idea so preposterous they discard it immediately. Even if what he tells everyone is well presented and credible."

Tucking his coins away, Angel offered Tommy a benign smile. The two hadn't always seen eye to eye. Tommy hadn't been sure of the man when he'd first captured the earl's attention, and Angel hadn't taken to Tommy either. But he'd more than proved his worth since.

"L'Esquire might be onto something." Angel shifted in his seat. "*Abracadabra* indeed, except a wand won't be necessary. 'Misdirection' is the term you are grasping for, I believe."

Tommy was unfamiliar with the word. "Er…possibly?"

Mr Angel nodded. "Misdirection is the cornerstone of any magic trick. What the eyes see, and the ear hears, the mind believes. Skilled magicians give everybody something to look at whilst the real activity is happening elsewhere."

"You'll have to explain a bit more," said the duke. "I'm a little slow."

"I mean that when Lyndon makes his big announcement, such a stir is being created elsewhere that his words are treated with the disdain and incredulity they deserve."

"That certainly has merit," mused Rossingley, nodding in thought. "Politicians do it all the time, slipping a piece of bad news in amongst the good."

"But how?" queried the duke. "Once the *ton* has its teeth into juicy tittle-tattle, it's like a dog with a bone."

"Very true," Rossingley conceded. "The misdirection must be truly spectacular if it's to distract them." He grinned impishly. "Any volunteers to set fire to the window drapes? My dearest Uncle Edmund did that as a boy to avoid broad beans at supper. The entire east wing required a rebuild."

Mr Angel smiled at him. "Perhaps we could dribble a few drops of arsenic in the ratafia. There are a few chaps I wouldn't mind losing as collateral damage."

"Ooh! Good lord! Ooh!" Francis clapped his hands together. "I think I have it! An excellent idea! Foolproof, in fact. Goodness, yes! I don't know why we didn't think of it immediately."

With a triumphant grin, he regarded the others as if the answer stared them in the face. "What we need is to convince everybody that my dearest brother Benedict is the least likely chap in the entire *ton* to ever have enjoyed the pleasures of a molly house. So that when Lyndon suggests it, everybody will think he must be insane."

"I'm not entering holy orders, if that's what you're suggesting." Benedict shook his head. "Speaking in front of an entire congregation? Absolutely not."

"In my experience," said Rossingley coolly, "Molly houses and the clergy are not mutually exclusive."

"Of course I'm not suggesting you join the clergy, Benedict!" Francis exclaimed. "My plan is even simpler than that!" He spread his arms expansively. "We must turn you into the *ton*'s most notorious rake!"

A disbelieving silence followed. The sort of silence so profound that Tommy fancied he could hear buds in the garden beyond, unfurling into blossom.

The duke was the first to break it.

"A rake," he repeated. And blinked twice. "That is what you said, is it not?"

"Yes," Francis clarified. "Your ears do not deceive you. A rake."

"A rake?" Tommy queried. "As in r-a-k-e?"

"Rake?" mouthed Mr Angel to Rossingley, a dark eyebrow arched.

Francis cursed. "Is there an echo in here? Yes, a bloody rake!"

Rossingley raised his own searching eyebrow. "You must mean of the gardening tool variety, surely. If you could pull that little magic trick off, it would most certainly divert attention, but I'm not convinced it is necessarily in Ashington's long-term interests."

"Of course not! I mean of the don't-let-him-within-sniffing-distance-of-my-daughter variety. Don't you see? Thanks to Mr L'Esquire's henchman, we have a fortnight's grace until Lyndon's face returns to its usual state of affairs. The Horton ball is a week later. In between now and then, we must ensure Benedict is seen to be seducing every eligible miss the *ton* has to offer. Perhaps a few ineligible ones too."

"Good heavens, that sounds...exhausting." The duke gulped back his brandy. "Not to mention horrifically frightening and also that this is probably a good moment to point out you may be confusing me with someone else. Someone rakish, for instance?"

"Yes, yes, yes," responded Francis, waving him off. "I know it's going to take some effort on your part. Starting with a whole new wardrobe and a new personality. But just imagine Lyndon's flabbergasted expression when he declares to a packed ballroom that you've been making the beast with two backs with some fella down Soho way, and everyone turns around to see you spread over the cheese trolley, knee-deep in the Marchioness of Cholmondley!"

Another three buds unfurled. With a cry of sorrow, a leaf floated down from a tree.

"I think this plan may need some finessing," murmured Rossingley, his face ashen.

"A *lot* of finessing," interjected the duke. "Especially the knees part. Francis, I have no idea where you get these coarse modern terms from, but really, I'm not sure I approve."

"Well, you should. And if you're going to be a rake by the end of the month, you'll need to get used to them." Francis smacked his head. "Good lord, I've come up with an even better idea."

"Surely not. My heart won't stand another."

"Even more misdirection," Francis said triumphantly. "A two-pronged attack of misdirection to match Lyndon's two-pronged attack on us. More gossip. More scandal. Honestly, Lyndon's big reveal will be such a side note, it won't even make the pages of *The Morning Herald*."

"Out with it." Ashington sighed. "And less prong chat."

"Well." Francis drew a deep breath. "As everybody here is all too aware, I am desperate to marry Lady Isabella Knightley, but Lord Ludham is insisting she waits until someone better comes along."

"Not possible," muttered the duke.

"And bravo for making this all about you," Rossingley purred.

"I'll pretend I didn't hear that. Anyhow, if by some teeny-weeny stroke of bad luck our turning-Benedict-into-the-biggest-rake-ever-to-squash-a-lump-of-cheddar plan fails, and everyone discovers he's a raving catamite, Lord Ludham will never allow me to marry Isabella. So, I need him to accept my offer of marriage *before* Lyndon attempts his big reveal. And I know exactly how."

"A switchblade to his throat?" supplied Rossingley, with, in Tommy's estimation, rather too much glee.

"No." Francis grinned. "I actually quite like the man, even if my current state of carnal inactivity is starting to feel like a terminal illness. We must create *another* diversionary scandal. We must find a couple of rogues to attempt to seduce Isabella. She will encourage them, and a furious Lord Ludham will realise his only sensible option is to accept my suit. We'll have it all happen on the same night. What with Benedict here excavating some poor woman or other's tonsils and Lady Isabella fighting off undesirables, the *ton* won't know which way to turn."

The dumbfounded silence following this outlandish plan was even more protracted than the rake silence.

Eventually, Rossingley found his voice. He cocked his head on one side. "Francis, my darling, you're an untapped well of surprises." His pale gaze skirted the assembled gentlemen, lingering suspiciously longer on Tommy and Mr Angel. "Now, if only we knew a pair of undesirables."

Tommy rolled his eyes. Spotted by the duke, they exchanged a brief, conspiratorial smile. When he wasn't in such a brown study, the man was unfairly beautiful.

"Obviously," claimed Rossingley, "I'd be the first to volunteer myself, if I wasn't so above reproach."

A few more seconds ticked by as the men contemplated the merits of the plan.

"I'm terribly undesirable," offered Mr Angel at last.

It was only the second time he'd properly spoken, and everyone turned to look at him, casually lounging in a burgundy Chesterfield, legs loosely crossed and one hand cradling his brandy balloon. Tommy concurred. Mr Angel was exactly the kind of chap a well-bred lady would and wouldn't like to meet alone in a shady corner of Vauxhall.

Aware he was under scrutiny, Angel tucked a few strands of his wavy black locks behind his left ear from where they'd escaped his ribbon. A single gold hoop glinted between those busy, coin-flipping fingers, and the lambent light from the coals in the hearth danced across his dark cheek.

"Not from where I'm sitting, darling," Rossingley cooed, loud enough for everyone to hear.

Tommy heaved a long-suffering sigh. The man was nothing if not predictable.

Lord Francis's eyes, meanwhile, popped out on stalks. "I say, chaps. I do believe I've been inhabiting a parallel universe all these years." Like a pendulum, his astounded gaze swung between Rossingley and Mr Angel, then back to his brother, trying to hide his amusement behind his hand but clearly failing. "Are you really…all of you? Weren't you…weren't you once married, Rossingley? And you…with Mr Ang…? Oh, I say."

"Spot on," said Rossingley warmly as if Francis's mutterings made perfect sense. "I couldn't have summarised the situation better myself. Now, if you would be so kind, Mr Angel, please attempt to convince Lord Francis here of your undesirability. His lips quirked. "Prepare to fail."

With a lazy half-smile, Angel held up a hand, counting off his fingers. "Firstly, I have very little in the way of family and only one home—not ancestral. There is enough colour in my skin to suggest Rom blood courses through my veins, and more importantly to the fickle folks for whom these matters have value, I have appeared in Society from nowhere. Furthermore, under direction inquisition, I steadfastly refuse to explain my origins; I refuse to flatter or engage the *ton*'s mamas in idle gossip. In addition to that, I dance despicably well, so I must be a foreigner, and I favour long hair and an earring. All things considered, I am perfectly undesirable in the eyes of every God-fearing father of the *ton*." He downed a large swallow of brandy. "Thank the Lord."

Laid out so comprehensively, it was hard to disagree.

"I'll save you the bother of pointing it out, Lordy." Tommy threw a wry smile at the earl. "But I fear I'm undesirable too. In fact, I'd go so far as to say I'm Lord Ludham's worst nightmare. I run gaming establishments and race stands. And—close your ears, Lord Francis, as I'm clean out of smelling salts—I own several brothels."

"Heavens above, pass the brandy," croaked Lord Francis. "I'm in the company of heathens."

"Yes, but think of all the fun you're having." Rossingley sighed happily. "So that's settled. By the time our new rakish duke has acquainted himself with the cheeseboard, and Mr Angel and young Mr L'Esquire here have done their very worst, Lord Ludham will be practically biting Francis's hand off, and Lyndon will be an insignificance. Now, talking of undesirable character traits, it's high time Mr Angel and I pushed off home."

"But we haven't discussed the horse nobbling yet," cried Francis. "We can't call it a night just as we reach the part where I might actually be of practical use. I've been nothing but ornamental so far."

"And may I say what a very handsome ornament you are, poppet," said Rossingley rising from his seat. "And, if I'm not mistaken, I suspect your big brother came up with a solution for the horse problem within minutes of hearing of it."

Modest as ever, the duke looked abashed and proud all at once. Tommy found it utterly charming. "Thank you, and yes, I have indeed. If I may beg just one moment longer of everyone's time."

He could have several moments of Tommy's time. All of them in fact. Something Tommy planned on making perfectly clear after everyone else buggered off.

Crossing over to the mantelpiece, the duke laid his hand upon the cool, solid marble as if garnering strength from it. In his fragile and tormented state, one could overlook he was a duke, but now, towering over them, he wore the first confident, hopeful smile Tommy had seen since, well, far too many years hence.

In turn, the duke regarded them one by one. "You are all being so terribly generous. I am truly humbled and grateful. At the same time, I am thoroughly humiliated that I lack the sufficient tools to remove myself from this circumstance without relying so heavily on the help of others." He directed the next part to Mr Angel. "Some of whom, I barely knew until very recently. And another whom"—his eyes dropped to the floor—"I...I have wronged but intend to spend all my waking hours putting it right."

"I think I speak for all of us," said Rossingley kindly, his gaze skimming to Tommy, "when I say there is no need to apologise for anything, Ashington."

"Be that as it may," the duke responded, "but for one error of judgement, I vow to apologise until the end of time."

He addressed the room once more. "What I am trying to say

is that you have all done so much for me already, and as Rossingley has so charitably remarked, I might humbly admit to having a modicum of expertise regarding matters of horseflesh. So, I'd like you all to leave the issue regarding Lyndon and my stables to me. I have the beginnings of a plan, and I'll wager it will surprise everyone."

*

"HOW ANYONE IMAGINES they can transform me into a rake is the devil's own guess. You'd have more luck with the Archbishop of Canterbury!" Flopping into a seat, the duke peered down his body. He plucked at his immaculate (but funereal) charcoal tailcoat in disgust. "Look at me! I'm the very essence of all that is dull and proper!"

Then it is fortunate that I'm not, Tommy nearly replied. And he *was* looking. Aside from Mr Angel's damned hypnotic coins, he'd hardly looked anywhere elsewhere all evening. As the others took their leave, he'd felt tempted to express interest in the fine etchings hanging above the fireplace as a flimsy excuse to linger awhile. But Tommy's desire for this diffident man had become too noisy and insistent a voice to waste time delivering pretty speeches about art. Actions spoke louder than words, and he'd craved an assortment of those ever since that surprise kiss in his study. And some actions, thanks to his inglorious past, he excelled at.

Covering the short distance to the door, Tommy turned the key. He then returned to where the duke sat in what was clearly, from how he appeared so at ease and how a side table was perfectly positioned with his brandy balloon within reach, his favourite armchair.

The duke stared beyond Tommy at the door. "You have locked us in."

"So I have." Tugging on the cuff of his tailcoat, Tommy slipped his arm out of the tight sleeve with the practised ease of a man long accustomed to surviving without the services of a valet. "Do you wish me to unlock it, Your Grace?"

When he performed the same manoeuvre with the other sleeve, letting his coat drop in a crumpled *fwhump* at his feet, the duke's shy eyes widened.

"Um…no. I don't believe I do."

Tommy's light fingers tripped down the elegant buttons of his waistcoat, hesitating over the bottom one. He rolled it under his thumb. The duke's restless gaze tracked the movement before dropping lower to where Tommy's swelling member made its presence felt at the fall of his breeches. Ashington shifted in his seat.

"Now, what was I doing?" queried Tommy, abandoning his slow undress. "Ah, yes. Delivering your first lesson on turning you into a rake."

The duke scraped together a rough laugh. "Currently, you are turning me into a puddle of want."

Tommy grinned as the duke wrenched a finger inside his own neckcloth, loosening the knot a fraction. "Then the battle is half won."

With unmistakeable intent, he sauntered towards the duke's armchair. From somewhere over his shoulder, a longcase clock marked out the passage of time, each earnest tick failing to drown out the hammering in his chest. He wanted this man, he realised, more than he'd ever wanted anything or anyone else. A few inches beyond the triangle of Ashington's long legs, he paused.

The duke hauled his dark gaze away from the outline of Tommy's stiff prick. He licked his lips. "You...I..." He made a hopeless gesture.

Again, Tommy circled the lowest button with the tip of his forefinger. "What would a rake do now, Your Grace?"

"He...he'd unbutton your waistcoat." The duke's voice rasped as he stumbled over the words. He gestured towards the garment. "May I ask you to—"

"*May I?* There's no place for prettily worded demands here, Your Grace." Tommy shook his head in mock disappointment. "Caution in this enterprise is fatal. Do your worst."

Ashington huffed a breathy laugh. "Come closer, man, so I can bloody well get my hands on you! Better?"

Tommy stifled a smile. "Excellent."

With a little sway in his step, he moved forwards until he stood close enough for the duke's delicious cologne to reach his nostrils. "Now, seduce me."

Even before the duke touched him, Tommy felt the caress of his lover's fingertips. Raw intent was written in the smokiness of his eyes, his heated cheeks, the part of his lips. Fabric whispered under his exploring fingers as he walked them, tentatively at first, over Tommy's narrow hips before drawing them along the slippery satin edge of his waistcoat. On reaching the line of buttons, the duke pulled each one apart clumsily. The most seductive thing about it was the desperate desire banked up behind his trembling fingers and in the tip of his moist tongue, poking out from between his lips.

"God," Ashington chuckled, "these were a rotten invention."

Tommy smiled at his fumbling, unable to resist. "Patience is a virtue with which you were clearly not blessed."

"It's a virtue I'd like to slap in the face! Ahh." The last fastening fell open. "Finally."

Cool air draughted across Tommy's belly as the duke tugged the snowy linen of his shirt from his breeches. His skin pebbled; he shivered, then let out a hiss as Ashington's palm, like a hot brand, smoothed the goosebumps away. The duke tilted his head back, his imploring dark eyes gazing up at Tommy. Bunching the linen in his hands, he gave it a tug.

"I want you down here. I need to kiss you."

Tommy didn't move, but God, how he wanted to fall on him and never clamber off. "Rake," he whispered. "Show me, don't tell."

A sharp jerk on the waistband of his breeches found Tommy tumbling onto the duke's lap with an undignified yelp. The man's predatory smile snatched the air from Tommy's lungs. "Like that?"

Their lips crashed together, Tommy's answer forever swallowed in a kiss. With urgency unbound, the duke prised his mouth open. His hot tongue plunged inside, his hands twisting in Tommy's hair, pinning him in place. Nipping, sucking, owning the kiss. Owning Tommy.

A vice-like arm took possession of Tommy's narrow waist. His gut clenched with want as a hand roamed under his shirt. An obscene heat grew between his legs. A raw, guttural sound came from the duke's throat, suffocating the thud of their combined heartbeats, strangling any last lingering resentment Tommy held for this man. A man who, with nothing more than this unstoppable kiss, was making him feel more alive than anything he'd known before.

Eventually, reluctantly, Tommy pulled away to catch a much-needed breath. Under him, Ashington nipped at Tommy's neck, moaning his disapproval.

"See, already I have you making disreputable noises," Tommy panted. "And you look…" He tailed off as the duke burrowed into the sensitive hollow behind his ear, emitting another rudimentary noise, laden with unholy promise. *You look like my raven once again* was on the tip of his tongue. *My beautiful, raven-haired lordling.* "You resemble a debauched rake."

In reply, the duke groaned. "How is your scent so sweet, Tommy?" He nosed at Tommy's jaw, his cheeks, his damp hairline. "I fear I am already bewitched by it."

Laughter ran through his gravelly voice, and he arched his hips, shamelessly pleasuring his clothed prick against Tommy's. His exploratory hands took a new path up the front of Tommy's loose shirt, pausing to scratch at a nipple. Tommy winced with the exquisite pain of it. "Rakish like this, Tommy?"

Not stopping for an answer, the duke's lips landed once more on Tommy's, and Tommy felt the press of a smile. As his other nipple took a turn for a scraping, it was Tommy's turn to utter a coarse groan.

"You're going to be an insufferable rake, Your Grace. I fear I have unleashed a monster."

They kissed deeply again. The rocking of the duke's solid prick became more insistent. As Tommy glided his palm across the jutting outline, pure mischief filled the duke's dark eyes.

"No, the monster is still caged," he whispered. Moaning with pleasure, he rolled his hips again.

"Oh God." Tommy almost giggled. "You believe yourself to be amusing, don't you?"

The duke tipped his head to one side, pretending to consider. "One tries not to fly in the face of public opinion."

This time, Tommy did giggle, a boyish, joyous sound he hadn't believed himself capable of.

Taking his wrist, the duke oh-so-very gently circled it with his finger and thumb before he dragged it across to his hip, over where the fall of his breeches lay. His mouth wore a cocky smile, and Tommy uttered a despairing moan.

"Where has my timid duke gone? I want him back."

His Grace's sweet mouth met Tommy's as Tommy's nimble fingers made light work of the fastenings.

"He's still here, Tommy," the duke whispered into his mouth. "And he's scared to death. But he's also fuelled by brandy and a desperate want for the beautiful creature in his lap, so he's saddling up anyway."

"Then he must be truly courageous." Tommy dipped his hand amongst the folds of white linen wrapped around the duke's prick, presenting it like a gift. With his other hand, he unfastened his own breeches.

"I want to pleasure you too, Tommy," said the duke through a hot breath, "As you pleasure me."

"Or—" Tilting himself forward, Tommy spat on his palm, then wrapped it around both cocks. "—we can do it this way."

"Oh, God, yes."

More than spit slicked them both. Too many bloody layers of linen were getting in the way for Tommy to see the damned things, but he could feel the duke's prick, rigid and scorching hot against him.

"By God, you feel good," Tommy said.

The duke clamped his own hand around Tommy's, and together, they found a jerky rhythm. Tommy nipped the damp skin at the duke's neck, suckling the sensitive flesh as their pricks rubbed against each other. He pulled harder, twisting up and over his lover's swollen crown.

"Oh," the duke rasped. "Oh, oh yes."

So *that* was how he liked it. "It meets with your approval, Your Grace?"

"I don't believe I have ever felt so hard."

"Iron sharpens iron," Tommy gasped. "Didn't you know?"

The duke let out a whimper. "Then I believe that iron has fast become my favourite of all the elements."

Both were close to spending, Tommy sensed it from the faltering of the duke's hips, from a tiny cry, fraught and wanting, carrying him back through time. A fresh wave of heat cantered down his spine, flooding between his legs. He sped up the shuttling of his wrist, licking the duke's neck, then sucking down hard. His lover cursed, tipping his head back for more.

"Now, Benedict, now."

"God, yes. Now."

They spilled almost as one, scrappily coating hands and linen. Uncaring. They spilled until the duke winced and stuttered and pulled Tommy's hand away. He held it up to his mouth, pressing his lips to it like a charm.

Tommy's eyes shuttered closed. He sagged, breathless and mindless, against the duke's broad chest, swaying as it heaved. In a moment, after permitting himself a few seconds to recover his senses, he'd recover his clothing and take his leave, a habit rooted in self-protection. One never knew when a madge could turn violent. Best to be out of range and closest to the door.

He made to clamber off and away from the mess cooling between them, but the duke hauled him back again.

"Where do you think you're going?"

"Nowhere, apparently."

The duke exhaled in a lazy, self-satisfied sigh. "Good. I haven't had my fill of you. You can stay there a while longer." It sounded very much like a ducal order.

"If your intention is a demand for seconds, I may have to demure, Your Grace," Tommy was still breathless. "I believe I have been bled dry. You have mastered rakery over the course of one evening."

"I have." The duke's eyes danced. He held Tommy's hand more tightly. "At least, with you. I...I feel I can do anything with you."

For a long minute, they contemplated each other. Tommy made good use of his pocket square, using one hand as best he could, considering Ashington was clearly reluctant to part with the other. As the duke toyed with Tommy's fingers, his gaze turned wistful. His smile faded. Now it was over, he seemed more like the diffident duke again.

"That's a melancholy face for a man who has recently had his ballocks drained," Tommy teased.

The duke chuckled softly. "Melancholy is not my intention.

I..." He ran his fingers down Tommy's arm, almost absently. "Given the juxtaposition of what we have shared and the invidious situation in which I find myself, I feel trapped between a rock and a...a place of utmost calm. And it is a most peculiar sensation." Cautiously, he glanced up as if braced for rebuttal.

Nothing was further from Tommy's mind. "That our lives have circled back to each other is a curious miracle, indeed, Your Grace," he agreed.

"Unwittingly, Lyndon has done me a huge favour." The duke toyed with Tommy's sleeve. "Despite the hellish mess he's created."

"If that were true, I would rejoice. But I cannot see how."

A mother-of-pearl button at Tommy's cuff commanded the duke's utmost attention. "If it were not for his actions, I wouldn't be here with you. He has forced me to cease being scared of the unknown and start being more scared of never knowing."

Tommy frowned. "Never knowing what?"

The duke shook his head. "Would you mock me, Tommy" — he moved his favours onto the next tiny button along — "if I confessed that I do not, that is to say, I have...I have never had a successful coupling with a woman? To completion?"

"No. In the course of my life, I have sought my pleasure lying with both sexes," answered Tommy truthfully. "But I would not make fun of any man who has had to endeavour to be that which he is not."

"You are a compassionate man." A sad smile played at the duke's lips. "Your forgiveness of me is testament to that. But what if I confessed that I have never been with a man either? I have... After we—after you and I were no longer— I...I have only ever been with you."

When the duke dared look up into Tommy's eyes, his own were full of anguish. "Would you mock me now? And mock the pretence I have just executed, pretending to be a rogue? When I am no closer to that than...than a Franciscan friar? The sting of my brother's bitter accusation wounds me ever more, does it not?"

Stunned, Tommy said nothing. He'd bedded countless men and women. In his distant past, he'd have done anything with anyone — man, woman, or beast — if they were willing to part with a few coins. Everything he was and everything he owned to this day had come at a high price.

Did he envy the duke's innocence? No. The horrors of his murky past had served Tommy well, making him stronger and more determined than ever. To never have done any of that? To have never known the sensation of skin on skin, that precious little death, that fleeting moment of perfection?

"Say something, Tommy? Please?"

Pushing back a lock of hair, Tommy looked down into a pair of brown eyes flecked with shards of gold. Eyes brimming with pain. He then pressed his mouth against each tender lid. "Why? Why have you not?"

"Because on that dreadful day, not only did I tie your sweet hand behind your head, but my own too. And I have lived with it bound tightly there since. Too guilt-ridden to set it free, too undeserving. And too aware of my own desires, desires unfitting for a future duke. Too fearful of what would happen if I did."

"But not now," urged Tommy. "Not now we have found each other."

How could someone feel so familiar, like a favourite pillow or the knotted wood grain of his desk, and yet so new? Like his home, and yet be part of a strange and untouched place, a place he'd yet to explore. But God, how he wanted to.

Tommy reached for the duke's wrist and kissed it as he had kissed his eyelids. Unbinding it in his mind, setting it loose.

"No." The duke allowed himself a cautious smile. "Though our timing is despicable. How can I woo women when my heart is wooing you? If not for Francis and Isabella, I do not think I'd have the strength for the plan."

"You don't believe you can appeal to Lord Lyndon's better nature?"

"I do not believe he has one."

Chapter Sixteen

STEP ONE OF public rakery commenced the following day with Rossingley strong-arming Benedict into his tailors on Clifford Street. It was the sort of expedition that, if it held any redeeming qualities, Benedict had yet to glean them.

Private rakery, on the other hand, had much to commend it. However, Francis's teasing as Benedict had helped himself to an ungodly amount of ham at breakfast made him wonder exactly how private his spooning with Tommy had truly been and also to ponder whether Lyndon wasn't his only brother adept at listening at doors.

As he trailed after Rossingley, feeling like a duckling shadowing its mother, Benedict replayed his intimacies with Tommy. His own behaviour had confused him. Faced with Tommy's beauty, his impulse was to possess it, to give it weight. To order it about! All the odder as it warred with his weak nature in every other aspect of his life. And that Tommy—clever, experienced, controlled Tommy—had gifted himself so pliantly was...

"Shield your eyes, my darling. These are not for you."

Truly in his element, Rossingley swept past fifty shades of charcoal grey cloth as though they weren't there. Wasting no time in ordering the tailor's apprentice to tidy them away, he proceeded to issue a lengthy prescription for all manner of garments and in a rainbow of colours and fabrics. Benedict prayed his friend was making some opportunistic purchases of his own. Alas, no.

For several long minutes, the earl fingered a length of emerald-green before laying it over a bolt of dazzling fuchsia-coloured silk. Nervously, Benedict waited. "Adds an air of assurance to any neutral palette," the earl commented finally. "Fuchsia is the new black, don't you know."

"I didn't know," Benedict hazarded, unsure whether a response was required.

A powder-blue and mud-brown waistcoat corseting the tailor's dummy snagged Rossingley's attention. Benedict held his breath. Already, he'd spent longer in the outfitters than his last three previous trips combined. With a wave of his elegant hand, Rossingley dismissed the waistcoat. Benedict breathed out.

"If that isn't proof those two colours should never be seen together, then I don't know what is," the earl declared.

Rossingley studied Benedict as the apprentice scuttled over to remove the offending palette. "A light shade of bilberry would be an excellent choice for you, darling, if only we could find the right one. I'm not saying for a minute that you're not *ravishing* in slate grey and black." He treated Benedict to the kind of smile that reduced him to a blushing youth again. "Far from it. But a pop of colour will ensure you are so much more *welcoming.*"

Before Benedict could mutter something about disliking the tartness of bilberries or, indeed, appearing welcoming, Rossingley pounced on a bolt of cloth named something or other complicated and tapped on it.

"Yes! This is perfect. It will effortlessly bring out the deep tones in your complexion and provide a most alluring look." Stretching the cloth out, he sighed. "You are lucky you can get away with it, Ashington. My dear Kit carries these shades off marvellously too. But when one is as fair as me and Tommy, it can be the devil's work ensuring one's colour isn't sapped by one's waistcoat. The two of us lament it often. But, on you, this Persian indigo, here, paired with that papaya silk, there, will have the *ton* positively salivating."

"Um…yes." Benedict nodded at the cloth, feeling a need to contribute. Focusing on the task at hand had proved difficult ever since Rossingley's mention of Tommy. He could have agreed to dress in a monk's habit trimmed with gold leaf, for all it would have dislodged the delicious memory of yanking the man down into his lap and Tommy's warm palm curled around—

"Papaya is so summery. It lifts one's mood even in the depths of winter, don't you find?"

"Um, yes. Absolutely." Benedict didn't care to admit not knowing the colour of papaya. It seemed too much to hope the fruit was an acceptable shade of dark blue. He ran his hand over both bolts of cloth as it seemed the right thing to do. "I have a navy cravat similar to this," he ventured.

"Persian indigo," corrected the earl in a voice brooking no disagreement. "And I think we should also have it made up into a tailcoat." Lips pursued in concentration, he made an unexpected lunge towards Benedict and ran expert hands along the shoulder seams of the duke's tailcoat, then tracked them down the length of Benedict's arms, something no man except his valet had done — ever.

"Hmm. Whilst this is exquisitely made, Ashington, I feel we should cinch you a little more tightly around here." Rossingley tugged at the material covering Benedict's sturdy biceps. "And perhaps here." He gave Benedict's middle a squeeze.

The earl's hands then trod a scandalous path over his thighs. "We'll also get you measured for two pairs of silk breeches and tighten them up here."

Benedict stared at the plain plaster ceiling above his head.

"That is if we really intend to draw attention to you, darling." The earl smiled again, showing all his pointy teeth. "And who doesn't love attention?"

*

THE MORNING DRAGGED on in a similar alarming fashion. By the end of it, Benedict had developed a theory that a rakish man's dissolute, louche appearance had nothing whatsoever to do with excessive indulgence. It was all down to interminable shopping trips.

When they emerged from the tailors, Benedict noted with surprise it was still the same day. More perturbingly, there was no mention of lunch.

"And now for a carriage ride," declared Rossingley, cheerily taking him by the arm. "We will be seen, we will be convivial, and you shall be an absolute honeypot with the ladies. And we must insist each and every one of them put you on their dance cards for Lady Wardholme's soirée this evening. Which we will be attending, by the way."

"We will?"

"We will. Don't pull that face, darling. She's a dreamboat once one looks beyond the wart." Rossingley clicked the reins. "And, between you and me, plenty of gentlemen have."

After the horror of the tailor's, the carriage ride was a welcome respite, even if Rossingley did maintain a constant stream of chatter. Mostly about Mr Angel.

Benedict marvelled at how freely he spoke of him. He spoke, too, a little of how they met. And then, because Rossingley was an inveterate gossip, they moved on to the subject of the disgraced baronet, Lord Gartside, and Tommy's minor role in bringing his downfall. He spoke of Tommy with great familiarity too.

"You were…were lovers. Weren't you?" Benedict asked daringly. He wasn't sure what made him think of it, but as soon as he gave it voice, he knew it to be the truth.

Rossingley threw him an extended, sideways glance, his pale gaze assessing. "Yes. On and off, during periods of time when we both needed something and the other supplied it. Such as when I lost my first true love, Charles. And when Tommy had lost…well, everything a few years before that."

Thanks to me, thought Benedict glumly.

They clip-clopped along. *Sorry* didn't fix broken lives any more than it fixed shattered china. They should invent another word, a nuanced, complicated one, something like those Prussian languages employed. Something that meant *sorry I selfishly left you to be arrested and potentially hung, but I'm a coward and not a day doesn't pass when my actions don't haunt me. And, incidentally, I still love you, and is there any way you could find it in your heart to love me back?*

"But have you guessed we're business partners too?" Rossingley's cultured tones dragged Benedict from his musings.

"Really? But he owns blackleg stands and gaming hells, and —" Benedict lowered his voice. " — brothels."

"Beautifully decorated brothels," Rossingley corrected. "So much fun to own, much more fun than cotton mills and draughty Scottish castles." His lips twitched. "Though I have those too."

"How on earth did you two meet?" As soon as the words left his mouth, Benedict regretted them. How did anyone meet a molly?

A smile played at the earl's lips. "You'll have to ask Tommy that. But we are old, excellent friends."

"He has few friends," Benedict observed. Indeed, he was unaware Tommy had any others, excepting perhaps Sidney. But that seemed less a friendship and more like mutual reliance.

"Yes." Rossingley nodded. *"Be wary then; best safety lies in fear."*

He smiled at Benedict's confusion. "The wisdom of Will Shakespeare. Tommy has faced imprisonment, poverty, and indescribable fear. He has learned to trust no one, and it has stood him in good stead. Hence the lack of close friends."

The earl's voice softened, though laced with amusement. "Secretly, though he has various convivial establishments, he prefers nothing more than quiet evenings at home with his ledgers and a good book. In that, you are well matched." He gave Benedict a sly nudge. "Amongst other ways."

Too busy blushing, Benedict missed Rossingley's next comment. But what with warts, papayas, Rossingley's revelations, and a reddened, lasting imprint of Tommy's mouth barely tucked below the line of his high collar, Benedict needed a moment to himself. Alas, it was not to be. A smart barouche pulled up alongside the earl's curricle, and two ladies, whom the duke should have known by name, fluttered their greetings. Fortunately, Rossingley was much more capable.

"Miss Caldicott and Miss Gresham! How delightful you are this fine morning! His Grace and I were only saying not five minutes hence how this overcast afternoon was in sore need of brightening with keen wit and vivacity. And here you both are!"

Two pretty, wide brimmed hats bobbed in unison. Two silk fans swished into action.

"Miss Caldicott insisted we admire the early spring blooms along the northern park border, my lord," cooed Miss Gresham. "The promise of that season's arrival is enough to survive the most bitter of winters, is it not?"

"Goodness, how marvellously you have conjured my own scattered contemplations into poetic verse." Rossingley produced a flirtatious smile. "You are a lady of hidden talents, Miss Gresham."

Something sharp pinched Benedict's thigh. "This is the part of the conversation where it's your turn to speak, darling."

Goodness, discourse was so much easier when the ladies he was addressing were Lady Isabella and the Honourable Beatrice Hazard. Their expectations had been set at a suitably low bar years ago.

Benedict girded his loins. "Uh...sadly, without rain, the

flowers will not flourish. According to a…um…botanical pamphlet from the Royal Society, the fallow months and rainfall are a necessary evil in order for the ground to build up good—"

"I trust our names are writ in bold gilt on your dance cards for the Wardholme soirée this evening, dear ladies?" the earl interjected, and Benedict's thigh endured another harsh pinch. "His Grace here is positively itching to accompany you both for a turn around the floor. Aren't you, Ashington?"

"Um…yes. Thrice! With both of you!"

The ladies tittered whilst Benedict tried to look like a man desperate to perform three polkas.

"Steady on, old chap," Rossingley murmured. "We're turning you into a rake, not a dancing bear. Issue our fond farewells, add something pithy and charming, and we'll move on to the next."

Benedict excelled at farewells. They were his favourite part of any social interaction. Doffing his hat, he bared his teeth in what he hoped was more a suave smile than a snarl.

"May the remainder of your afternoon ride be edged with sunshine and illuminated with beauty, ladies," he declared, pleased with himself. "And I very much look forward to our reacquaintance this evening at Lady Wart—*Ward*holme's."

Rossingley was still tittering when they paused to exchange pleasantries with the occupants of the next carriage. And the next, and the one after that. By the fourth encounter, Benedict was struggling to maintain a polite façade too.

"So," Rossingley surmised as they turned into the home straight. "Our plan of campaign for this evening—Eat heartily, as you have committed to practically every dance. Special attention, however, will be paid to the delightful and Honourable Beatrice Hazard, our dear, blemished Lady Wardholme herself, and the divine Mrs Catherine de Villiers."

"I am not well acquainted with the latter."

"You shall be," responded Rossingley with a glittering smile. "In fact, the *ton* will believe you to be most *thoroughly* acquainted with her before the night is out. And trust me, nothing would amuse that delightful lady more."

"She may reverse that opinion after time in my company."

Ignoring him, Rossingley carried on. "My valet informs me that Lord Lyndon has no plans to appear at any evening soirées for the foreseeable future, as he has travelled down to the south coast to nurse a twisted ankle and some unfortunate facial bruising. So, we have several occasions during which to firmly establish your rakery."

"My enthusiasm knows no bounds," muttered Benedict.

"Meanwhile," continued the earl, "Tommy and my darling Kit will spend their evening overtly seeking and monopolising Lady Isabella's attentions whilst Lord Francis mopes from the sidelines yet behaves impeccably. On board so far?"

Benedict was on board with an intent to sail off into the sunset (having first kidnapped Tommy), never to be seen again, thereby resolving all his problems in one fell swoop. He wondered if the Prussian's had invented a fancy long word for that.

Chapter Seventeen

TOMMY TOOK PERVERSE joy in attending smart balls in private houses. Especially when, strictly speaking, he hadn't been invited. Other gentlemen guests acknowledged him, of course, even if the majority sneered at any person who worked for a living. They didn't do so in his presence, naturally. They were too well bred for that and enjoyed the ambience of his club too much to risk being blackballed. Furthermore, sneering was damned awkward when he was a guest of not only the eleventh Earl of Rossingley but also the fourteenth Duke of Ashington. The handful of older ladies who recognised him (from back in the days when he never did anything he shone at for free) were as familiar with a part of his anatomy tucked behind the fall of his breeches as his pretty face. Thus, they tended to steer clear of him.

Tommy sensed the moment the duke arrived, even before he was announced. The atmosphere shifted; the burn of his dark gaze raised the hairs on the back of Tommy's neck. His rehearsed cool salutations dried in his mouth.

"Mr L'Esquire." The tiniest of naughty smiles played on the duke's lips. "Good evening."

"Your Grace."

As was his due, and with the *ton* looking on, Ashington accepted a small bow.

Tommy's mind went for a swim in the duke's deep brown eyes as if a string had been plucked midway between his knees and his heart. And a terrifying, wonderful truth hit him. *My desire for this man will never stop. I shall desire him if I see him never or if I see him each morning.*

The duke's exquisite navy waistcoat, paired with a tangerine-coloured cravat didn't help Tommy's cause. He cursed Rossingley's excellent taste in choosing them. Obviously, the earl wouldn't have used such an ordinary term as navy to describe it. He'd have given it some ridiculous puffery, like Peacock-neck Magenta or Yesterday's Empty Inkpot. In actual fact, it was the navy of a perfect starry sky and currently hugged the duke's solid frame in such a manner Tommy hungered to trade places with it.

Benedict seemed equally dumbstruck until the petite brunette on his arm issued a polite little cough.

"I don't believe I have the pleasure of your acquaintance, sir. Perhaps, if we loiter here long enough, His Grace might summon sufficient social polish to introduce us."

"Ah, yes. Apologies. Tom—Mr Thomas L'Esquire," the duke stammered. "May I present to you the Honourable Beatrice Hazard, only daughter of Lord Michael Hazard, Viscount of Wilmhurst. Lord Michael is a very dear friend of my late father.

And may I also present, before her impatience gets the better of her and she stamps her foot, Beatrice's close friend, Lady Isabella Knightley. Youngest daughter of Lord Ludham."

He regarded both his companions fondly. "They tend to come as a package, and I seem to frequently find myself playing the role of the string knotted around. Usually when I'm searching for a little peace and quiet."

"If we didn't disturb him, then most days, he wouldn't utter a single word," retorted Miss Knightley indignantly, whilst the Honourable Beatrice Hazard regarded Tommy with a curious half-smile.

"Pleased to meet you, Mr Thomas L'Esquire," Beatrice said.

"The pleasure is all mine," said Tommy gallantly. "And I beg to further my acquaintance with both of you during the dancing later this evening."

"You might live to regret that, Mr L'Esquire," ventured the duke. "Lady Isabella here pesters me endlessly about the goings-on in a gentleman's club. She will use the slower pace of the 'Duke of Kent's Waltz' as a perfect opportunity to chew your ear off."

"Then I shall be sure to make it worth her while." Once more, Tommy held the duke's gaze. "I have plenty of tales to make her swoon. Although I am of the opinion some of our more *private* affairs should forever remain behind locked doors. Don't you?"

"I believe you and I have this dance, Your Grace," Beatrice murmured with a subtle tug on a flushed Ashington's arm.

"And given that Mr Bannister hasn't yet shown his face, the scoundrel, I shall ask Mr L'Esquire if he would do me the honour of taking my arm too," said Lady Isabella. "Otherwise, I shall be forced to join mama." Without giving Tommy a moment to excuse himself, she carried on. "But I warn you now, my pumps are new and pinch dreadfully. So, I ask your forgiveness in advance if I step on your toes."

"Brace yourself, Mr L'Esquire. Lady Isabella is a ferocious interrogator. She will have your extended family tree and your preferred watchmaker before the evening is out."

"And you are awash with nonsense, Your Grace." She bobbed her tongue. "Come, Mr L'Esquire. Let me interrogate you far away from this annoying, fustian duke."

Trotting around a ballroom with the delightfully coquettish Lady Isabella proved no chore at all, though the quizzing began even before the musicians struck the first note.

"Lord Francis informs me he has devised an elaborate plan to win my hand in marriage. You and Mr Angel are to pursue me until my father collapses at Lord Francis's feet, begging him to plead his troth. It is the most exciting scheme imaginable, and you will have my full cooperation. I have been giddy since I heard of it."

"Giddy enough that I shall I have to hold you up?" Tommy answered as they took their position on the dance floor. "Very tightly? With one hand here?"

"Goodness, yes. And whilst we dance, you ought to gaze into my eyes and compliment me on how extraordinarily pretty I am. And then confess, loudly, as we glide past papa, that you cannot survive another day without me."

Her voice dropped to a furtive whisper. "Except I rather think we should skip that and talk about you instead. You own Squire's, am I correct? How thrilling! Tell me all. Is it terribly depraved? Do the gentlemen brawl? Are there fisticuffs?"

Two dances flew by before Tommy delivered her into the capable arms of Mr Angel, whose toes and ears would no doubt take an equal bashing. Alone again, he hoped to run into Benedict at the refreshments table and suggest they wander off into one of the murkier corners of Lady Wardholme's garden for some much-needed cool air and perhaps whatever else took Benedict's fancy. No such luck; he found himself leading the duke's other female companion—the Honourable Beatrice—onto the dance floor instead. And she proved to be as exhausting as Lady Isabella but for entirely different reasons.

"You appear to be very well acquainted with His Grace," she observed. Her hand gripped his coat sleeve with surprising firmness. "As a rule, he is of a reserved nature but is quite forthcoming in your company."

"As I only ever experience his manner when he is in my company, I am not in a position to comment on his behaviour when I am absent."

Tommy felt rather pleased with his sidestepping reply.

A feeling which only lasted as long as the opening bars of the quadrille.

"Mmm. It's most odd, but I have the distinct sensation that you and His Grace are friends of old, Mr L'Esquire." The honourable lady executed a neat turn. "In fact, a stranger observing you both might go as far as to surmise that you and he have a much-shared history." She fixed him with a narrow stare. "And yet, though I have known him since my childhood and spend many an afternoon in his company, I do not recall him ever speaking of you."

A little too late, Tommy realised he had underestimated his dance partner. Beatrice Hazard's eyes were sharp enough to see through a millstone, never mind rummage through his thoughts. "Forgive me," he tried, "but how could one possibly deduce all that from a brief exchange of pleasantries in a receiving line?"

"Because I miss very little, Mr L'Esquire," she confirmed unnecessarily. Once again, she impaled him on the end of her inquisitive blue gaze. "And because, having the misfortune to be of the weaker sex in the company of men, one is expected to say little of any value and think even less. Thus, one's powers of observation are frequently dismissed as inferior."

Beatrice accomplished an elegant *chassé* before continuing. "For instance, I have observed, Mr L'Esquire, that whilst you and I have been performing a creditable quadrille, your regard has landed on my perfectly acceptable features only once, and on my modest decolletage not at all. And if I were to ask you to close your eyes and describe the colour of my ballgown, I don't believe you would have the foggiest. And yet, you would be able to tell me His Grace's exact location to within a foot of where he is currently pretending to woo Mrs de Villiers. And also, the precise number of buttons adorning his very fine new waistcoat. And if I could also add—"

"I think, my lady, you have added quite enough," spluttered Tommy, his stomach dropping to the floor.

Alas, the blasted woman hadn't yet finished.

"Mr L'Esquire, I beg you not to interrupt—it is a habit gentlemen have around ladies, and it is most tiresome."

"Please accept my sincere apologies."

If, at that moment, he'd dared look into her rather fine sea glass eyes, he would have detected amusement brimming there.

"Accepted. I was only going to finish by adding that I don't give two figs that you are hopelessly besotted with him. I only hope you make him happy. Because God knows nobody else can."

*

TOMMY STAGGERED INTO the garden, immediately heading away from the lamplit terrace to make a beeline towards the shaded flower beds, where he might find a few minutes alone to compose himself. It wasn't often someone managed to wrong-foot him, but Beatrice Hazard had done it with ease. And so charmingly too.

"Here to admire the begonias?"

A thrill ran through Tommy's veins. "As long as that eagle-eyed woman isn't following me, yes. My head feels like a bouncing ball."

"You have my sympathies," the duke commiserated. "Beatrice has that effect on most men. It's a deliberate ploy to ensure she maintains her spinsterhood."

"She's…ah…at no risk of having that purloined by me."

Tommy looked up to where Benedict casually leaned against an old stone wall, dappled in clouded moonlight and hidden from anyone glancing out from the terrace. A half-empty glass of claret hung from one of his hands, the other tucked in his pocket. Tommy suddenly found himself grinning.

"You know," Benedict observed, casting his gaze around. "This spot was created for a lover's tryst."

Breathing in the cold night air, Tommy took up a position next to him, then rested his head back against the cool stone. "Yes, it is perfect for a romantic rendezvous."

"I am famous for contriving them." Benedict laughed. "In my own head, at least. There, I have dreamed up thousands. In reality, this is the first."

Tommy twisted to look up at him. His handsomeness stole the words from Tommy's mouth. He couldn't understand why every woman in the place didn't find themselves similarly mute. Or maybe they did, but the duke was oblivious. "You were loitering here in hope?"

With a swallow of wine, Benedict shook his head before passing the glass to Tommy. "Truthfully? No, though I could be persuaded." He took a deep inhale of the cool night air. "I came out here to escape. I've gallivanted around that damned ballroom so many times with so many different partners, I've made myself seasick. He wiped his fingers across his brow. "Not to mention I'm baptised in my own sweat."

With a chuckle, Tommy handed back the glass. "You are becoming less romantic by the minute, Your Grace."

"I'll happily drown in a bath of everyone's sweat if all this dancing and coquetry prevents Lyndon tarnishing our family name, allowing Francis to marry Isabella." Benedict let out a long sigh. "Though it's damned hard work."

"Be cheered that it appears to be having some impression. In the receiving room, I overheard one matron discussing you and Mrs de Villiers in a suitably scandalised voice. To which her companion remarked—disapprovingly—that you had also been paying close attention to Lady Wardholme. Which was courageous of you."

"The woman is terrifying. She has an extra, hidden set of

hands especially reserved for the polka." Benedict's own warm fingers slipped between Tommy's. "My courage should be rewarded, should it not?" His voice was barely above a whisper. "Perhaps a reward of the romantic tryst variety?"

The duke's lips were soft, cool, and moist. He tasted of claret and smelled of fresh rainfall. As his strong arms looped around Tommy, Tommy hungrily sank into the kiss.

"You called me by my name," whispered the duke around his mouth. "Benedict. You said it once. Like a sigh. As you spilled into my hand. I shall never forget the sound of it."

Anything more than this single hurried kiss was fraught with danger. Even that was foolhardy.

"And I fear I shall do both again if you kiss me like that," Tommy answered, "and insist on laying your hands there."

With a final lick of his tongue into Benedict's sweet mouth, Tommy groaned and pulled away. He halted the path of the duke's hand, trailing down his belly, by bringing it up to his lips. "We must go," he urged. "Your absence will soon be noted, seeing as you are cutting such a swathe through the ballroom."

"You are right. But this snatched moment is not enough." Benedict squeezed his hand, bringing it to his lips. "You...we have much time to make up." He hesitated, his eyes twin bright spots in the dark. "If that is something you want too? After...after everything?"

"Yes," Tommy breathed. "Yes."

Benedict smiled his slow, wary smile, the one that melted Tommy's bones. The one Tommy had believed lost to him forever, set in amber for all time, perfectly stored. The smile of the youth — of Tommy's lost lordling, innocent and shy and so damned sweet, perfuming the very air Tommy breathed.

Tommy returned it with his own exceptionally ordinary one. "I find I can deny you nothing, *Benedict.*"

"Aah," Benedict kissed each knuckle. "I like how that sounds on your tongue."

The doors to the terrace were flung wide. As chatter drifted across the garden, the duke peered over Tommy's shoulder.

"Listen," he said urgently. "I have a small hunting lodge, only a two-hour ride southwest from here. Ordinarily, one doesn't visit until the Glorious Twelfth, but it is not unheard of for me to drop by after a long hack. To be hacking with a gentleman friend would not be so peculiar. We could ride out there tomorrow if you… I could send a groom on ahead with a message to set fires, to ready the house, to do ah…whatever is entailed before my arrival. My household comes from the village each day—they do not stay overnight. We…we would be quite alone. Or if tomorrow doesn't suit, then perhaps a weeks' hence. Or even a month, two months. A year!"

After that hurried, long speech, the duke sucked in a deep breath. "Say yes?" he pleaded.

A shiver swept through Tommy at the picture Benedict painted of dark wood-panelled rooms, a log fire, cosy nooks, a private bedchamber. Of the duke's long, solid body laid out under him, on top of him, wrapped around him with no one but Tommy within miles to hear that gut-wrenching tiny noise he made in the back of his throat just before he—

"I have business engagements tomorrow which can't be postponed," Tommy said, and when the duke's face fell, quickly added, "But the day after, then, yes."

Chapter Eighteen

"YOU HAVE BEEN quite the twinkletoes this evening, Your Grace," Beatrice observed as they performed a (thankfully) sedate waltz. Any faster, and Benedict might collapse in a heap. Afternoons sparring at Gentleman Jack's were much kinder on the feet. And the jaw.

At least with Beatrice, he could give the inane chatter a rest. "And you have been quite the harridan," he admonished. "Poor Mr L'Esquire is terrified of you."

Beatrice laughed. "Oh, come, Your Grace, he's made of sterner stuff than that. Isabella is already enchanted by him. And by the Earl of Rossingley's chum, Mr Angel, also. He is outrageously charming. Between the two of them, Lord Ludham will be greasing Lord Francis's fist with double Isabella's allotted portion before the week is out. I sat beside him at supper, and I swear he had fewer grey hairs at the start of the evening than by the finish of dessert."

"Then we must hope Francis's ridiculous plan is working." Benedict stepped forward, rising on his right foot as his partner stepped back with her left. "Isabella is perfectly safe with both gentlemen, by the by, in case you were at all concerned."

"Not a jot." Beatrice nodded to a passing acquaintance. "I sense that both Mr Angel and Mr L'Esquire prefer their *amours* to be of a more rugged nature." As one, they performed a neat spin. Beatrice brought her lips close to Benedict's ear. "As, I believe, do you."

Rich claret turned to stone in his belly. How did one respond to that? His face burned as if in fever as, with an ungainly lurch, he stumbled over his next step, nearly sending them both crashing to the floor. A move far too adventurous, even for a newly anointed rake.

"Oh, do not fret, Your Grace," Lady Beatrice murmured as she righted them both. "I have suspected for some time."

"I have..." Benedict groped in vain for a sensible riposte. "I hoped...really?"

"Really." She smiled. "But I am a steadfast keeper of secrets. Especially when they bear considerable weight."

"It is a secret I planned on taking to the grave. I was...I was not born to stand out in such a way, to be of a different nature. I do not have the nerve for it."

"I'm afraid one cannot fight it, Your Grace." She regarded him so tenderly that tears plucked at his eyes. "Only dead fish go with the flow. And we have but one life. My dear father has always drummed into me that one must not waste it being a facsimile of what one is not. It is excellent advice, no?"

"Yes." Benedict blinked rapidly, then swallowed. "And I...I have come to realise that in recent days." Very gently, he squeezed the small hand clasped in his. "And also, that I have many friends."

They danced in perfect accord after that, almost like lovers. Indeed, if the duke had been granted more than one life, then sharing it together as husband and wife would have been a most amicable way to spend it. As they floated around the dance floor, Benedict became increasingly aware their happiness in each other's arms was under scrutiny.

Beatrice smiled up at him. "Your situation and our close friendship serve us both excellently, does it not? We can sully my good name with the gossipmongers so that I will not be obliged to attend these blasted cattle markets next season. I can retreat into happy spinsterhood. And you will gain the reputation as a dastardly duke of the lowest morals. Which means you and your delectable Mr L'Esquire may continue your discreet trysts until either one, or both of you, is thoroughly sick of the other. Which I suspect will be never."

Her beatific smile turned sly. "He's the person, isn't he? The one who has held your heart all these years. Whom you once wronged?" She leaned closer conspiratorially. "You don't have to say yes if it's too difficult. Simply blink twice."

Hiding one's face in one's hands was not an option with a dance partner in hold. Benedict groaned, the next best thing. "Even now, Beatrice, as you flail my secret desires wide open, you have the capacity to bring me joy. Will it appease your inquisitive mind if I confess that man sparks something inside me that I have never felt with anyone else?"

"It is mere confirmation of what I already guessed, Your Grace."

As they performed a tricky closed change, a dense fog of smug satisfaction radiated from Beatrice's slight form. Every now and again, she caught Benedict's eye, raising a shapely eyebrow.

"You, too, deserve every bit of happiness you can find, my dear Beatrice," he said at last.

Twice, they had sashayed past an entire row of matrons pointedly whispering behind fans, and twice, he'd moved his body scandalously closer to his dance partner's. With the taste of Tommy's lips still on his, Benedict was tempted to give them all a wave.

"And if it pleases you," he continued, "finding it between the pages of some ghastly tome harping on about fossil reptile discoveries, then I shall do everything in my power to make it happen. Starting with gazing oh-so-sincerely into your eyes as we sweep past Lady Butterworth and the Countess of Horton, then allowing my hand on your shoulder to drift...ah, just so."

*

THE FOLLOWING AFTERNOON, safe in the haven of his second study, Benedict indulged in a serene spot of thumb twirling. Ignoring his usual mountain of correspondence, he mulled over the previous evening. Especially the part where he and Tommy admired the begonias. He then skated over the chapter towards the end, where he had been hounded by Lady Wardholme, three cups of ratafia to the good. Never had the phrase 'pushed from pillar to post' felt so apt. Until the sublime Mrs Catherine de Villiers heroically rescued him, the woman literally had him backed up against a pillar and searching for a suitable post as a weapon to facilitate fighting his way out.

Interrupting his peace, Francis barged in without knocking and flung himself into a chair. "Joe Jonas stopped by ten minutes ago to inform us that Sam Leonard, the jockey riding Ganymede in the Gold Cup on the Thursday of the Horton ball, has been offered twenty pounds by Lyndon to throw the race."

Benedict hummed. He continued to twirl his thumbs. "Good. Tell him he must take the money."

"Tell him *what*? Surely not! Lyndon can't get away with it!"

"And he shan't," replied Benedict stoutly. "I have it in hand."

"*In hand* would be marching over to his rooms right this minute and confronting him!"

Benedict huffed, shaking his head. "No. That would be a waste of all our energies. He'll outright deny it. You and I both know our brother lies as well as an Aubusson rug. Send a message to Jonas that the jockey should take the money."

"If we let him get away with it this time, he'll simply carry on!"

"I have it in hand, Francis." Rarely was Benedict stern, making when he was so much more effective.

"Ugh." His youngest brother drummed his fingers on the arm of his chair. "I hate this. Why does he have to be such a bloody arse?"

"If we knew the answer to that, none of us would be in this mess. But be reassured that I will embark on a discussion with Lyndon in due course. When he returns to London."

Benedict had reached that conclusion last night whilst watching Tommy so elegantly leading Isabella through a waltz. They all deserved a shot at happiness; it was high time Benedict stopped being so timid and made sure it happened.

"I'm going to insinuate that we have an idea what is afoot regarding his plan to expose me and then offer him an opportunity to reconsider."

"But we have a scheme in place to counter his accusations. According to this morning's *Herald*, 'The fashionable world will not be surprised to hear that a young and very rich nobleman of the highest rank danced twice with the blooming and beautiful widow of a late distinguished French general'."

"Three times," Benedict corrected. "I was avoiding Lady W."

"And the *Post* describes Mr Angel tripping on the light fantastic with 'the accomplished and deservedly celebrated beauty, Lady Isabella Knightley'." Francis frowned. "*My* Lady Isabella Knightley. Our plan is bearing fruit."

"So it would appear," Benedict agreed. "But it is not foolproof, and I prefer we don't have to use it. And...he's our brother." He sighed heavily. "And we were once friends. No one is irredeemable, no matter how far they are prepared to fall."

Francis made an anguished, groaning noise. "You're bloody right, of course. I know that, but...God, it's hard." Shaking his head, he rose to his feet. "You have a big heart, Benedict. Sometimes, I fear it is both the worst and the best of you." As he reached the door, he hesitated. "Though I'm still befuddled as to why you won't call him out on nobbling our jockey."

"Because no one is irredeemable," Benedict repeated. "If, and when, he sees the error of his ways, I would prefer society judges him less harshly. Therefore, as it impacts no one but us, the bribery is a matter I wish to keep private. It is enough that, after the race is run, it will be clear to him that I knew of the bribe yet did not expose him. Trust me on this."

Screwing up his nose, Francis nodded his acceptance. His astute gaze narrowed as he studied Benedict. "Something about you has changed, dear brother. Since you...you know, revealed your...um...truth. You are surer of things. Of yourself. Of being the duke." His face relaxed into a grin. "That tangerine cravat, for instance, paired with the navy."

"I think you'll find the cravat was papaya and the waistcoat Persian indigo. And I'm considering having the same waistcoat made up again, but in a honey-yellow. Perhaps with a few flowers embroidered. What do you think?"

Francis chuckled. "I think, *Your Grace*, that the fourteenth Duke of Ashington is well on the way to becoming the finest and fairest of all the Ashington dukes. Also, may I say, the feyest."

With his hand on the door, he paused again. "And a little bird told me he is off for a lengthy hack tomorrow, which may take him away overnight."

"He is," admitted Benedict, refusing to meet his brother's eye. "I have an idea to stop over at...um...the lodge in Hampshire. Even us rakes need a night off from wooing the ladies, Francis."

Francis replied with a casual shrug, and Benedict relaxed. He'd got away with it. "Then I wish you a safe ride. Not sure much is happening tomorrow night, anyhow." His brother shrugged again. "No soirées that I'm aware of. I'll probably just wander over to Squire's for a jar or two, I expect."

He had the door open now and was halfway through it. "Mr L'Esquire won't be there, of course. *Hacking*. Honestly, Benedict, as if I'd fall for that."

Chapter Nineteen

TOMMY WAS QUIET on the long ride on account of an unfamiliar emotion suspiciously close to nervousness. And nudging on irritability. The stink of cow shit had kept them company for the last half mile, liberally spread across the fields in every direction he looked. If that wasn't enough to make him long for the festering fug of London town, then, ever since they crossed the river Rye at Ashtead, a persistent horde of gnats were making it their short life's work to build a home in his mouth.

He remembered, a little too late, that he loathed the countryside almost to the same extent as he loathed Lord Lyndon Fitzsimmons.

Tommy was out of his depth, of course, he reflected miserably as they trotted along at a pace a little faster than an occasional amateur rider such as he was used to. Making opportunistic love to Benedict in London, a grimy town with rhythms as familiar to

Tommy as his own nose, was one thing, but trotting out to his *hunting lodge* was another kettle of fish entirely. Nothing exposed the thinness of his respectable veneer like falling in love (and how insufferably!) with a duke in possession of a hunting lodge.

Regardless, love seemed determined to drag him there by his bootlaces.

Riding with great ease alongside, Benedict was quiet, too, no doubt brooding. On their return, he would meet with his brother and suggest he alter his course, together with a modest offer to increase his annual income. Tommy hazarded it would fall on deaf ears. He'd grown up in the stews. He knew people. He knew how they ticked. How petty jealousies matured into feuds, how envy and resentment simmered for years, how weak, clever creatures such as Lord Lyndon desired nothing more than to draw those they despised down to their level.

Which meant the half-baked scheme they'd laid most of the groundwork for had to succeed.

"How do you plan to tackle Lord Lyndon's assault on your stables?" Tommy enquired of his companion. He'd saddled up Rossingley's fine grey mare, a creature he often borrowed when riding through the parks at leisure with the earl. She was placid enough, but after an hour, he was convinced the saddle was stuffed with rocks. Surreptitiously, he shifted his aching buttocks.

"It's a secret," answered Benedict, then chuckled. "I am permitted *one*, aren't I? If only to drive Francis and Rossingley insane."

"For those reasons, you certainly are," Tommy agreed. "Rossingley prides himself on always being one step ahead."

"I am in awe of his wit as much as I am yours. I imagine the two of you make an excellent business team. You have accrued several investments together, I understand. When did you begin?"

Two years after I was freed from the pillory? Nine months after I stole a man's silver watch? One month after a madge beat me to a pulp? For all that he sensed Benedict was hungry to fill the gaps, his inglorious past didn't belong here, amongst fresh spring blossoms and dewy green grass.

"Several years ago," Tommy answered, shortly.

Bestride his beloved Nimbus, his lover sat straight-backed and severe. Even Tommy's inexpert eye recognised Benedict was a superb horseman. Windswept, flushed, and so solidly in his element, the longer he spent on horseback, the farther the diffident, uncertain duke receded. And the wider the crevasse between them gaped.

"He told me you were once lovers, too," Benedict pressed.

"Did he?" Tommy tightened his hands on the reins. "How very…forthcoming of him."

"More a lucky guess on my part. You…you do not hold a candle still?"

"No."

Tommy spat out a gnat, more single-minded than its companions. The foreshadowing of a sneeze tickled his nostrils. "We…I have had more than my share of lovers, Benedict," he said testily. "My sordid chequered past can attest to that. Do you care for me to enumerate them?"

Tommy couldn't have startled Benedict more if he'd pushed him off his mount into the clusters of stinging nettles lining the road.

"Apologies, Benedict," he managed stiffly, then sneezed twice in rapid succession. "I'm a little out of sorts."

"You are ill?" Concern limned Benedict's soulful eyes. "You are coming down with a cold? Have I ridden too fast?"

"No. I am perfectly well." Another sneeze, even more explosive than the first two. "Perhaps a little fast."

"Then tell me what ails you. Please, so that I can prevent it."

"It is nothing. I must apologise for my short temper."

Yet still, those bloody brown eyes gazed at him from within their damned fluffy lashes, mirroring the strength of the man's sincerity, his gentleness, his absolute goodness. And, despite himself, Tommy's deprived, velvet fist of a soft heart was enchanted. "I am...not at ease in the country," he admitted. "Nor indeed, in hunting lodges, though I have never had cause to visit one. What with once being a molly boy and all."

There, he'd said it. Benedict could make of it what he would.

The duke replied with a sharp clicking sound. He pulled on the reins, Nimbus stopping in an instant. "Let us pause a moment and dismount. Here."

"I am quite all right. Forget I said anything. Indeed, I have looked forward to our trip."

"I said we're stopping." Benedict dismounted with a smoothness belying his size. "We have gone too long without each other to let snappish words and misunderstandings go unheeded. You are unhappy. Or uncomfortable. Or...something."

He helped Tommy down, which was damned embarrassing, unnecessary, and yet also indescribably wonderful. He secured the horses whilst Tommy succumbed to a sneezing fit.

"I'm going to give you some riding lessons this autumn,"

Benedict declared as much to himself as Tommy. "And I shall acquire a suitable mount, especially for you, to keep at my stables." As if fitting him for size, his eyes raked over Tommy, from the top of his head where his annoying cowlick was most likely doing its thing, down to the shine of his riding boots, still creaky from underuse. A satisfied smile reached from one corner of his mouth to the other. "I shall enjoy that very much."

"Alas, it will take more than a good seat to make a true gentleman of me."

"I know," answered Benedict, taking Tommy's hand. "And I don't care. Come here."

Being neither oak nor beech, the tree Benedict selected exceeded the extent of Tommy's botanical knowledge. Tall and sturdy, with oval-shaped green leaves, it was a commonplace sort of tree, the kind a child might draw. And yet, when Benedict gently pushed him against the trunk and its crusty brown bark warmed his back, Tommy forgot about ordinary trees and gnats and his chafed arse. Because Benedict was kissing him as though his hand was already around Tommy's prick and his head resting on a goose down pillow.

"I have neither enjoyed nor suffered much in this life," Benedict murmured between kisses. He smoothed back Tommy's errant lock of hair as his eyes, fringed with lashes the colour of the damp earth under their feet, levelled with Tommy's. "I have been surrounded by creature comforts, yes; I have wanted for nothing. But believe me when I tell you this. It has been a life lived in grey twilight. Until now. Until you."

He tipped Tommy's face up to the leafy canopy above and smiled before planting a kiss on the tip of Tommy's nose, which

Tommy loved, although it made him squirm. "And I shall embrace you and cherish you, young Tommy Squire, because of our differences, not in spite of them."

And then, looping his arms around Tommy, Benedict hugged him.

The man was very much like a warm solid tree trunk himself. He smelled of the earth, of horse, and of a handsome raven-haired youth. Tommy couldn't recall ever having been the recipient of a hug like it.

"There are so many questions I want to ask you, Tommy, I scarcely know where to begin. They spring into my mind, unbidden, when I should be focussing on mundane matters. For instance, whether you have a favourite season? Why you favour red ink? If you like crocuses? Thunder? What is the origin of the scar on your left wrist? Your preferred dessert?"

Tommy couldn't help a short laugh. "Those things sound terribly immaterial."

"Not to me."

He lost track of how long they stood that way, Tommy's body cradled in his lover's arms, his head nestled in the hollow of his neck. This hug was a little thing, too, immaterial, like his penchant for red ink. And yet it told Tommy so much about the man.

When they reluctantly pulled apart, Benedict fished out his pocket square and offered it to Tommy. He beamed as though bestowing a gift.

"Your nose. It is dribbling."

"As you can see, no part of me is fond of the country." Mortified, Tommy dabbed it. "But my nose will learn to tolerate it. As will the rest of me. For you."

Conversation flowed more freely when they resumed their ride. Benedict pointed out a few unusual landmarks and places he'd visited, and, as they came nearer their destination, places and land he owned.

"You are so grand that I feel I should be offering you a tithe of my harvest," Tommy teased as they passed yet another swathe of forestry belonging to the Ashington estate.

"At the risk of imitating every pompous, shallow nobleman that ever lived, it is a monumental headache. Ever since my father passed, I've become increasingly of the opinion us Ashington brothers were born in the wrong order. Francis, for instance, would have made an excellent duke. He has our father's quick intelligence, yet he is kinder and fair with it. And more importantly, he will beget children." Benedict looked across at Tommy, his expression sombre. "I, on the other hand, whilst fair-minded enough, have insufficient wit to manage our affairs without it taking up the lion's share of my attention. And" — at this he threw Tommy a small, intimate smile — "I have no intention of producing issue. Of that, since stumbling across you again, I am certain. Dukedom be damned."

Why did that make Tommy's heart sing so freely? Ever since his reacquaintance with Benedict, his mind had whispered their affair was nothing more than fleeting. Or, at best, an occasional tupping when his future duchess failed to satisfy his urges. With the weight of Benedict's responsibilities, not to mention the horror of the title falling into Lyndon's hands should he never have issue, how could it be anything else?

"But the Ashington title and lands would pass to Lord Lyndon or his future offspring on your death, would they not?" Tommy confirmed. "As the next in line?"

"Yes," Benedict clarified, not seeming too concerned. "But I plan to rehabilitate him or, if that fails, outlive him."

"On his current trajectory, the latter is more likely."

"Sadly, for him," replied Benedict with a nod, "I concur. With a bit of luck, he'll not sire any legitimate offspring, and on my death, everything will pass over to Francis. If so, then I should die a happy man knowing our affairs are in safe hands."

"But not too soon, I hope."

They exchanged a smile.

"I have recently begun to hope that too," answered Benedict. "So, you see, though I have all this—thousands of acres of land, hunting lodges, fine crystal, silks, pots of wealth, priceless art— none of it is mine. Not really. I'm simply a custodian, and a very average one at that, passing through. In years to come, the four- teenth duke shall be nothing but a brief, dull footnote in the long, distinguished history of Ashington." Leaning forward, he patted Nimbus's withers. "And, when I'm astride this majestic beast or one of his stablemates, all of whom are truly mine, I understand that. I see it very clearly. And it brings me both endless comfort and boundless joy."

*

"A *SMALL* HUNTING lodge?" Tommy scoffed, greatly amused. His anxiety had withered around the time his lover had offered him his pocket square and kissed his temple. Again. The sneezing hadn't ceased, but it seemed a lesser foe.

As they rounded the final corner of a shady, twisting lane, a sprawling redbrick manor house came into view. Row upon row of paned lead windows twinkled in the rare late afternoon sunshine, as if welcome candles had been lit in each. A striking stack of chimney pots dominated the rooftop, all four puffing out smoke. Ivy crept around the doorways and snaked up the walls.

Benedict's eyes twinkled too. "Forgive me, I was comparing it to the one in the grounds of Ashington House."

I'm in love with a duke in possession of two hunting lodges, Tommy thought. Lord, just strike me down now.

"This one hardly sees much use outside of the shooting season," Benedict continued. "Not my thing, really, taking shots at defenceless animals. But, come the winter months, I suppose hunting and billiards are the only goings-on keeping us idle men of leisure occupied."

The *only* goings-on? Tommy still tasted Benedict's hot kisses under the shady bower, not an hour since, and how his fingertips had cupped Tommy's face as if it were precious.

"Let us stable the horses, and I'll show you inside."

Whilst as lavish as Tommy expected, for all its grandeur, the place had the empty, melancholic air of a home barely inhabited. Hovering in the entrance hall as if trying to ascertain his bearings, Tommy wondered if Benedict felt it too. While bold and garrulous in the saddle, Benedict seemed to shrink into himself inside the lodge. As if now he had Tommy here, he wasn't sure what to do with him.

"It's a lot, isn't it?" Tommy said quietly. "Bringing a lover home to seduce."

"I...um, yes. And only now am I discovering it." He shot Tommy a curious look. "For the first time, we are entirely alone, you and me. And I haven't a clue what to do next."

Tommy could compose an entire list. "One's education, no

matter how grand, doesn't generally include it."

Benedict smiled faintly. "I'm going to make a cake of myself, aren't I?" He huffed a laugh. "I assumed I would bring you here and, well" — his face coloured — "do what comes naturally. And I do want to do that, of course. But also, I can't help feeling saddened that this…this subterfuge and a two-hour horse ride are necessary for us to be alone."

"Surely it is better than the alternative."

"Yes, but…" Benedict made an exasperated sound. "I don't want snatches of you, Tommy, where we…we make love, then hurriedly put ourselves back together. We've waited too long. Although, just to be clear, I do want that too. But I also want to laze around my bedchamber with you, or my study. Or your study. Visit parks and friends and my stables and so forth. As good chums, like Francis and Isabella do. As well as…be lovers."

"Rossingley manages it," Tommy ventured.

"He does," Benedict agreed. "Awfully well. But he's…well, he has… He's beyond reproach, isn't he? He has a dead wife, bless her soul, and two sons. Angel hides in plain sight too. Men regard him askance, convinced he's out to bed their wives, whilst the wives look at him praying for the same thing. And with a sly glance here and a flutter of his eyelids there, he is careful not to disabuse them."

Benedict made another despairing noise. "Anyhow. Be that as it may. I daresay you're famished. I…um…if I'm here alone, I fend for myself."

Goodness knows how Benedict hadn't expired from starvation, Tommy observed, as he led him downstairs to the kitchen. An inviting, freshly baked loaf sat in the middle of the rough-hewn table, still warm. Platters of cold meats, fruits, and cheeses circled it, enough to feed an entire shooting party. Tommy's mouth watered; Benedict seemed baffled.

"Cutlery," he said eventually, gazing about him as if a maidservant might miraculously appear and thrust the correct implements into the correct hands. "And plates. We need plates."

Such was his bewildered, helpless expression, like a little boy lost, that Tommy took pity on him.

"Sit." Pushing on his shoulder, Tommy plonked him in a chair. "You can make yourself useful by opening this claret."

Then, gathering utensils, he fussed around with napkins, dishes, bread knives, and such, passing them to the coddled duke one at a time, tempted to explain their purpose—doing everything but eating the damned food for him.

So, yes. Differences. They had enough to fill a kitchen three times the size of this one. But as they sat opposite each other and exchanged a look, they still had the same beating hearts.

"This is terribly awkward, is it not?" Benedict laughed distractedly; it wasn't a laugh at all, really. "You must feel as if you are visiting a bedridden maiden aunt or like a child forced to play with another whilst the mamas gossip and drink tea."

"It's the most entertainment I've had all week. I've decided that as payment for my riding lessons, I'll teach you how to make a pot of tea. And peel potatoes."

"Potatoes? Really? Do they have skin on them?" With a grin that lit up the room, Benedict poured them both a generous glass of claret. "I have no practical abilities at all outside the stables. I…didn't exactly think it through, did I? I'm a spoiled, idle Corinthian, and you're a—"

"An upstart who's barely set foot outside the borough of St Giles?"

"I was going to say a person with vastly more experience than me in these situations. Boasting many, many more useful skills. And infinitely more desirable."

"None of those statements carries an ounce of truth, Benedict." It was funny, but now Tommy had begun using his Christian name, his mouth couldn't forgo an opportunity to speak it. "Your physical virtues far outweigh mine, and as you know, this is my first trip to a *hunting lodge*. I'm making it up as I go along."

"My *reserve* hunting lodge."

"You are leaving room for my aspirations."

Tipping back his head, Benedict took a swallow of claret. Tommy imagined it slipping down his long throat, and he wanted to lick the length of it himself. "Apart from the obvious," Benedict said, swirling the drink around in his glass, "there's very little to occupy one in the countryside out of season."

The obvious was perfectly fine with Tommy.

"I suppose we could always get drunk," he added. "Tends to be the usual fallback for most of my chums."

Or we could indulge in mind-blowing, glorious fucking? Perhaps there was an etiquette to staying in a hunting lodge that Tommy was unaware of. No fucking until nightfall. Or perhaps his virgin lover was simply waiting for Tommy to make the first move. "Not the worst suggestion I've ever heard," he said neutrally.

The duke pushed away his plate. "Do you play billiards?"

Really? Those games could go on for hours. "Badly," Tommy admitted. "Rossingley once tried to teach me but gave up. His house rules are unorthodox, to say the least."

"I imagine he's sickeningly good."

"At everything," Tommy supplied. "Except being a patient billiards tutor." *And teaching me hunting lodge etiquette.*

"Then allow me before the best of the light fades."

How large must the billiards room be in the bigger hunting lodge? This one could double as a cricket square. Even in here, a fire merrily simmered in the grate. The duke's absent household had anticipated his every need.

Both men removed their tailcoats, and Tommy took up a winged leather chair with a view of the table. Dusting off two cues, Benedict offered one to Tommy, then leaned across the baize to set up the three balls. With such an excellent view of Benedict's breeches, moulded to his muscular arse, Tommy suddenly became quite fond of billiards. And as the white linen of Benedict's shirt pulled tight across his strong shoulder blades, all in all, the game could quite become one of Tommy's favourite pastimes.

"I tend to play two points for a cannon and three for a hazard," Benedict explained, "with a one point deducted for a foul. First player to reach twenty-one wins." He brushed a speck of fluff from the table. "But we can forget points if you are a bit rusty. Or I can start with a handicap."

How typical, thought Tommy, admiring the beautifully made cue. And how dare Lord Lyndon even consider kicking his brother down. Benedict's modesty was both his most charming and greatest flaw.

"I'll be the dot ball," continued Benedict, scratching his cue tip with a piece of chalk. "Would you like to kick things off?"

"You carry on." At ease, Tommy crossed his legs at the knee. "I'm perfectly fine here for a moment, absorbing it all. Watching your technique." *Watching your arse.*

As in all areas of his achievements, Benedict had down-played his skill with the cue, effortlessly racking up early points until, in a typically Benedict way, Tommy had the distinct impression he was holding back so as not to humiliate his opponent. Tommy cared not whether he won by a margin, drew, or lost, but he knew that if he pointed out Benedict's talent, the other would try even harder to hide it.

In fact, Tommy decided, as Benedict apologised for defeating him and set up the balls for another game, the diffident duke was a little like a billiards table himself. When viewed from afar, it seemed a flat, bland expanse yet hiding many deep dark pockets, which one didn't discover until one was right upon him.

A position Tommy was very much looking forward to. Especially when the man draped himself across the baize right beside him to reach for an extended pot. With his delicious backside within fondling distance and two generous measures of brandy down, on top of the claret, the temptation for mischief proved too great.

"That was an excellent solid stroke," he observed as Benedict potted yet another ball, racking up two more points. "You have such a smooth cue action. Your wrist, it's like this." Naughtily, he demonstrated with a suggestive up and down movement, bordering on obscene.

Evidently not having moved in the same social circles as Tommy during his youth, Benedict took his comment at face value. "A fluid wrist action is key," he agreed. He blew a little chalk from the end of his cue, his handsome face a picture of innocent concentration. "And regarding my cue, I find I am most effective when I use just the tip."

Bending forwards again, he lined up for his next shot. Dark eyes narrowed on the ball, he drew his arm back and took careful aim.

"I bet you are," murmured Tommy.

The shot pinged off two cushions, missing the hole by miles.

"Take it again." Tommy insisted expansively. "Think *hard* about that tip action."

Still bent over the table, Benedict snorted. "Should I pull out my long cue?"

Now it was Tommy's turn to laugh as he held up his hands. "You'll have no complaints from this quarter."

Still chuckling, Benedict lined up another shot. His eyes grazed upwards, once, to meet Tommy's before dropping back down to the baize. "Of course," he added as, with a deft flick, he sent the ball cannoning into the heart of the pocket, "you could always come over here and take it out for me."

Straightening, he abandoned his cue and hefted himself onto the table. He leaned back on his hands, legs swinging invitingly. "What say you, Tommy?"

Tommy's cue clattered to the floor as he sauntered over. "I say we shouldn't waste any more time."

Their first kiss felt soft and new. Small nips, tender presses, as if they were compiling an inventory of each other's mouths, memorising the shape and texture. Tommy dropped his hands to Benedict's broad thighs. He sketched the shape of those, too, the span of his hand measuring the meat of them.

Benedict's palms cupped Tommy's face, tugging him closer. His thighs fit around Tommy's narrow hips, holding him there as he took his fill. A small moan slipped from his lips as he deepened the kiss. His hands glided down to Tommy's arse, and the heat of his cock rubbed up against Tommy's belly.

"What do you need?" Tommy whispered. "Tell me what you want."

With nimble fingers he pulled at Benedict's cravat, letting it slide to the floor. Dark pupils flaring, Benedict dipped his gaze to watch.

"I need you." Benedict's fingers were at the fold of Tommy's breeches. "I want...I want a night that lasts for days. Weeks. Years. Here. With you."

Two sets of boots came off. Later, Tommy wouldn't be able to recall how. Nor how he ended up on the billiard table, on his back, naked. A shirtless Benedict crawled between his legs. Like a blind man picking his way, his fingers led and his lips followed, hugging the slope of Tommy's calf, the shallow bend of his knee, the curve of his thigh. Worshipping indifferent, functional, inglorious pieces of him and bringing them alive.

He greeted Tommy's cock with a gust of hot air and a thirsty sigh. "Missed you, old friend," he whispered. Benedict softened his spit-glossed mouth against it in the gentlest of kisses. Tommy shifted his hips as it leaked a reply.

"But still, you remember what I like," he breathed as Benedict sealed his lips around the tip.

Tommy's fingers tangled in his raven's hair, twisting the strands. Benedict's cock-sucking was a torment—a lengthening, a withdrawal, a provocative hint of more. With every push and pull, the satin heat of Benedict's throat closed tighter around him, dissolving his mind and his bones, edging him heavenward. A pressure built in his ballocks, and heat spilled down his spine. He pushed Benedict away, squeezing himself.

"Not yet," he panted. "I do not wish that yet."

Smugly—and the tilt of Benedict's swollen lips could not be mistaken for any other expression—he snuggled his hips in between Tommy's thighs, making himself a home.

"You taste of sugar there too," he whispered.

Tommy rolled his eyes. "I fear your romanticism is incurable."

Benedict's hot tongue nibbled behind Tommy's ear. "Dirty, delicious sugar."

Tommy would remember forever the feel of Benedict there, like that, the hard warmth of his chest against Tommy's smooth, hairless one. The tickle of the coarse black curls covering it, the scrape of his whiskers along the hinge of Tommy's jaw. The burning hunger in his velvety, jet-black stare. And the tenderness of the unkillable smile climbing Benedict's cheeks as he rested on an elbow, how familiar it was becoming and how much he'd never tire of it.

"Of all the amorous seductions I played in my mind during our ride here, this wasn't one of them," Benedict confessed. He pressed his lips to Tommy's forehead. "The soft bed in my chamber featured in all." His gaze slanted across to the abandoned cues, the ocean of deep blue baize. "But here we are, adrift in the middle of a billiard table."

A laugh at the absurdity of where they'd ended up erupted from Tommy's throat. "Even Rossingley's heretical billiards rulebook states one should always maintain a foot on the floor."

Throwing his head back, Benedict joined him in laughter.

"My house, my billiard table, my rules." And then, "My dearest lost love."

They fell into each other. Desperate, open-mouthed kisses littered Tommy's throat. Somehow, as they both caught their breaths, Benedict's breeches also made their way to the floor. His hard cock milked the groove of Tommy's thigh, his teeth latched onto Tommy's neck. Digging his heels in, Tommy clawed at his lover's back, his own needy cock forging a damp path along Benedict's belly. A molten knot formed in the pit of his own as Benedict drew back.

"I fear I may spend," he gasped, "too soon."

Tommy ran his fingers lightly down the curve of Benedict's spine. He had not travelled far from spilling himself. "Who knew billiards could be such fun?"

Benedict's answering boyish grin stole the bones from Tommy's knees. Tommy tasted himself as their mouths briefly joined. Sinfully, Benedict rolled his hips over Tommy. "We're touching balls. A new billiard rule for the second-best hunting lodge." With another smug tilt to his lips, he added, "I'm a duke, don't you know. Apparently, I can make up new rules just like that."

Winding his arm around Benedict's neck, Tommy pressed a hard, punishing kiss to his mouth. "My duke," he whispered.

Benedict's hand found a passage between their damp bodies; he wrapped them both up in his palm. Three swift strokes, four if they were generous, and Tommy whimpered before pulsing hot and harsh between them. His lover, on a low groan, was but a second behind.

It took them a long while to part. In the warm dip between

Tommy's neck and shoulder, Benedict discovered a cosy spot for his head, burrowing in and collapsing there. Every now and again, little contented sounds broke the velvety silence. If Tommy hadn't been so squashed between the hard leaded board underneath him and the equally hard but more magnificent one atop, he fancied he could have stayed there until morning. When Benedict finally clambered off, daylight had all but gone, taking the heat of the room with it. Tommy shivered.

"Come." Benedict held out a hand, hauling him up. "You're cold."

He appraised Tommy's slight, naked form with a naughty gleam. "You never did have much meat on your bones." Unbothered by his own nakedness, Benedict swamped Tommy in his linen shirt, a gesture as sweet as any lovemaking.

"Your staff are in for a treat in the morning." Tommy eyed the damp patch in the middle of the baize. "We may have damaged it."

Lazily, his arm resting across Tommy's shoulders, Benedict peeked over. "Billiards table be damned." He cupped Tommy's jaw, delivering a savage kiss. "It's mine to do with what I want."

"What happened to 'I'm simply a custodian passing through'?"

"I've changed my mind." With a final kiss, he pulled away, giving Tommy's hand a determined tug.

"Bedtime, I believe. At the second-best hunting lodge, we keep country hours."

Chapter Twenty

LEADING TOMMY TO his bedchamber, washing them both clean—even taking it in turns to piss—then pulling aside the counterpane and slipping under together felt the most natural thing in the world. As though all the pieces of himself were finally aligned and working together. As if his head, his heart, his lungs, hands, and cock—even his feet, tangled with Tommy's—were thinking, doing, feeling, thumping, *reaching* towards the same harmonious thing.

Tommy reclined against the pillows while Benedict fiddled around like a maidservant until he was quite comfortable. Now, he lay on his belly beside him, pillowing his head in his arms whilst Tommy's hand rested on his nearest arse cheek, petting it. Benedict had believed the happiest moment of his life had occurred a half hour earlier as he'd lain over Tommy on the billiard table. Already, this one pipped it.

He reached out to finger the commonplace key hanging from a thin silver chain around Tommy's neck. The metal had a warmth to it from lying next to Tommy's skin.

"Is this the key to your heart?" He curled it in his palm, and Tommy closed his hand around Benedict's.

"No." Tommy sounded amused. "You already have possession of that. And have done for many a long year." He accepted the brush of Benedict's mouth against his. "Even though, this evening, you have kissed my lips sore."

Benedict traced the line of them with his thumb, and then, because he could, and they were his, he kissed them again. "They are superlative. I cannot resist."

He tapped Tommy's ribs with the key. "Then it must be the key to a treasure chest."

Tommy's deliciously reddened lips curved. "Of a dull sort. It unlocks my desk, containing my accounts ledgers for all my businesses."

"My lover is a rich man!" declared Benedict, grinning. He imagined Tommy's accounts were meticulous. And if he was fishing to unearth more about his lover and his extraordinary past, then he wasn't sorry.

Tommy raised an eyebrow. "All things are relative, Your Grace. Though Rossingley and I enjoy expanding our little empire."

"Rossingley has fingers in many pies. He continues to make large profits from his cotton mill." Benedict hesitated. "But he has experienced sadness, too, I think. Like you."

Tommy's fingers walked up Benedict's back, counting the vertebra one by one and then, as carefully, down again. He seemed lost to his thoughts.

"Rossingley saved my life," he said softly. "And then he became my lover, and after that, he supplied most of the capital for my first investment." His finger tapped at the base of Benedict's spine. "And now he has Kit, and I have you."

Benedict turned the key over before letting it drop. "May I ask how? How he rescued you?"

Tommy's eyes slid in his direction. "Through pure chance, would you believe. Nothing more. The day of the raid, chance led him down Vere Street. He was making a detour; a carriage had overturned in Margaret Street. His own rode by as I was being dragged in cuffs out of the Hart. Though he had never visited, he knew of the place and what it was. Then, because he's kind and decent and one of our sort, he arranged my release as soon as he was able." Tommy's fingers recommenced their slow count. "He bribed someone for a paltry sum." Staring up at the ceiling, again, he blew out a long exhale. The cool breath ghosted over Benedict's spine. "My life was worth a mere three guineas."

"I have spent more this year on treats for Nimbus."

"Last season's cravat fetched almost as much. It was still around my wrist when I was carted off. I sold it to a tailor."

Kings, queens, and dukes be damned. Chance was the real monarch, reigning overall. Even the mighty floundered in a sea of it. An ugly thought penetrated Benedict's mind, and he immediately hated himself for it.

"Did you become his lover out of obligation?"

Tommy gave a soft laugh. "God, no. I didn't see him for several months after that. His wife died; he was occupied with the estate and his children. Though he kept tabs on me from a distance. His valet, Pritchard, used to appear every now and again to make sure no harm befell me."

"How did you live? Did you...?" Benedict had a feeling he already knew the answer.

"Yes. When I had to. I stole things too. But then I joined a theatre troupe — an actor I befriended introduced me. They were looking for a pretty boy to play the role of a starving young girl." He barked a laugh. "I was half-starved and my hair long and unruly; very little acting was required. My career treading the boards continued from there. I accrued a little blunt, Rossingley watched a performance, we rekindled our acquaintance, and, well, here I am. An idle gadabout in a duke's second-best hunting lodge."

A decade of pain and struggle concertinaed into a handful of sentences. Benedict wouldn't press for more, not now. One day, perhaps. Instead, he rolled on top of Tommy, pulling him into his arms. "A man as courageous and beautiful such as you deserves all the good things life has to offer."

Tommy slipped a hand around Benedict's neck, playing his fingers through Benedict's hair. "Pretty words, Your Grace." A sly smile tilted his sublime lips. Cupping his mouth around Benedict's ear, he whispered. "But they mean nought until you tell me I'm your very special pomegranate."

Benedict snorted with laughter. He straddled him, pinning him to the bed. "Yes! You are my most special, my most perfect pomegranate." He laughed again at the joyful folly of it. "Hard on the outside, Tommy Squire, but by God, your seed is succulent!"

"And you are a ridiculous, starry-eyed fool."

Benedict swooped down for another taste, and even more

capricious flights of poetic jabber filled his head. Ones he'd die clutching to himself rather than share with his lover and risk making even more of a cake of himself. But there they were, buzzing around his head like bumble bees drunk on nectar — whimsical nonsense itself. How else could his mind interpret the delicious rush to his cock and the ache in his ballocks?

"Make love to me," Tommy murmured as their mouths parted. Hunger gleamed in his blue-grey eyes, and Benedict's swarm of bumble bees scattered as his belly lurched with pleasure. "Spill your seed inside me. For weeks, there has been nothing I have desired more."

"God, yes. But you must show me how."

"Your body will know how." Tommy held Benedict's face in his palms. "For men as in tune as us, it is as natural as breathing." His eyes flicked to bedside table. "We have hair oil, do we not?"

"Hair…oh. *Oh*." Benedict's voice turned inexplicably hoarse. "We…yes. I would do that gladly. I…" His speech faltered. Already, his prick felt more unyielding than a marble bust. "I…do believe there is not a drop of blood left in my head for thought. Hair oil. Yes, here."

"Make good use of it." Tommy's eyes crinkled. "You must permit a new rule for the second-best hunting lodge. Just when you think you've added enough, add a little more." He arched his hips up to meet Benedict's, eliciting a shiver from deep in Benedict's core. "I have not had a man inside me for many a year. And a duke, never."

Tommy's fingers, coated in hair oil, disappeared between his legs. With his other hand, he fondled himself. Benedict watched, torn between putting his fingers where Tommy showed him and mesmerised by Tommy doing it to himself.

"I have never seen or done..." Benedict moistened his lips. Tommy's cock was as hard as his own. "Do you find that to be pleasurable, or is it merely essential?"

In answer, Tommy guided Benedict's fingers into the shallow slippery divide. Then, relaxed and loose, he sank back into the pillows as Benedict copied what he'd seen. Tommy closed his eyes, shamelessly rolling his hips to greet every movement of Benedict's fingers. His cock dribbled, darkening his fair curls. Tiny noises left his lips, pleased humming sounds that made Benedict's spine tingle and his ballocks ache.

With his other hand, Benedict gave his cock a desperate squeeze.

"Now, my love." Tommy's voice sounded husky. He spread his legs impossibly wider. Benedict hesitated.

"I have...have seen dogs and...they turn like so, no?"

Tommy's laugh was throaty and warm. "Yes. But we are not dogs, though I am panting for you like one. And we will turn. You shall take me every way, in every manner. But for now —" he shoved a pillow beneath him — "like this. So I can see you."

Tommy's legs gripped his back as Benedict lined himself against Tommy's hole. And then, feeling as if he might burst, Benedict inched forwards. His body tingled and heated as if not only his cock, but the entirety of him plunged blindfolded into a hot, hidden world, like a wild seed burrowing deep into succulent earth.

"I have never, in my stormiest dreams, imagined you would feel like this," Benedict gasped.

Tommy's eyes were half-closed, his mouth pinched. Sweat

glistened on his brow, and his fingernails bit into Benedict's flesh.

Benedict instantly stilled. "I'm hurting you."

"No…never," Tommy puffed. "Just…ah." His heels carved new dimples in Benedict's back, his hips shifting under him. "You are stretching me wide. We are… Yes, that's better."

Around Benedict's shaft, something softened, slipped, unlocked. Tommy's lips parted on a low broken moan as, in a rush, Benedict slid deeper. His ballocks tightened; an inhuman gasp escaped him. Every fibre of his being screamed for him to plunder and ransack.

"That," Tommy breathed shakily. "Just…stay…like that… That is perfect."

Benedict's skin, all of it, was taut as a bow string. He moaned again. He cursed. "I beg, Tommy, do not make that sound. Perfect—ah, how inadequate that word is—will be but a fleeting memory if you do."

Tommy's huff of laughter squeezed Benedict like a vice. A stream of curses burst from him.

"Also," Benedict gasped again, "oh lord, there is another hunting lodge rule. One I shall pass immediately. Do not, with me here at the mercy of whatever you are doing to my prick, laugh again. I beg you."

Predictably, things sped up a little after that. Amusement and discomfort vanished from Tommy's eyes, replaced by a restless burning desire. He pushed up against Benedict, swallowing Benedict deeper still, shattering his last shred of control. With urgent need, Benedict thrust into his lover as his lover thrust back. Together, they drove towards release, whirling out beyond the boundaries drawn for them by others, beyond ones Benedict had drawn for himself. He poured his love into Tommy with every snap of his hips, feeling it returned, hearing it sighing in every harsh breath.

Tommy's hand pumped between them as his white throat heaved. And then he shuddered his release, his channel clenching and unclenching around Benedict until he, too, was spilling, hot and endless and —

"I…ah…yes…" Benedict managed, collapsing on his lover like a weighted blanket. A very weighted blanket. And he stayed that way.

*

"I MAY HAVE lost a few moments in time," Benedict observed a while later.

Under him, Tommy huffed a laugh, the movement causing Benedict to slither from inside. Wincing, Tommy brought his legs down.

"You are sore," Benedict stated, alarmed. He lifted his bulk away from him. "I was too rough."

"No," Tommy shook his head in protest. "You were…you have nothing to compare yourself to, but you are…dominant in your lovemaking." Blowing a cool gust of air through pursed lips, he wiped the back of his hand across his damp forehead, then brought his hand to his nose. "Your scent is everywhere. Even my sweat contains traces of you."

"That is a good thing?"

Tommy brought him down for a kiss. "An excellent thing, my love. For me."

Benedict liked the word 'dominant'. Perhaps lovemaking

would become the only area of his life where he strongly excelled. Perhaps he could become expert in caring for this man; God knows very few ever had.

"I want you to teach me everything you know," he declared. "And, for when we ride out here again, some of those kitchen skills you mentioned too. Where plates are located when not on the table. How the tealeaves get to the pot, for example. And how to boil water for a bath. So I can pleasure you even more."

Tommy laughed sleepily, Benedict's favourite sound in the entire world. "Tea, a hot bath, and lovemaking. How perfect."

Chapter Twenty-One

BENEDICT WHILED AWAY the next four afternoons drinking lemon tea (made by someone else) and perusing *The Morning Post*'s excellent racing commentary in the relaxing and comfortable surroundings of Mrs Catherine de Villiers drawing room on Cumberland Place. And replaying his night with Tommy over and over in his head, like the lovesick youth he used to be. They'd made love again during the darkest hours—coming together whilst still half asleep, and in the morning, too, a lazy mutual cock rubbing which left Benedict swearing he'd never leave the bed. They did, of course, and by the time his staff arrived, they were up and dressed and pointedly discussing horseflesh.

The charming Mrs Catherine de Villiers, accepting of his poor, distracted company, used the time to complete a rather intricately designed coverlet for her niece's trousseau and taught him the rudiments of lansquenet, a card game she'd learned during her years as the bored young wife of an elderly French General. His card-playing valet, she confided to Benedict with an impish smile, had been younger and vigorous.

Tongues had wagged, Francis reliably informed him. Especially by the fifth afternoon, when the *Post* dedicated an entire column to a description of Benedict escorting the spirited widow *and* the Honourable Beatrice Hazard in his landau around Vauxhall Gardens on two separate occasions during the same day.

What the *ton* failed to read about on the sixth afternoon was a rendezvous at Beatrice's home between Beatrice and Mrs de Villiers. The two ladies got along famously, according to Francis, who heard it directly from Lady Isabella, who herself had quizzed Beatrice until she threatened her with Bach.

"A cunning plot is afoot," confided Francis on the seventh afternoon when Benedict had been granted a reprieve from lansquenet. He'd yet to win a hand; Mrs de Villiers's young French valet had taught her well. Uninvited as usual, his youngest brother made himself comfortable in the second study. "Individually, Mrs de Villiers and Beatrice are forces to be reckoned with. Together, I fear they could rule the world."

"Albeit a topsy-turvy world," agreed Benedict, "where men occupy themselves with nothing more arduous than shopping for hats whilst womenfolk manage household finances and debate our foreign policy in Parliament." With a sigh, he surveyed his cluttered desk. "Bring it on, I say. They wouldn't be able to make any more of a hash of things than the current government."

"Until that utopian day comes, they are putting their excellent brains to finessing a plot set to unfold at the Horton ball." Francis smirked. "Designed to display the devilish Duke of

Ashington at his most daring and dastardly. The finer details of which I must, on no account, share with you."

"Because you don't know them," observed Benedict drily, tapping his quill against his ink pot. He had changed his usual black ink to a dramatic dark green and was quite taken by it. So much so, he'd ordered a similar coloured cravat. "Beatrice doesn't trust you not to blab. That woman's wisdom knows no bounds."

"Mmm," confessed Francis. "Damned annoying."

Benedict threw him a grave look. "Do you think the plot involves cheese?"

For a startled moment, Francis actually contemplated it. Had Benedict always been such a bore that even his rare jokes were misconstrued?

"Who knows." He heaved a sigh. "I'm dreading it, to be blunt. The whole bloody evening." In a rare show of annoyance, he banged his fist on the arm of the chair. "Isabella and I shall elope if we have to. Lord Ludham's views on it be damned. I refuse to let bloody Lyndon ruin her life. Mine and yours, too, come to that."

"So do I," said Benedict. "In fact, you have my word that I shall not allow it. You will not need to elope. You and dear Isabella shall have the finest wedding the *ton* has seen since Peel's lavish affair at Westminster. I promise. If it's the last thing I do."

*

WAS IT POSSIBLE to hate and love the same person in equal measure? No, Benedict didn't believe it was. And anyhow, he wasn't a man capable of hate. He might pity someone, perhaps, though still love them all the same. He could balance those emotions against one another. His sympathy for the bitter demons occupying Lyndon's head was bottomless. Those demons drove Lyndon to pit his wits and rage against his twin, the firstborn son, forever set to gain everything, thanks to a few minutes. An accident of fate. And yet, despite the campaign Lyndon raged against him, Benedict wanted nothing more than to forgive and forget, to cast the other cheek. And he would, if his role wasn't to protect Francis and Isabella, innocent victims of all of it.

As far as practical dealings with Lyndon were concerned, honesty was best. In Benedict's experience, it afforded one the advantage of surprise. Having never employed that virtue as a tool himself, Lyndon never expected it.

Afternoon visits were advised too. They increased the likelihood of finding Lyndon awake.

"Only just returned from Brighton," he informed Benedict after he'd been shown through to the small drawing room by a housemaid. The same drab woman, matching the drab furnishing, proceeded to procure tea. At least Lyndon wasn't squandering money he didn't have on staff and belongings he couldn't afford. "Spent a fortnight in bed. Staring out to sea and fucking my mistress." His upper lip curled into a sneer. "Good fun. You should give it a go."

He certainly didn't look as though he'd spent a fortnight having fun. He looked weary and pale. And alone. The bruising around his eye and jaw had healed though.

With effort, Benedict allowed the comment to wash through him. If he played this game with Lyndon, rising to the bait, his brother's cleverness would win out, leaving Benedict feeling small and inadequate. And now he had Tommy and the friendship of Rossingley, not to mention the support of Francis, Angel, and his dear confidante, Beatrice, he knew he was neither of those things.

"I come in the spirit of friendship, Lyndon," he began. "And brotherhood. Our father, rest his soul, would hate for his sons to be at war with one another."

"If only he'd taken that into consideration before he disinherited me."

"He did what he thought right to help you to help yourself. Can one ask any more of a conscientious parent?"

Smirking, Lyndon cupped a hand behind his ear. "Did you hear that? I swear he's still in the room."

Benedict pushed on with the speech he'd prepared. "You still have your entailed house in Norfolk. You could go there, make a fresh start. I could…I am prepared to assist with any necessary renovations. Setting you up with suitable staff and so forth. A change of scenery might suit you."

Lyndon threw him a disdainful look. "What, and miss all the merriment here?"

"The season is soon drawing to a close. Next Thursday's race at Ascot and the Horton ball are the last major events on the Society calendar until autumn."

"Matters of which I am fully aware. And I wouldn't miss them for the world. I intend to have a flutter on the horses, then drink myself into a stupor on Countess Eveline Horton's free sherry. Which reliably flows freely. And after that, who knows what will transpire?" He threw Benedict one of his sly looks, perfected back when they were still in short trousers. Funny how it didn't elicit quite the usual nervousness. "Loose tongues are worse than loose horses. Isn't that what they say, Your Grace? You'd know, what with owning all of those ever-so-lovely nags."

Never mind hearing his father's echo, Benedict fancied he heard his heart, slipping down into his boots.

"Don't do this, Lyndon," he pleaded quietly. "I know you are the anonymous sender of the list. Do not deny it."

"I have no need to deny it." If Lyndon was shocked that his underhand behaviour had been discovered, he showed no sign. "Why would I? It comprises nothing but the truth, and unless my share of our family's wealth is fully restored to me, I intend to reveal it."

Benedict tried again. His brother was only a lost cause after everyone had given up. And Benedict never would. "Then, I beg you to reconsider. I do not ask for my sake but for Francis's. And for the sake of our mother. However low your opinion of me, they are not deserving."

Lyndon examined his nails. A smile toyed at his lips, of a sort that a man less mild than Benedict would have smacked away with his fist. Yet Benedict could no more have raised a hand to this man than he could to a newborn lamb. What was it Francis had said? His big heart was both the worst and the best of him. Ah, well. So be it.

Eventually, Lyndon spoke. "I'm afraid that's not possible, Your Grace."

A profound sadness wrapped around Benedict's chest as he regarded his twin brother. All this, over some damned pilfered teaspoons.

Except it was so much more than that. It was about the impact of a few minutes on years of a life. The whimsy of primogeniture. Chance, a cruel monarch, ruling over them all yet again, sorting the pair of them into the duke and the not duke. The heir and the spare. No judgement, no ambiguity. No choice. Their identities had slotted into a crisp hierarchy from the moment they'd sucked in their first sobbing breaths.

And, in the only ways he knew how, Benedict's clever, capable, brother rebelled against it by seeking out external pain, a matching twin for his inner grief.

With nothing to lose, Benedict attempted one last time. "This will not end well for you, Lyndon," he said, gently. "Please. I implore you to reconsider."

For a long minute, he stared into a pair of dark eyes so similar to his own, even if the rest of his twin's bloated body and mind had long since slid beyond recognition.

"So you say." Rising to his feet, Lyndon gestured to the door. "Begging your pardon, Your Grace. I have another appointment. You can show yourself out."

Chapter Twenty-Two

A PERSISTENT AND delicious image of Benedict mooching around his stables in his shirt sleeves, between pretending to woo two very agreeable ladies, convinced Tommy he had the raw end of the deal. He was a busy man, juggling several business interests. He needed to while away four afternoons trotting around Regent's Park in a phaeton with Lady Isabella Knightley like he needed a new aperture in his cranium. Nonetheless, he fell on his sword and, by the end of the week, was rewarded with rumours of his amour detailed in the *Mirror of Fashion* column, alongside a puff piece about the enigmatic, brooding Mr Angel and his competing pursuits of the delightful Lady Isabella.

The point being, he barely saw Benedict. Of course, he could have paid him a call at his imposing, lavish home on Park Lane, but even if he did, Tommy couldn't exactly lunge at him on the drawing room settee and cart the man off to bed. A friendly ride through the park would prove equally frustrating. And whilst a brief liaison in Tommy's rooms above the club was entirely feasible, anyone spotting the duke tripping up and down the staircase would find it most odd. Of course, all that assumed Benedict found a spare moment to visit Squire's in the first place. So far, since their return from the hunting lodge, the broadsheets reported his evenings had been taken up with soirées, musicales, and an expedition accompanying his harem to the bloody opera.

Rossingley bore the brunt of Tommy's ill temper. With one knee neatly crossed over the other, he sat in the spindly chair (which didn't as much as whimper) across from Tommy's desk, picking through a jar of sherbet twists.

"Since falling in love, darling, you've become a terrible bore." Rossingley licked at a sherbet. "Benedict this, the duke that. Honestly, Tommy, I'm beginning to question why I still endure your company."

"Says the man who not so long ago sat in that very seat and treated me to a detailed account of precisely how Angel's double-jointed tongue succeeds in pleasuring you so thoroughly. As I recall, it's a similar technique to how you're making love to that blasted sherbet."

Rossingley pouted, then attacked the sherbet with even more gusto.

Restlessly, Tommy threw down his quill. "Oh, Lordy," he sighed, swiping a sherbet for himself. "I'm heartsick is all. Is it too much to ask that one might spend a few nights under the same sheets as one's lover without having to skulk about?"

Rossingley regarded him with a thoughtful look as he demolished the sweet. "No, I daresay not."

"I can't just drop everything and hare off to one of his bloody hunting lodges every time the urge takes me. I have too many obligations in town. As does Benedict. And I like town. I don't sneeze in town."

Rossingley procured another sweet. "My brother, Robert, a first-rate countryman, would advise you at this juncture that the answer is at the tip of your nose."

"My runny nose," Tommy interrupted. "When I'm in the country."

"Quite," said Rossingley. "And then, after boring you with an unsolicited diversion into the joys of animal husbandry, he'd pronounce that successful shepherds persuade their sheep so their interests might align with their own."

"Then thank heavens bloody Robert is not here," replied Tommy testily. "Really, Lordy, I can't see the relevance. If you're simply tolerating my brown study to scoff my sherbets, you can bugger—"

"You're the shepherd," cut in Rossingley, his silvery eyes glittering with amusement. "And our club patrons are your sheep. Now—" He paused whilst he unwrapped his sweet. "—ask yourself this. How could my nightly craving for a tumble with my handsome duke possibly align with their needs?" He licked his lips. "Their needs for a nearby bed when foxed, for instance."

He gazed around Tommy's cosy study, then drifted his eyes lazily up to the ceiling. "If I'm not mistaken, there are quite a lot of rooms above here, aren't there? For a single man? Imagine, all those empty bedchambers. Going to waste."

"Baa," bleated Tommy irritably. "You really can be bloody smug sometimes, Lordy."

*

"I'M MISSING YOU," he murmured close to Benedict's ear.

For a minute or so, a small twitch of Benedict's lips was the only indication he'd heard. To all and sundry, the duke appeared to be studying the procession of horses being led slowly into the parade ring in readiness to race for the Gold Cup.

"I miss you too," he answered, his dark gaze fixed on the handsome creatures lining up to be inspected. "But only when I'm breathing. And I would like nothing more than to shout that from the Royal Stand."

It was Ladies Day at Ascot. And the day of the dreaded Horton ball. The typical, dry June afternoon held the power to change the course of Benedict's future forever and, with it, the path of Francis, Isabella, and Tommy. For a man bearing such a heavy load, the duke appeared remarkably calm. But then, he was surrounded by his beloved horseflesh.

"Sidney informs me Lord Lyndon is betting heavily on Tuppence Tilly, Bannister's piebald mare," Tommy informed him. "She's running against Ganymede. He's spreading his bets across several blacklegs, not only mine."

"Is he now?"

Scant rain had fallen during the week and the fair weather set to continue. With the completion of the new Royal Stand, a crowd of thousands had gathered to watch the main event.

Benedict hummed, lifting his shoulder in a dismissive shrug. "She's a decent runner and most definitely suits this hard ground. I'd put fifty pounds on her myself if I thought she had a hell's chance of besting Ganymede."

Tommy was taken aback. "Has your jockey not accepted Lord Lyndon's bribe?"

"Goodness, yes. I advised Sam to accept the money two days ago."

Benedict raised a polite hand to a group of acquaintances. The ladies in the party giggled behind their fans. "I also instructed him to treat Mrs Sam and the children to something special with it."

"I see."

He didn't see at all, but his lover seemed utterly unbothered. Whilst Tommy digested this snippet of information, hoping for more, another group passed. The ladies bobbed blushing curtsies in the direction of his companion. Benedict had become a far more interesting object of late. Acknowledging them with an elegant bow, he groaned.

"I'll be glad when this blasted ball tonight is over, and I can go back to being nothing but a dull part of the *ton* furniture."

Tommy wished fervently for that, too, being much preferable to the alternative. A sick feeling gnawed at him every time he thought of it. "I have prayed every night and most mornings for that satisfactory outcome."

"Does He listen to prayers from men such as us?"

"Probably not." Tommy chuckled. "I'm hedging my bets, regardless."

Tipping his head up to the clear skies, Benedict filled his lungs with a deep breath, then let it out slowly. "Strangely, I find myself at peace with the world. I'm feeling...lucky." Again, he tilted at more well-wishers gathering for the race. "This excellent clear weather is an omen for things to come."

Tommy fervently hoped he was right. As Benedict surveyed the scene laid out below, Tommy snatched a glance at him. Tall and proud, he wore a new navy greatcoat, and his bejewelled signet ring flashed in the watery sunshine. He stood every inch an untouchable, commanding duke.

Sensing Tommy's eyes on him, Benedict turned, his own crinkling. "Don't worry, my love. I have a feeling everything will turn out just fine. Starting with this race."

Tommy shook his head, wishing he had half the confidence and wondering from where his timid duke had gleaned his. Perhaps it came from the knowledge he was much-loved, from being unashamedly his true self, at least amongst those who cared for him.

"You're loving being mysterious, aren't you?" said Tommy, unable to tear his eyes away.

"Mmm." Benedict smiled crookedly. "Rossingley and Francis are pestering me at all hours of the day and night. Rest assured, none of you will have to wait much longer. Ah, there's Sam, leading Ganymede into the ring now. He's looking in excellent form, don't you think?"

Tommy couldn't help but agree. All sinews and sleek chestnut coat, the beast restlessly pawed the ground. Its bunched muscles rippled with barely contained power, like stacks of musket balls, ready to explode. "He's in the form of his life."

Leaving Ganymede to his admiring audience, Tommy's gaze flitted over the onlookers, vaguely searching for people he knew, then lurched to a sudden halt. On the opposite side of the parade ground, utterly still and alone, stood the unmistakeable tall, broad, redhaired figure of Lord Lyndon Fitzsimmons. Tommy was too far away to see his expression, though he sensed his tension, coiled up, a furious, living thing. He hoped Benedict, still studying the horses, had not seen him.

A hush descended on the crowd as the master steward invited the stable owners into the parade ring for the traditional inspection. Belonging to some of the *ton*'s wealthiest families, they were as much a spectacle as the racehorses themselves.

Benedict turned to Tommy, not as unhappily as Tommy would have expected. "That's my cue," he announced cheerfully. "Wish me luck."

Before Tommy could question why, his lover strode away. He watched, inordinately proud, as Benedict slipped into the weighty role of dutiful duke, waving at some folks and nodding at others as if nothing gave him more pleasure. God, how Tommy, longed, prayed, *begged*, that tonight would give them cause to celebrate tomorrow.

"Lord Lyndon ain't going to be best pleased with young Sam Leonard if he don't throw the race," observed Sidney, sidling up to him. For once, Tommy was glad not to be alone. "I wouldn't want to be in the lad's shoes," Sidney prattled on, "if he goes and wins the damned thing. He'll be looking over his shoulder for weeks. Not to mention having to dodge the crap Lord Lyndon will fling the way of the duke's stables. I wouldn't put it past him to get someone in there with a bit of poison." He nodded to himself. "I reckon your duke's high in the instep brother knows a few men in low places, don't you?"

"I suspect so," agreed Tommy. "If Sam Leonard goes on and wins this wretched thing, there will be hell to pay. A point I made to the duke several times whilst visiting his lodge."

Sidney grunted. "Need to work on yer pillow talk, Tommy.

No wonder you only stayed the one night."

Tommy's vulgar response was cut off by Sidney's low appreciative whistle.

"His Grace looks good in that black clobber though, don't he?" Sidney said.

"He's not wear— What the devil is he doing?"

A minor commotion was underway in the centre of the parade ring. Having inspected Ganymede with utmost care, stroked his hand down the beast's withers, even checked his hooves, the fourteenth Duke of Ashington was in the process of donning a black velvet huntsman's cap. With a flourish, he removed his greatcoat, carelessly handing it to a grinning Sam Leonard.

Tommy gasped sharply. "He's...no, he can't be."

"What the...?" Even Sidney's mouth hung open. "He bloody is, you know."

"Come on," urged Tommy. "Quick! Let's get closer."

He barged his way to the front rail, Sidney limping after him. Ignoring the curses in his wake, Tommy arrived just in time to hear Benedict's rich baritone, ringing out across the assembled owners.

"Ganymede is in perfect form for today's flat race, Sam," he declared. One finger at a time, he pulled off his fine kidskin gloves and tossed them into Sam Leonard's waiting hands, exchanging them for a thicker pair of riding gloves. "I've examined the turf— the going is quite excellent," he added. Surveying the track beyond the parade ring, he shielded his eyes with his left hand. His right was occupied with unfastening the buttons of his emerald-green topcoat. "So good, in fact, I am of a mind to ride him today myself."

Every eye at the racetrack was fixed on the impromptu strip-tease.

"Bloody hell," swore Tommy as a collective inhale gusted around him. Then he swore again. "The bloody, bloody...rake-hell!"

As if doing nothing more than taking a stroll through his walled garden, the duke wandered over to Ganymede, and, in one fluid motion, mounted him. His mouth closed in on the horse's ear, his lips moving as he spoke to the creature, words inaudible to the watching crowds.

"You're my treasured turtle dove," murmured Tommy, and a thrill ran through him.

"And you're my prettiest stewed dumpling." A wheezing Sidney drew alongside. "Never knew you cared so much, Tommy." Still cackling, Sidney tugged on his arm. "When you've put your peepers back in yer head, take a gander over there." He gave Tommy a nudge. "Someone ain't too happy."

If looks could kill, Lord Lyndon would be arrested and hung from a gibbet outside Newgate, and the fourteenth duke's body trampled to mincemeat under seventeen hands of prime race-horse. As it was, with his black silk shirt billowing like a sail in the breeze, Benedict and Ganymede were making their way to the start line. His face pale as death, Lord Lyndon brandished his cane, defending his position on the front row as if his life depended on it.

His ability to afford his own breakfast tomorrow morning certainly did, if his heavy bets were any indicator.

"I've seen the duke race, once," offered Sidney as they waited for the riders to assemble. "He was riding Nimbus then, his horse that won the St Leger umpteen times. Never seen anything like it. Like the wind, the pair of them. Don't think he raced him again after that."

"He didn't," said Tommy. "He retired from racing after their sixth win to give the others a fair chance."

"Decent of him."

Tommy wouldn't have expected anything less from his humble lover.

"Of course, I didn't realise back then that the bloke was *your* duke," Sidney rambled on. Tommy didn't wish him ever to stop. It was possibly the only thing keeping him from undignified tears. "He was the marquess of something-or-other fancy then. And I was so far back in the cheap seats, he could have had three eyes and a nose covered in festering warts for all I'd have recognised him."

Tommy and Sidney left the parade ring at a brisk march and moved to the finishing straight, once more elbowing racegoers aside. Sidney's massive shoulders came in useful. As they took up position, only a narrow stretch of turf separated them from Benedict's twin.

"Flew like a whole wild night was in pursuit of him," continued Sidney, oblivious to Tommy's internal chaos. Drymouthed, he gripped the rail, his heart no doubt beating at a similar tempo to Lord Lyndon's, though for entirely different reasons.

Sidney rested his meaty forearms next to Tommy's. "Or half the town's runners, at any rate. Never seen the like before nor since."

Lord Lyndon, now on the opposite side of the track, was still alone. Watching intently. One gloved fist covered his mouth as if trapping a scream.

The competitors formed a higgeldy, restless line, the horses pawing and whinnying in anticipation. Benedict sat high atop Ganymede, a foot or two back, keeping clear of the melee. His lips moved again as his hand fondled the beast's silky ears, no doubt whispering more of the same sweet nonsense he whispered to Tommy.

As the race starter stepped up, the excited chattering crowd fell silent. Tommy held his breath as, like a declaration of war, the starter's pistol shot ripped through the air. And it was, for the few that knew. Two jittery horses reared at the blast; one dug its heels in and refused to budge. The rest cantered away.

Ganymede might as well have been stone deaf for all the effect the harsh firing crack had on his nerves, and for a few moments, Tommy lost sight of both the horse and Benedict, swallowed up in the thick of the race.

"Two miles, three furlongs," commented Sidney, squinting into the sunlight. "Mostly flat, bit of a climb in one section."

Eighteen horses stretched away from them, galloping up a slight incline towards the first bend. In the whirl of mud and clattering hooves, picking out Benedict's black silks was nigh on impossible, though Tommy spotted Tuppence Tilly, the piebald mare, haring up the inside, a length ahead of the rest. He gripped the rail harder.

"Don't fret. His Grace'll be pacing himself. Young Tilly will weary over the last quarter. Just watch. Yer fella will come good in the last third. That Ganymede is the best stayer in the field."

Tommy's heart was in his mouth. He wished he had an ounce of Sidney's confidence. Benedict hadn't raced in years.

What if he took a tumble? A rider had been trampled to death at Newmarket last year, his neck snapped under the weight of fifteen thoroughbreds stamping on it. As the riders disappeared behind a copse over the far side of the track, Tommy blew out a long breath, searching the sea of faces for Lord Lyndon.

The duke's brother remained rooted to the same spot as if cast from stone. This close, Tommy could almost smell the venom. He prayed Benedict knew what he was doing.

A rallying cheer went up as the race came back into view. Cursing he wasn't taller, Tommy craned around the shoulders and broad chest of the man to his left.

"Can you see him?" He pawed at Sidney's arm as if trying to scale him.

"Yes, they're neck and neck! Come on, lad!" Sidney's fists clenched as tightly as Tommy's. "Yer fella and the mare, out front by a couple of lengths. The field's thinned out. Two riderless horses. A couple of fallers, too, by the looks of things."

But not Benedict. Thank the Lord. As the racers pelted along the back straight, the air filled with the *galalop galalop* of hooves. They bore down towards the finish line, drumming louder still, the ground reverberating as if the very pit of the earth were rising. Benedict, black as night, sat up out of the saddle, his taut, muscular frame hunched over Ganymede's flowing mane. Like a poised black comma, his mouth whispered in the horse's ear, pressing them forwards, urging him on.

Tommy clutched Sidney's arm, and his friend's low chuckle was lost in the clamour of a thousand voices hollering. A whistle shrieked. A child screamed. Gloves, fans, pocket squares, and scarves waved madly. Feet stomped.

And Ganymede's nose inched ahead. The piebald mare was tiring, her jockey standing out of his seat, too, the whip in his spur hand a dark, ugly blur of motion.

"Go on, my lad, go on," bellowed Sidney. "Sock it to 'em!" And as Ganymede's neck pulled clear, "Go *onnn*!"

Tommy could hardly bring himself to watch. He certainly forgot to breathe. A whole body length separated the two front runners—daylight flashed between them as Ganymede, with the scent of victory within his grasp, pulled away, unstoppable. The cheering crowd knew it, too, pushing Benedict onwards to the finish line.

And then, as soon as it had begun, it was all over. The fourteenth duke crossed the line, modest as ever. Not even raising a triumphant fist, simply easing up and cantering past the winning post like he was riding through another daisy-freckled pasture. Like he and Ganymede were out for a hack, racing through the countryside for the sheer thrill of being alive.

Sidney mopped sweat from his brow with a filthy, chequered pocket square. "Bloody brilliant," he declared, then beamed his big, gaping grin. "I told yer he'd do it, Tommy, and he bloody did!"

Tommy hugged him. It was that or collapse in a dead faint. They'd taken it in turns to hold each other up over the years, and today was Tommy's. "Yes! He bloody did, Sid, he bloody did!"

With his earthy bulk and strong arms, Sidney hugged him back before gently depositing him back on the ground. "I warn you now, Tommy." He chuckled then dropped his voice. "If His Grace loves you as much as he loves that there horse, your bum's in for a right pummelling tonight."

Tommy barely managed an obscene gesture, never mind a witty riposte. He still felt as if he'd run the race himself on two wobbly legs. His heart shot through with pride as he searched the crowd for Lord Lyndon. Then searched again.

"He's buggered off," Sidney remarked. "If he's bet as heavily with the other blacklegs as he's bet on ours, he'll be five hundred quid out of pocket by the end of the afternoon. He'll be singing for his supper."

He'd be singing something, that was for sure. There would be no stopping him now. Singing it loud and clear and making sure the whole *ton* heard his voice.

Chapter Twenty-Three

AT SEVEN O'CLOCK that evening, the fourteenth Duke of Ashington alighted from his carriage outside the Earl of Horton's sprawling townhouse. Gritting his teeth, he straightened his evening coat and stared up at the myriad of lights sparkling from the tall windows.

The afternoon had been nothing but a dress rehearsal, albeit a faultless one. This evening, the curtain would rise on the grand finale.

"Feeling rakish?" an amused voice enquired.

"Hardly."

His beloved Tommy slouched against Rossingley's carriage. "You certainly played the part well this afternoon," Tommy continued. "It was a heart-stopping performance. Literally." Though the gentlest of teasing smiles played at his lips, anxiety flitted across his gaze. Mirroring Benedict's own soul.

"Thank you," Benedict acknowledged. "I'd be lying if I didn't admit I thoroughly enjoyed myself. But now?" He glanced back to the Earl of Horton's solid red door. "Bloody terrified."

Benedict's joy from his spectacular romp to victory had long fled. Disquiet for the evening ahead manifested as a throbbing in his temples, twinned with a hard, cramping knot in his belly. However, the sight of Tommy, elegant in full evening dress and fondly smiling at him, lessened his afflictions somewhat.

Benedict would give anything to hold him. Alas, his gaze alone would have to be enough, if only for these few minutes. To gain strength from him. To declare his love. Because who knew how tonight would end?

"Do you know what terrifies me the most?" Glancing around, checking they were alone, Benedict took a step closer. "It's about more than simply walking into that ballroom." He lowered his voice. "It's...it's never feeling the rest of my whole life how I felt as I made love to you in my bed at the lodge." *Safe. Cherished.* "I'm scared of my heart. How it stops and starts, simply at the very sight of you. And losing that sight forever."

A thousand emotions slid across Tommy's dear face. How Benedict wanted to hold it between his hands and kiss every part of it.

"Benedict."

That single word was answer enough. The rawness of it. The crack in Tommy's voice. The way he dropped his head, shielding his eyes. How, with that single word, Benedict knew his love was returned without measure.

Tommy levelled his gaze. "Tonight, Benedict, you must know this," he continued softly. "All night, it will beat in perfect rhythm with mine."

*

"RARING TO GO, chaps?" Adjusting his top hat the minutest of angles, Rossingley waggled a gloved finger. "Be prepared, Ashington, for every eventuality." He raised a beautifully manicured eyebrow. "I hear the ladies have been plotting. And I sense that Lady Isabella has an exceptional talent for taking simple plans and contriving to complicate them."

Benedict's neckcloth inched a little snugger. "Your senses do you credit. Have you been furnished with any clues?"

"More a list of instructions." Lightly, Rossingley cleared his throat. "If my memory serves me well, at this very moment, my dear Kit will—according to a rigid timetable—be spinning Lady Isabella like a top around the dance floor. Meanwhile, Lord Francis should be looking on in abject misery, whilst standing beside Lord Ludham, also in abject misery and, hopefully, not fighting an incipient *crise cardiaque*."

He indicated to Tommy. "You, my darling, are to raise the stakes—and Lord Ludham's blood pressure—by cruelly cutting in and demanding Lady Isabella take your arm. During the waltz, Kit will rudely cut in on you, and so on and so forth, until Lord Ludham either spontaneously combusts or hurls his wayward daughter into Lord Francis's waiting and open arms."

Rossingley smiled his most criminal smile, displaying his two neat rows of small pointy teeth. "You must glower at Kit frequently and with menace, Tommy. Is your acting ability up to glaring at a rival whilst also wooing a lady?"

"It will be my most vexing role to date," responded Tommy

sourly. "The wooing part, at any rate. I've been wanting to throw daggers at your annoying lover for some time."

"I do believe the feeling is mutual, darling."

Relieved nothing was required of him, Benedict breathed an inaudible sigh. For all of three seconds.

"Ashington?" Rossingley waggled an elegant, gloved finger. "My spies tell me Lord Lyndon and his chums are currently showing off their hollow legs over at Bootle's but will be heading to the party any time in the next hour. You are under strict orders to do whatever Beatrice and Mrs de Villiers command."

Almost as an afterthought, he added, "And watch out for Lady Wardholme. Your reputation as a rakehell has most certainly gathered wings and taken flight, darling. Allegedly, she is hankering after a piece of it and has a very strong arm." His pale eyes glittered. "My advice is to, under no circumstances, enter a discussion regarding home furnishings. It will not be what it seems."

*

STREAMS OF DANCERS flowed in dizzying numbers around and around the dance floor like a swollen river, threatening to burst its banks. The room smelled brackish, too, brimful of hot bodies and competing fragrances. Wisps of steam spiralled above, condensing into drops of water on the too-low ceiling, then damply plopping back down onto unsuspecting heads. Benedict felt as if he was suffocating. It seemed as if every single member of the *ton* was crammed inside the too-small ballroom.

A balcony leading to the outside ran the length of the room, with both sets of tall windows shut tight on account of the poor foxed chap who plummeted to his death a couple of years earlier. As the first uncomfortable trickle of moisture snaked down Benedict's spine and settled in an unmentionable area, he cursed his high collar, his evening coat, well insulated ballrooms, and the *ton* in general.

A footman thrust a welcome glass of wet something-or-other into his clammy palm, and he gulped it down before snatching a second. And only just in the nick of time. Not too dissimilar in size, like the prow of an ocean-going liner, Lady Wardholme's ample bosom advanced on him.

"The minuet, Your Grace," she boomed in a voice striking the room like a thunderclap. "I insist. Miss Gresham and Miss Caldicot vow that a girl floats in your strong embrace like no other."

Benedict suspected sturdy Lady Wardholme would float about as elegantly as a brick. Sharply, he reminded himself he was a rake, at least for this final evening. His two snifters of something had begun working their magic and, with a brave smile, he took to the dance floor.

"There is mischief afoot tonight, Your Grace," his stately partner declared. Her powerful fingers clamped around his upper arm.

"Is there?" he asked weakly, unsure whether he wanted to hear it. He had a feeling she'd inform him, nonetheless.

"Oh, yes." She leaned in closer, affording Benedict an eye-watering whiff of lavender. More bothersome, he found himself in the invidious position of either staring into her eyes, at the portion of her face below her eyes (where one unfortunate feature inexorably drew his eye), or down her cleavage. As they sailed past the string quartet, he plumped for the latter, as any rake worthy of the name should.

"Not to put too fine a point on it, Your Grace, but on the other side of this room, it is blindingly obvious to everyone watching that Lady Isabella Knightley is in over her head with those two cryptic rogues and doesn't know which way to turn. *The quill yearns for ink as the ink, alas, kisses the foolscap*, as they say."

"Um...do they?"

Flummoxed, Benedict missed his footing, stubbing his toe. As far as he was concerned, the other side of the room only contained more dancers, squashed together like flower stems wrapped in a tight bouquet. One couldn't have slid a sheet of foolscap between them, let alone a quill. "I...um...and if you were to put a finer point on it?"

His dance partner was either suffering from an acute attack of ague bouts or quivering with excitement. "A triangle *amoureux* has developed," she exclaimed, "between that flibbertigibbet Lady Isabella Knightley, the dashing Mr Angel, and mysterious Mr L'Esquire! I wouldn't be surprised if Mr Angel doesn't challenge Mr L'Esquire to a duel before the night is out!"

In a vain attempt to quell her obvious glee in the whole thing, she tutted. "Your poor, poor brother has the face of a raincloud, the dear chap. Not once did he imagine his childhood sweetheart would have her head turned so." She threw him a cheerful smile. "And yet here we are!"

Lady Wardholme's strong arm was not to be underestimated, and the claws around his bicep imperilled the blood supply to Benedict's hand. Moreover, though happier skirting the edges of the dance floor, Benedict suddenly found himself thrust into the melee.

"It's Lord Ludham and his darling wife I feel sorry for," Lady Wardholme continued, her tone highly suggestive of the opposite. "If one of her suitors doesn't offer his hand tonight, Lady Isabella might find herself at the centre of quite the disgrace."

For the briefest of moments, she paused, but only to suck in a waspish breath before launching into the next chapter. "Although, I do believe another scandal might trump her this evening."

"A-another?" Benedict's insides twisted painfully. "Is... ah...?"

"Oh, yes." Evidently about to betray a confidence, Lady Wardholme leaned even closer, serving as a reminder to Benedict that full-breasted ladies, or indeed, ladies, weren't quite his thing. "Apparently, something even more disreputable. She pursed her lips in a futile attempt at disgust. "A distinguished male member of the *ton* is about to be *exposed*."

At least on such a packed dance floor, Benedict couldn't keel over. There was nowhere to keel. "Exposed?" he repeated unsteadily.

"Exposed," she clarified. "Your Grace, are you quite well? I do believe you have segued into a cotillion step whilst we are still in the midst of a minuet."

Benedict shook his head in a valiant effort to clear it. There was a plan, he reminded himself. A great plan. Falling in a panicky dead heap would be of no use to Francis and Isabella whatsoever. And he was a duke. And a rake. With dear friends who cared for him. And he had a lover worth more than life itself.

Bracing his shoulders, Benedict issued a firm, ducal stare.

"Forgive me, but I do not dwell on idle gossip, my lady." And then, because, first and foremost, he was a rakehell, he mustered something he hoped approximated a debonair smile. "How could I? When all your exquisite loveliness floats in my arms?"

"Oh, Your Grace, how right Miss Gresham was!" Lady Wardholme fluttered her lashes. Benedict's hand had turned numb and tingly in her strong grip. "You make a girl feel quite giddy. Like an innocent debutante. Forgive my prattling. Let us talk instead of other things. Have you any preferences for wallpaper patterns? I am of a mind to refurnish my breakfast room."

*

"HOT UNDER THE collar, Your Grace?"

"You have no idea." Benedict sagged against a cool wall. "The sight of you, my dear Beatrice, is truly a balm for sore eyes."

If Benedict weighed less, he would have enjoyed floating off in Beatrice's sensible arms for a while. Off and down the street, if at all possible. Instead, he had to make do with allowing her to demurely curl her hand around one of his and lead him to the fresh air of the blessed balcony, wondrously open and miraculously empty.

"I have a key," his companion explained as if being in possession of a key to someone else's balcony doors, and seemingly the sole owner, was perfectly normal. Frankly, he lacked the strength to query it.

"From your flustered demeanour, I'll wager Lady Wardholme began discussing wallpaper." Beatrice nodded to herself as Benedict drooped against the wrought iron balcony rail. "You're not the first."

In sharp contrast to the dazzling chandeliers of the ballroom, inky blackness swathed the garden and the balcony. Benedict blinked a few times as his eyes adjusted. Then, realising the guests inside couldn't see out, not unless they squished their aristocratic noses to the glass, he loosened his cravat *and* the top two buttons of his waistcoat.

"Apologies, Beatrice. But consider this lapse in decorum preferable to me dissolving in a puddle and then streaming out over the side. Those flower beds are a considerable distance beneath us."

Beatrice waved him away. "Unbutton a couple more, Your Grace." She wasn't paying attention to him anyway, too busy studying the gallivanting on the other side of the glass. "Decorum and I parted company years ago. As did a fascination with the male of the species. And anyhow, a dishevelled cravat is a marvellous touch of improvisation; I should have thought of it."

Tearing herself away from the goings-on inside, Beatrice cast her gaze over him. "You don't look quite the thing, Your Grace. Lady W didn't take undesired liberties, did she? She has the most dreadful wandering fingers, according to Francis."

"Lord, no." Benedict shook his head. "Nothing like that. Just stiflingly hot, that's all. And…and Lady Wardholme also hinted regarding Lyndon. Not by name, thank God. But it's clear the ladies have caught the scent of something brewing in the air. In amongst the stale sweat."

"Ah." Beatrice nodded calmly and resumed watching the ballroom. "Yes. I see him. Lyndon's just arrived with some chums. From the sway of his shoulders, he's utterly spangled."

"Oh joy."

"He's on his toes, craning his neck. Searching for you, I'll be bound." She stepped a pace back from the window, unperturbed. "Good. Now we simply wait here until the bell rings for dinner. I say, what lovely rhododendrons these are, growing up this back wall."

Chapter Twenty-Four

UNQUESTIONABLY, LADY ISABELLA Knightley was having the time of her life. For the last hour, she had been tossed between Mr Angel and Tommy like a prettily embroidered pin cushion. Lord Ludham, on the other hand, was not enjoying his evening. Tommy had seen less gloomy cats stuck in rainstorms. He felt quite sorry for him; the chap didn't seem a bad sort.

Nonetheless, his distress mostly passed unmarked, as not only were Isabella's antics keeping the *ton* entertained, but a new rumour gathered pace around the ballroom. According to Miss Gresham, the gallant fourteenth Duke of Ashington had thwarted a determined Lady Wardholme's advances by employing a neat trick called *disappearing into thin air*. Moreover, he'd taken the high-spirited Honourable Beatrice Hazard with him.

"Pssst!" Francis hissed as he and Tommy refreshed their glasses. "Look over there. Lyndon has appeared." Mr Angel joined them, with a creased and pinkly glowing Isabella hanging on his arm. All four downed their drinks in one. The incendiary heat had turned the ballroom into an airless crush.

"Of course he has," answered Isabella. "He reliably turns up in time for the free supper."

Tommy followed the direction of Francis's gaze in time to see Lord Lyndon Fitzsimmons confirm his entry into the fray by stumbling through a set of doors and knocking over two potted plants. Tommy tightened his hand around the glass. Where in hell was Benedict?

"Then the stage is set," murmured Mr Angel. "All we need now is the remainder of the cast. Has anybody seen His Grace?"

"I haven't set eyes on Ben—His Grace—for quite some time," Tommy said uneasily. "Any ideas, Lord Francis?"

"None, I'm afraid."

"*His Grace* is precisely where he should be," Isabella informed them. "Hidden away for the moment. And there's no point quizzing Lord Francis because he wouldn't have been able to resist sharing it with someone. Would you, Franny?"

"You know me too well, my love." Francis surveyed the assembled throng, still smiling. "Now, if you'll excuse me—oh! I do believe…look over there! Oh, good lord… Me? Is he pointing to me? Lord Ludham is beckoning me over. He's s-smiling at me. I…oh…"

Isabella let out the sort of sanity-depleting squeal that would still be echoing around Tommy's head by the same hour tomorrow. Francis looked stricken. "Do you…do you think he's…?"

"Perhaps you should have a wander over there and find out," Mr Angel suggested smoothly. "Lady Isabella, Mr

L'Esquire, and I will continue to ply the worthy matrons with gossip whilst keeping an eye out for that devilish duke. And focus Lord Ludham's mind."

"You won't find him," Isabella trilled as Lord Francis fairly sprinted to Lord Ludham's side. "His Grace has been kidnapped by Beatrice! It's all part of the plan."

Tommy never imagined a day would arrive when his entire fragile future rested in the delicate hands of a clutch of society ladies. Before he could fully absorb the precariousness, the deep, sonorous *clang* of a gong announced supper was served. Which gave him and Mr Angel plenty of leisure to refill their glasses.

"Nothing reinforces one's lowly position in society as much as seating arrangements at supper," observed Mr Angel as the diminutive Countess of Horton and her husband headed a hungry procession towards the dining room. He sipped calmly. "Don't you find?"

"I suspect you and I will form the rear guard," agreed Tommy.

As was the due of the highest-ranking lady in the room, the Earl of Horton abandoned his wife's side to acquaint himself with the arm of the Dowager Marchioness of Cranborne. His own wife, the countess, hovered patiently behind to follow him in on the arm of the highest-ranking male.

Who didn't appear.

One row behind her, in their correct placement, Rossingley was making small talk with the Countess of Ringwold.

Tommy registered the duke-sized gap, and his heart skipped a beat. "This should be amusing. Or horrific. One way or another."

Mr Angel's dark gaze flicked his way. "Indeed, L'Esquire. I do believe the play is about to begin."

As an awkward, shuffling queue formed, the Countess of Horton rose to her toes to peer over the shoulders of her guests. She whispered something to her butler. Then, she looked back at the empty dining room, at the space beside her, and then back to her guests.

The highest-ranking gentleman was still missing.

A few long minutes ticked by, during which several members of staff were dispatched to locate the fourteenth duke. The hungry crowd was getting restless.

"Just waiting for His Grace," the countess declared brightly to no one in particular. "I'm sure he'll be along."

Tommy wasn't so certain. The look he exchanged with Mr Angel informed him that Mr Angel was of the same opinion.

Abandoning the marchioness, the elderly Earl of Horton marched stiffly back to his wife. "Where the devil is Ashington?"

"I haven't the foggiest," she answered. Her forehead creased into a little frown.

"He's rather a rogue these days, is he not?" The earl pursed his lips. "If he's busy swiving some chit, then he damned needs to hurry it along. The soup will be cooling."

"So charming, the upper classes," muttered Mr Angel.

"Should I be anxious?' Tommy queried under his breath. "He's been missing for quite a while now."

"Isabella reassures me not." Which reassured Tommy not at all.

Resplendent in chartreuse silk, Rossingley stepped forward. "I may be utterly mistaken, of course, but I recall him mentioning something about the…ah…balcony?"

Tommy's smirk was answered by that of Mr Angel. To those who knew Rossingley well, the hint of mischief in that helpful, innocent interruption was unmistakeable.

"The balcony, you say?" Lord Horton's frown matched that of his wife. "It's locked."

A disturbance near the front of the gathering heralded Lord Lyndon, clumsily shoving aside some fellow guests to take his rightful position. Even in his inebriated state, as the brother of a duke, he was entitled to be there. Some poor woman would have to sit next to him during dinner; whoever she was, she had all of Tommy's sympathies.

"Out there with another chap, is he?" Lyndon sneered, slurring his words. "Sharing the night air?"

"My balconies are not accessible to guests this evening," the Earl of Horton informed him stiffly. "I do not wish disaster to befall this house."

He looked longingly back at the dining room tables, laden with food, and at the dowager marchioness, seated in splendid isolation at the far end, staring straight ahead. "I daresay he will be along shortly."

Lyndon swigged from his glass. "Doesn't take one long, does it?"

A dribble of amber liquid ran down his chin. He carelessly wiped at it with his sleeve. "I'd wager one of your footmen is missing too. One of the comely lads."

"Oooh," commented Angel, "that's thrown the cat amongst the pigeons."

Sure enough, like wind sweeping through a pile of autumn

leaves, a murmur susurrated along the queue. Silk fans materialised from within the folds of skirts, faces were madly flapped.

"Lord Fitzsimmons." The Earl of Horton drew himself up to his not very impressive full height. "I'm not entirely sure I know what you are insinuating." His gaze flicked to Rossingley for support, who nodded gravely, managing to look both haughty and as if thoroughly enjoying himself.

"May I remind you," Lord Horton lisped. "This is a private ball, not the back room at Bootle's. Please note there are virtuous ladies present."

Lord Lyndon took another gulp before lobbing his empty glass into the only pot within range still standing vertical. "I assure you, my lord, they have nothing to be worried about."

Lord Horton banged his cane on the floor. "So where the devil is he? Where's Lord Francis? Does he know? Is the duke unwell? Has he departed early, without a by your leave?"

"His carriage is still outside, my lord," offered a butler. "At the head of the line."

"Precisely where its owner should be!" thundered Lord Horton.

Never one to be excluded, Lady Wardholme pushed her way to the front. "He was with me not half an hour gone! Complimenting my choice of neckline."

"I very much doubt that," scoffed Lyndon. "Hate to break it to you, my lady, but you are not quite his cup of ratafia, if you catch my drift. Too…" He made a lewd gesture with his hands as if weighing grapefruit. Tommy stifled a snort.

Lord Francis bounded up. "Lyndon. For God's sake! Control yourself, man. Do you want to be thrown out?"

Rossingley laid a delicate hand on Francis's arm before bowing to the Countess of Horton. "As amusing as this speculation is, and an endless source of gossip for the coming dull months in the country, all that dancing has made me quite peckish. At the risk of rewriting centuries of decorum, shall we begin dining without him?"

"No!" The countess stamped her foot. "I'm unhappy that the duke has vanished, and his brother is causing a rumpus! I want it resolved immediately."

"He's on the balcony," said a clear, cool voice, floating over everyone's heads. "Rossingley was right the first time."

As though pulled by strings, every single guest turned to where Mr Angel stood next to Tommy, lolling against a pillar.

"You knew all the time?" hissed Tommy. "And you didn't tell me?"

Angel shrugged. An indolent, disreputable smile played at his mouth. Two ladies craning their necks to get a good look at him fanned even harder. "I overheard him demanding one of the footmen escort him to the balcony, as he sought some air," he added. "One of the *younger* footmen, I believe. As to the chap's comeliness, I cannot comment."

Tommy turned away, covering his mouth with a hand. The bugger. He and Rossingley had been in on the ladies' plan all along. Everyone was playing their part beautifully, even those with no clue they were on stage, such as the irate Earl of Horton.

As Mr Angel's words sank in, all eyes returned to Lyndon before swivelling to the dark balcony and then back to Lyndon again, drinking in his smug expression. If he listened carefully, Tommy fancied he could hear shiny pearls clacking against shiny pearls as they were clutched to bosoms. One could power a cotton mill with the collective *whoosh* of flapping fans.

The Earl of Horton was the first to find his tongue. "Jackson!" He flung a finger at his head butler, standing guard at the doors leading to the dining room, patiently awaiting the guests to be seated. "Open up the balcony. At once! Let us settle this farce once and for all."

Chapter Twenty-Five

"THE DINNER GONG can't be too far off," observed Benedict as he leaned on the railing, looking out across the dim garden. Blessedly cool now, he was mostly recovered, and his belly rumbled. Beatrice had stopped rabbiting about the flora and fauna ages ago. Now that the light had completely gone, there was naught to see but dark, gloomy trees.

He checked his pocket watch. "I should probably get myself back in there, shouldn't I? There's nothing more annoying at one of these shindigs than hanging around, famished, because one arrogant duke or marquis decides he's not quite ready to dine yet."

He spoke from years of experience. His father had been a past master. On taking up his title, Benedict resolved never to become that person.

"In a few minutes hence, Your Grace," remarked a totally different voice to the one belonging to the woman he'd escorted out here, "I doubt anyone will be giving their hungry stomachs a second thought."

Benedict jerked around to find Mrs de Villiers hastily unpinning her hair and doing something fiddly in the region of her bosom, which involved pushing it much farther from the confines of its corset than was decent.

"Who...what? Where's Beatrice gone? And what on earth are you doing?"

Mrs de Villiers flashed a quick glance inside, and Benedict followed her gaze. Fewer people milled about the dance floor. None, in fact. They all appeared to have gathered at the far end in a bunched-up semicircle as if something, or someone, held their entire collective attention.

"You'll find out soon enough, Your Grace. Beatrice is awfully sweet, but she really doesn't need her reputation totally besmirched. And I believe you would hate for that to happen too." Mrs de Villiers gave each of her cheeks a hard pinch and then rubbed at her lips. "Only a widow could get away with some scandals in this perfidious town. Now...come here, Your Grace. Stand like this. I need you to place this hand here, put that leg there, and your lips here on my —"

Her last instruction was swallowed by Benedict's mouth. And superfluous. Their lips smooshed together as one of Mrs de Villiers gloved hands pressed forcibly around the nape of his neck and the other yanked him into her grasp. Caught off guard, he staggered backwards, but a thoroughly committed Mrs de Villiers reeled with him. Wind whipped at her dress. Their feet tangled; she tripped over his. He flailed madly, and they careened into the railing. In an instant, Benedict felt himself tipping and overbalancing, tipping and overbalancing. He hovered in mid-air. Shards of the past flashed before his eyes, tossed like playing cards: Lyndon's childhood laughter, his first race with Nimbus, a billiard table as a makeshift bed, Francis wrinkling his nose at Isabella. Last season's cravat. And Tommy, his dear, dear Tommy, loving him without measure.

With a choked cry, he scrambled for purchase. The tips of his fingers grazed something soft and silky, like peach skin. With both hands, Benedict grabbed at it, clinging on for dear life.

At that precise moment, the doors behind him wrenched open.

"Good heavens, Your Grace!" squawked a voice. "Put her down! Now! Put. Her. Down!"

A thrilling silence echoed around the stunned onlookers. Time slowed to a crawl; Benedict fancied it stopped altogether.

"Put. Her. Down!"

Summoning the shreds of his dignity, Benedict extracted his hands from the twin cushions of Mrs de Villiers pert breasts. Tenderly, carefully, he put her back on her feet. His own felt as if they'd been swapped with those of a newborn foal. His heart had been exchanged for that of a frightened rabbit. This was the plan, he told himself, over and over. It was all part of the plan. He was a rake, a rake, a rake.

"Thank you, Your Grace," Mrs de Villiers purred breathily. Her gaping decolletage heaved in time to his own, yet otherwise, she appeared no more distraught than if he'd rescued her slipper from a muddy puddle. As if unaware of the *ton* scrambling over one another to glimpse a better look, she straightened Benedict's wayward cravat and moved to his waistcoat to refasten it. Then, most audacious of all, she winked at him. He took the moment to slow his racing thoughts.

At last, bobbing a small curtsey, Mrs de Villers stepped away. Her luscious mouth twisted into a smile. "As always, Your Grace, that was most…magnificent."

A ringing slap against his left cheek sent Benedict barrelling back against the railings.

"How jolly dare you, Your Grace!" The Honourable Beatrice Hazard's familiar, clever countenance was inches from his own and had morphed into a mask of flushed, affronted horror. "You promised! Scoundrel!"

"What? I…ow!" Dazed, Benedict scrabbled to his feet in time for another smart spank to his right cheek. Like a thunderclap, the sound resounded through the crisp night air.

"Rogue!" she wailed in a high-pitched voice. "Philanderer! Lothario! You made a promise!" A third vicious smack followed. "Rakehell!"

"Ow!" Benedict's cheeks smarted. His eyes watered like garden cans, not that he had a second to notice. Now, both women loomed over him, Mrs de Villiers managing to look awfully indignant whilst Beatrice desperately tried her best not to laugh. He braced against the railing.

"I thought you were my one true love," Beatrice howled. A little overdramatically, if Benedict was being perfectly honest, though at least no more bodily assaults seemed forthcoming. And judging by the collective gasp of horror circling the crowd of onlookers, no one else noticed or cared.

"Scapegrace! Varlet!" she added for good measure. Yes, he knew that look. His good friend, currently demonstrating her unmatched command of synonyms, was thoroughly enjoying herself.

With a strategically placed dinner napkin, Mrs de Villiers threw him a last, sultry look, then allowed the Countess of Horton to usher her away. Beatrice, affecting an imminent swoon, rushed from the balcony, too, quickly swallowed up in a swarm of ladies. Gingerly, Benedict fingered his burning cheeks.

A robust figure barged through the crowd. Benedict swallowed. Oh Lord.

"Your Grace," Lady Wardholme declared, accompanied by another ringing *smack* as she put that splendid strong arm to use. Benedict swore; his cheeks would never be the same again. Hands on capable hips, she glared at him. "And to think I believed myself unique!"

"You are, my lady." Staggering to his full height, Benedict performed a wobbly bow. "Truly, unique. In every single blessed way."

The Earl of Horton joined her, also glaring. "Dinner is served, Your Grace. Though the entrees will be stone cold. Nonetheless, we should not keep the Dowager Marchioness of Cranborne waiting any longer."

"Absolutely not," Benedict managed. "Quite right."

Fishing out his pocket square, he mopped his brow. "You and she have my most sincere apologies. Time and—" He floundered. "—stepping out here to admire the begonias ran away with me. The marchioness and, indeed, your dear wife, the countess, have my sincerest apologies. All ladies everywhere have my sincerest apologies. I shall trouble none of you anymore. And I apologise if your evening has been ruined."

Could one ever apologise enough? If he repeated the word would everyone forget the scene they had just witnessed?

"Trust me," he added as fervently as he'd ever spoken. "It shall never happen again. I promise and humbly apologise. You have my word as a duke."

"Bravo, Your Grace. Bravo. Apology accepted." Lord Horton gave a brisk nod, then leaned closer. "If I was but ten years younger, my boy, I'd have been duelling you for those two ladies, you mark my words. Fine fillies, the pair of them. Bravo!"

For the briefest of interludes, Benedict imagined that would be the last word on the matter. His relief was short-lived.

"But I haven't finished with him yet!" declared Lady Wardholme.

"I think, poppet, you'll find that you have," contradicted a cool, commanding voice. Considering he cut such a slight figure, Rossingley had a forceful presence. Benedict heaved an enormous sigh. Finally, *finally*, someone to take charge.

Rossingley patted his arm. "I do believe, Your Grace, that the earl and countess and each of the ladies present this evening accept your fulsome apology."

He made an expansive gesture, encompassing the assembled throng. "The night is warm, the punch has flowed freely, and we've all had a terribly exciting day." His upper lip curled with mischief. "And we've all been guilty of overindulging in the delights of the fairer sex, have we not? Now…" Turning away from Benedict, Rossingley searched for a particular person. "Ah, yes. Lord Lyndon. There you are, my darling. What is it you were wittering on about earlier? Something about the duke having a dalliance with…with a…a young *footman*?"

A few titters broke out while several gentlemen snorted. More notably, a few of Lyndon's chums edged away from him.

A picture of waspish disapproval, Rossingley addressed Benedict's bleary, confused twin. "Do I take it you were referring to *this* duke?" He pointed to Benedict, that gesture somehow encompassing his creased collar, rumpled waistcoat, flushed, damp face, and askew hair. Askew, Benedict thought, described exactly how he felt.

"Incidentally, Your Grace," Rossingley murmured, "you have a touch of rouge on your shirt."

For the benefit of the folks straining their necks at the back, Rossingley tutted loudly. "No, no, no, Lord Fitzsimmons." He shook his head. "It can't be *this* duke. I fear you have erred greatly."

"I've never heard such a preposterous suggestion in my life!" Francis butted in. "Lyndon, don't be an ass. Retract at once. If His Grace wasn't our esteemed brother, for this slight of character, he'd want pistols at dawn! Wouldn't you, Benedict?"

What Benedict really wanted was a chair to sit on and for everyone to stop looking at him as if he were some exotic bug that had crawled from under a rug. As that wasn't happening any time soon, he mustered his last reserves of ducal gravitas.

"Quite possibly." Clasping his trembling hands behind his back, he pushed on. "But I am your brother. If we duelled, my weapon would not be a pistol. But forgiveness. We are all at the mercy of foolish mistakes when foxed." He brushed himself down and vainly tried to rearrange his hair. "A lecture I should be delivering to myself this evening. None of us is immune. Our dear father, rest his soul, used to say there are no mistakes, only lessons."

With herculean effort, Benedict nodded to his brothers, then stepped away from the balcony. "I have had an excellent day at the races. You find me in excellent humour. Thus, on that note, I shall forget you ever entertained such nonsense and will put this matter to bed. A lady's bed," he added as he caught Rossingley's amused expression.

Benedict rested his eyes on the Countess of Horton. "My lady, I do believe I have kept your delicious banquet waiting long enough. It would be my greatest pleasure to take your arm and escort you in to supper."

Chapter Twenty-Six

SUCH WAS HIS social insignificance. Tommy was practically seated in the servant's quarters. He didn't know the young woman on his left, and he never would; whatever the bespectacled chap on *her* left was saying must have been riveting. Over the (cold) entrees, the (cold) soup, the meats, the stews, and the desserts, Tommy became more familiar with the angular line of her right shoulder blade than the contours of her face.

A low door opened to his right, possibly leading to a cellar if the welcome draught was a marker. Tommy's dinner companion wouldn't have noticed if he fell through it.

An immaculately restored and composed Mrs de Villiers sat diagonally across from him, the envy of nearly every woman in the room. Her self-satisfied smile hinted she was fully aware of that fact. Angel sat not too far away, steadily chomping through everything placed in front of him and washing it down with claret. Tommy even caught occasional glimpses of Rossingley's blond head, off in the highfalutin distance. But he was far too far down the pecking order to see Benedict.

Tommy felt him though. He'd felt the waves of relief flooding from him as the plan had unfolded, as the tide of uncertainty swung in his favour. As Lyndon's friends distanced themselves, shuffling away until he stood alone, malevolent, drunk, ridiculed. The scheme could scarcely have gone any better.

But Tommy sensed Benedict's pain, too, at having to endure such a public pantomime, at having to behave in the kind of grubby manner to which he was ill-suited, for no other reason than that his blameless life and that of his blameless brother, Francis, and his one true love, could continue undisturbed.

But, even more, Tommy felt Benedict bleeding out for his lost brother and his unconditional love for a troubled man unworthy of even a fraction of his love and his forgiveness but freely offering both anyway. And Tommy knew Benedict would continue trying to persuade his twin to accept them long after all this hoo-ha had died down. As surely as the *ton* would hold extravagant balls and the scandal mongers would find something to tattle about, he understood these things.

Was Tommy attending his last ball ever? He damned hoped so. And the sooner it was over, the better, so, at last, he could be reunited with Benedict and perhaps escape somewhere private with him.

An insistent rattling sounded in the distance from a spot towards the important end of the table. All around, the chattering voices quieted. Even the woman next to Tommy paused for breath.

A very-pleased-with-himself, Lord Ludham, stood up to speak.

"Your Grace, my lords, my ladies, and gentlemen," he began in a ponderous fashion. "Good evening to you all. And thank you, Lord Horton, for allowing me to speak." He nodded a bow. "As you all know, I'm not a man of many words."

Tommy's heart sank. In his experience, that line presaged all the longest speeches.

"Brevity is the soul of wit," Lord Ludham continued, his booming baritone probably reaching the ears of the good citizens of Piccadilly. "As you'll soon learn for yourselves on the tenth page of my discourse."

Tommy relaxed. He knew he liked the man.

"And, I think we can all agree—" Lord Ludham's gaze skirted the assembled gathering. "—this evening has been eventful enough. However, there is just one more announcement before the ladies withdraw."

His long, contented sigh echoed around the packed dining room. "Our dearest Isabella, the youngest of my and Henrietta's offspring, has been a most wonderful daughter. We thank her for the nineteen years of unbroken joy she has bestowed on us." He flashed a surprisingly roguish grin along the length of the table. "I am fully aware she turned twenty November last, but I'm not counting the few months since because, frankly, there was nothing joyful about endeavouring to follow her exploits."

Hoots of laughter followed this declaration amidst shouts of *hear, hear*, the majority from Lord Ludham's wife. As the merriment died down, he carried on.

"So, it is with utmost pleasure that I announce her

impending nuptials to Lord Francis Oswaldo Edward John Fitz-simmons, third son of the late thirteenth Duke of Ashington. Welcome, Lord Fitzsimmons, to the family!"

At this, he offered up his glass, all following suit. "Over the years, dear Francis, I've come to think of you as the dear son we never asked for. A toast to the both of you! Hip, hip, hooray!"

Chapter Twenty-Seven

BENEDICT'S TIREDNESS SEEPED through to his bones. He was foot sore. Head sore. Back sore. His thighs burned too; it had been some years since he'd crouched up in the saddle. God, that race seemed a lifetime ago now. Rich food, late in the evening, had his belly aching. Even his nerves were frayed from being flattered by ladies and from flattering them in return. Far from becoming a social pariah after being caught on the balcony with Mrs de Villiers, his currency had increased tenfold.

Finally, Benedict heaved himself into his waiting carriage. His eyelids drooped. With a grateful sigh and a very ungentlemanly, loud belch, he sank back into the plush seat.

"Is there space in there for another?"

Benedict's skin couldn't even summon the reserves to blush. "I...ah...didn't anticipate anyone would hear that."

"Hear what, Your Grace?"

Benedict's lips, sore from ceaseless talk, would never be too sore to break into a smile upon hearing that dear, amused voice.

"So," the voice asked again, its wild honey timbre coursing through him like a balm. "Is there room?"

"In my heart?" Benedict prised his eyelids open. The effort was worth it. "No. You already occupy every square inch."

The carriage door closed as Tommy took the seat beside him. Like a seamless puzzle, his smaller fingers slotted neatly between Benedict's. His warm thigh rested loosely alongside.

"I'm so sorry," Tommy whispered, squeezing his hand, "that you had to endure all of that."

"Yes," agreed Benedict, the one word encapsulating his thoughts. "But it is done. I am free from scrutiny, and Francis is set to marry." He heaved a sigh. "And yet…Lyndon…his happiness, his mind, his sanity… He is a constant worry to me."

A cushion of stillness settled around them as they jolted over the quiet cobbled streets. How marvellous it would be if Tommy could accompany him home, lead him to bed, and wrap Benedict up in his arms. To wake him early and make love. Soon, he would ask Tommy to join him on another trip to the lodge so they could do just that. For now, though, he would make do with the pad of Tommy's thumb gently soothing across his knuckles, curing his aching head. Savouring it, sinking into the lull of his horses' hooves, Benedict's eyes drifted closed.

*

"THIS IS NOT my house," he observed thickly, roused by the sudden quiet. Benedict wiped a hand across his gritty jaw, blinking into the night. "Nor is it your club."

"No." Tommy untangled their hands. "We are outside Rossingley's town house."

More company? Benedict needed his bed, not drinks and conversation, no matter how comforting. Instead of climbing down, Tommy shifted in his seat, turning towards him.

"There is something I must tell you, Benedict. I have…I have a few empty rooms above Squire's. Four, to be precise. As we speak, three are being furnished and turned into bedchambers, which will be available to my patrons should they require an overnight stay."

Benedict nodded. On the vanishingly rare occasions he'd overindulged, he'd done the same himself, at White's. Though he didn't know what this had to do with Rossingley. Or himself. "And the fourth?"

Tommy hesitated. In the dim light, Benedict fancied his skin took on a rosier hue. "It is being furnished as a bedchamber also. But, should it please you, reserved for your use and mine. The presence of the other bedchambers means you may come and go as you please, at night and in the morning, and nobody will think anything of it."

Benedict sagged back in the seat. A bedchamber, here in London. To share with Tommy. Night after night. Year after year after year. Such a glorious thing, squeezed in amongst his fatigue and despair. More wonderful than any Gold Cup, more wonderful than a dukedom. A small, tired smile crept across his face.

"As a single man without wife and issue," he ventured, "it would not be so unusual for me to spend several nights a week at my club."

"Not unusual at all," agreed Tommy. "Nobody would think

anything of it." He brought Benedict's hand to his lips. "I believe we are employing a strategy referred to in the magical trade as *misdirection.*"

"Misdirection." As a declaration of love, Benedict's romantic, poetic mind couldn't find fault. "How I wish I could kiss you properly right this minute."

Tommy's kissable lips widened into a grin. He opened the carriage door. "If you wait another few minutes, you can. And more, if His Grace wishes it. Our own bedchamber is not yet ready, but I believe I can offer you the next best thing."

Benedict faltered. "You've lost me."

"Rossingley runs an unusual household." Tommy glanced up at the solid, austere property. "His staff is… 'Specially curated' is how he describes them. Put more simply, they comprise the biggest bunch of fruits in the whole of London town, this side of a molly house." Lest Benedict's groom overhear, he pressed his mouth to Benedict's ear. "Frankly, *poppet*, you and I could fornicate on the stairs, and no one would take a blind bit of notice."

As Benedict's chin dropped in wonder, Tommy added, "But, don't fret. That won't be necessary. I have reserved us a sumptuous bedchamber for the night."

*

FUNNY THING, TIREDNESS. There one minute, dashed off the next. Benedict had every confidence the bedchamber was magnificent—Rossingley didn't stint on luxury. But for all he cared, it could have been a tiny garret at the top of a molly house, accommodating nothing but a narrow cot with a single mean pillow. The simple reason? His beautiful Tommy was in it, and he was removing Benedict's evening coat, his waistcoat, his cuff buttons, his shirt. He crouched at Benedict's aching feet, detaching first one dance slipper and then the other. Stockings unfurled and breeches followed. Throwing aside the coverlet, he laid thick towels in its place.

"I have a bowl of hot water, soap, and many more towels. Lie back, close your eyes."

Tommy washed him first—his face, dabbing and drying in turn, sprinkling kisses across Benedict's clean cheeks, his nose, his eyelids, his forehead. Kissing his mouth, Tommy lingered awhile to taste him, to love him.

He took his hands, one by one. Tommy cherished the palms and each finger, cleansing where so many had grasped them that day, so they were new and Tommy's alone. Leaving a trail of lather and soap, his strong fingers glided under Benedict's arms. He bathed the nape of his neck until it no longer itched with dried sweat. Benedict's body thrummed back to life; he smelled the citrussy, almondy fragrance of the soap; and he began to smell himself, his own heady arousal.

And then the washcloth and the soap travelled lower, to the dark pelt of his chest, so different to his lover's and yet so loved by him. They moved across the planes of his belly, soft and tender, and its thick arrow of coarse hair. Tommy lingered there, too, until Benedict's hips shifted. His prick rudely vied for attention. It was rewarded with a tiny peck on the tip.

"Patience, my love."

Water droplets tickled the hairs on Benedict's shins as Tommy's lips caressed the inside edge of one knee and then the other. He nudged apart Benedict's thighs. He flexed his knees, bent his hips, exposing Benedict's shadowy, most intimate groove. The warm cloth slipped in there too.

And then the pad of a soapy finger pressed against his hole. Benedict tensed.

"You must stop wriggling." Tommy's lips curved into a grin against Benedict's thigh. "You are a veritable worm."

"I cannot." His face burned, and he squirmed some more. "Even my bones are mortified."

Tommy cut his objection short by crowding the damp fingers of his free hand against Benedict's lips. "Hush, Your Grace. Let me worship you. Every part of you." His grey eyes crinkled. Benedict could barely meet them. "Shall I have to distract you with more misdirection?"

"What? Yes, no! But surely, there are some parts that—"

Sharp teeth bit down on Benedict's thigh.

"Ow!"

Tommy's fingertip slid inside.

"Oh. Oh, I…"

"Shh." Tommy's other hand muffled Benedict's protesting words. His obscene mouth closed around one of Benedict's ballocks, suckling on it like a tit. Benedict did not think he had ever felt so utterly *hamstrung*.

And then, Tommy's mouth left his ballocks to fit over his jutting prick. Burying him to the hilt. He drew his teeth back along Benedict's shaft, circling—nay, teasing—the head and swallowed again. Swallow, bury, repeat, swallow, bury, repeat as though measuring the length and checking for accuracy. Or, as though hell-bent on his lips forming an unholy union with that criminal, inquisitive finger. He swept back and forth, back and forth, imprinting over and over upon a singular sensitive nubbin, a diabolical nubbin that had Benedict cursing, writhing, and begging for more. In fact, if not for the fingers of Tommy's other hand, lewdly jammed in Benedict's mouth, it was exceedingly possible the entire household would be privy to his pleasure.

Was that…was it two fingers? Oh Lord, it was. It was two fingers. And one mouth, one bleeding, scorching tunnel of a mouth. Benedict felt skewered, like a fish dangling on a hook, except with no desire for escape. Quite the opposite in fact. Leaning into it, he clutched the short strands of Tommy's hair, shoving his hips up and Tommy's head down, burying his lips into the tight curls at his groin.

The pressure of his release swelled. "I'm…I'm…"

Truth be told, he didn't know what he was; words and conscious thought dissolved in a miasma of need and want and Tommy's mouth. And in his fingers; those damned undignified, magnificent fingers. With whitened vision, a spine-tingling shudder, and an even more undignified roaring noise, Benedict's embarrassment dissolved in a tidal wave of release. Demanding, unstoppable, it pulsed from him in the blink of an eye to last, infinitesimally, for years.

"Benedict," said Tommy softly from his spot between Benedict's quivering thighs. Benedict had a suspicion he'd already called his name a few times. Silvery threads of spend speckled his lover's reddened upper lip as though he'd looted a spider's web. Benedict's prick jumped alarmingly when Tommy swiped it with the tip of his tongue.

Tommy's eyes flicked down to it. "Again? So soon?"

"If so, then it is a miracle, and the only organ of my body left alive," Benedict croaked.

Very deliberately, Tommy crawled up Benedict and straddled his hips. With long, slow strokes, grinning down, he fisted
himself. His other hand reached behind.

"I have not...I did not know." Benedict gesticulated
vaguely. If the pretty man on his lap wasn't doing *that*, he would
have screwed his eyes shut. "That...one could...that a finger..."

"Two fingers," Tommy pointed out.

Two fingers. "That it felt...that I could...like that." Hysteria
edged his breathy chuckle. "I fear that, for all these years, these
lonely years, I have been eating eggs without salt."

Tommy's abbreviated laugh ended on a soft moan. A solitary pearl of wetness glistened at the tip of his cock, like a tiny
shimmering piece of him. On instinct, Benedict reached out to
catch it, then touched his finger to his tongue.

Tommy moaned again, dampness glimmering on his brow.
"Touch yourself, Benedict. Watch me as you touch yourself."

"I can look nowhere else." Unbidden, Benedict's hands went
to his groin, his sensitive member already stiffening. "The devil's
own serpents couldn't drag my eyes away."

Like a voyeur at a paper peep show, he frigged himself hard
as Tommy, lost in pleasure, teetered on the precipice. His fist flew
back and forth; his chest heaved ragged, harsh breaths. A crimson
flush spread across Tommy's smooth chest. Benedict followed the
path of it with his palm to pinch the flat disc of a nipple, then
pluck at the other.

Tommy's crisis rolled though him. The first spill seared Benedict's cheek, the second plastered his neck, the third splashed his
belly. The fourth mingled with Benedict's own. If any more issued

forth it was lost between them as Tommy slumped in his arms. This time, neither of them moved.

Chapter Twenty-Eight

ASHINGTON HOUSE, SET in too many acres of rolling Hampshire countryside to compute, had overseen many a wedding. None so gay as Francis and Isabella's, perhaps. Nor arranged so hurriedly. From the plump, rosy glow of his betrothed cheeks, Benedict suspected his youngest brother's *urges* might have been assuaged sometime before the date was set. For a chap with a sore head, he'd been awfully chirpy the morning after the Horton ball. Then again, so had Benedict.

"Do you think Lyndon will come?" Tommy asked.

They were seated around the fireplace in the Ashington library, a grand old and draughty corner of his vast ancestral home that Benedict didn't especially care for. Not being much of a reader, he rarely ventured inside. Few did, which meant he and Tommy were blessedly alone.

"One can hope." Benedict checked his pocket watch. "He's

still only fashionably late. The church ceremony isn't until three."

Four weeks had gone by since the Horton ball, during which most of the *ton* had decamped to the countryside. For Benedict, the visit was fleeting. He would be returning to town after the celebrations, whereupon he'd enjoy a quiet season in town with his lover. He was counting down the hours.

A footman's scratch at the door announced Lyndon's arrival. No one spoke until drinks were served and the footman departed. With his back to Benedict, Lyndon inspected the shelves as if totally alone. He looked better, Benedict thought. Less dissipated.

"Why is he here?" Lyndon queried, running his finger across a row of dusty, burgundy spines.

"Because I requested it," answered Benedict. *And because I can hardly bear leave his side.* "I hear you have been staying in Norfolk."

"Yes." Selecting a volume, Lyndon turned, weighing the book in his hand. It was one of the ancient ones, beautiful to look at but never opened, and trimmed in delicate gold leaf. "I shall return tomorrow."

"Is the house sufficiently comfortable? I have not visited for many a year."

"Yes," Lyndon confirmed. "If one is an enthusiast of flat, bleak wetlands and a social diary rivalling that of a garden slug. Also, it drizzles incessantly." His eyes flicked to Benedict's. "A feature of the Norfolk climate not even a grand duke such as yourself can bend to suit his wishes."

He weighed the book in his hand again, deliberating. For an awful moment, Benedict thought he was limbering up to throw it.

"Though who knows?" Lyndon continued. "You succeeded in bending the minds of the *ton*, after all. Well played, Your Grace."

"They saw what they saw," Benedict replied evenly, "and drew their own conclusions."

"Did he put you up to it?" Lyndon jerked his chin. "Tommy Squire?" The corner of his top lip curled as if smelling something rotten. "Naturally, I know who you are, *Mr L'Esquire*. And I know what you do." His gaze drifted around the vast library, up and across the miles of shelves. "Since when did a molly boy acquire such a taste for luxury?"

"Around the time I acquired a duke as a lover," Tommy replied.

"If you refer to Mr L'Esquire's past in those terms within my earshot one more time," Benedict cut in, "I shall scratch you off without a penny. He is a gentleman of business, running successful gaming establishments, brothels, and blackleg stands. Nothing more, nothing less. And if I hear you are insinuating anything different, then—"

"Yes, you'll set me free from your apron strings without a pot to piss in." Lyndon sighed irritably. "Was there a specific reason you requested my presence, Your Grace, or was it simply to parade your well-used male lover?"

The objective was fast becoming to punch the light from his brother's eyes if he carried on much longer in this supercilious vein. Which would serve no purpose whatsoever, except to temporarily soothe Benedict's temper and give Lyndon the satisfaction of witnessing him loose it. Under his breath, he counted to ten.

"I have a proposition for you, Lyndon, one you may not like, but which is for your own good."

Lyndon smirked. "Your transformation into our father is complete, brother."

In some situations, poor behaviour was better ignored. Though damned difficult. Benedict had already spotted Tommy's fists curled into tight little balls. He knew what was coming. Tommy had listened, expressed his misgivings, then supported Benedict's decision anyhow.

"I would like you to spend the autumn in Norfolk. The estate manager tells me there is much work to be done, and ideally, a family member needs to oversee it. That member shall be you, and I expect monthly reports. Mr L'Esquire's man, Sidney" — at this his brother's eyebrow rose — "will periodically surprise you with a visit to ensure all is well. It transpires he has family that way."

"I'll be sure to kill the fatted calf," murmured Lyndon. "Though I seem to recall he mentioned something about pigs, so perhaps a loin of pork might suit his palate more."

"If you follow that instruction to my satisfaction — and I have modest expectations — I shall return your full allowance and give you use of the rooms in Portland Street." Before Lyndon's next dollop of sarcasm, Benedict added, "There are conditions."

"Of course, there are." Lyndon's eyes rolled. "I must dole out alms to the poor each Wednesday, join the Tuesday ladies' sewing circle, and pay a visit to the church every morning. Twice on the sabbath."

"No. Nothing as draconian as that. Though I'm not stopping you. I'm simply asking that, on your return to London, you

restrict your club membership to Squire's—you must rescind Bootle's and White's. That way, I can keep tabs on your gambling habits. Furthermore, you must use Squire's stands to place your wa-
gers for the same reasons."

"Must I only fuck his chits too?"

"Actually, they're the only ones you are prohibited from
fucking, my lord," answered Tommy smoothly. "I'm quite fond
of them."

"Oh, and you must stop using the word 'fuck' in my presence," interrupted Benedict. "Especially when you dine with me
and Tommy, which—again on your return to town—shall be
every Thursday evening at six. It's childish and vulgar, and Francis and Isabella will periodically join us."

"On balance, I think I preferred father's rules. Less prissy.
Anything else?"

Benedict and Tommy exchanged a look. "No," said Benedict. "I think that's enough to be getting on with, don't you?"

Halfway to the door, Lyndon paused, toying with the heavy
book as if deliberating. Benedict waited.

"Indulge my curiosity, Ben," he said at last. "How did you
do it? Convince the *ton* you were a scoundrel of the highest order?
Word of your exploits is still reaching my ears all the way up in
Norfolk."

Benedict permitted himself a small smile. He imagined his
thwarted nosy brother pacing the wooden floors of his gloomy
Norfolk home, his clever brain increasingly frustrated.

"I recently discovered, since finding Tommy again, that I am
not alone in my predilections. There are…ah…quite a few of us
knocking around." Unbidden, a picture of his dear Beatrice,

strolling through the walled garden only a few hours earlier, arm in arm with Mrs de Villiers filled his mind.

"Some have been under our noses all along, if only one knew where to look," he added. Rossingley's slight frame flitted across his vision, but as he'd been when Benedict was a boy — a bright, dazzling bolt of colour in his stuffy, dreary boyhood.

"And the funny thing is," Benedict continued, his gaze never wavering from his beloved Tommy, "despite our differences, we are allies. Which is a roundabout way of saying that I have more friends than I ever imagined. And they are a strong bunch. I would recommend not taking them on. Only, I think you've possibly worked that out for yourself."

Even clever Lyndon had no answer to that. As he reached the door, Benedict spoke again.

"The book, Lyndon. It belongs to the Ashington estate, and you appear to still be holding it. Do leave it on the table on your way out. *Poppet.*"

*

"HE CALLED ME Ben," Benedict said excitedly. "Did you hear? He never calls me that. Not since we were very young. It gives me hope, Tommy."

Tommy shook his head, though he was still smiling. "Hope was never lost, my love."

He rose and sauntered to the door, carefully locked it, then sauntered over to where Benedict lounged on a settee plenty big enough for two. Settling himself, he snaked his arm around the back of Benedict's neck, drawing him close and kissing his temple.

"I've never fucked in a duke's library," he observed. "A

hunting lodge, yes, and in a bedchamber, of course. Also, on a drawing room chair, on a spindly study chair, which is sadly no more, and quite recently, across the bench of a duke's coach and four." He kissed Benedict again, no doubt recalling how they whiled away the hours travelling through Hampshire. "But I've never fucked in a duke's library."

Benedict chuckled. Already, he was loosening his cravat and fumbling with the fall of his breeches. "It's a funny thing, Tommy. I don't find that coarse word half as unpleasant spilling from your mouth."

"What else do you like spilling from my mouth, Your Grace?" His fingertips traced slow circles up Benedict's thigh. Benedict pulled him into his arms.

"The church service is not for another hour. Why don't we find out?"

Epilogue

"WHERE IS EVERYBODY?" demanded Francis. "I turned around to find only myself and my darling new wife remaining on the dance floor! And now, her mother has pulled her aside to say her goodbyes to the northern side of the family. I'll be embroiled for hours if I join her; they'll make me promise all sorts of dreary treks to Yorkshire. I don't have the constitution for northern living."

He peered over Benedict's shoulder as if expecting a contingent of elderly aunts armed with cuffs and chains. "I can usually rely on Rossingley to show a half decent leg on the dance floor, but he's buggered off too. So, I need to appear terribly occupied over here for the next few minutes."

"Rossingley and Angel retired an hour ago," Benedict answered. "To their bedchambers in the east wing."

"Angel was muttering something about soft furnishings, I believe," added Tommy blandly.

"Oh, right..." Perplexed, Francis scratched his head before noticing Benedict's mouth twisting into a smirk.

"Listen, you chaps," Francis blustered. "I know I'm being terribly grown up about this, but honestly, I've just gorged on a huge slice of my own wedding cake. As things stand, it's going to be a devil to digest without that imagery."

"What imagery would that be?" Full of innocence, Tommy's grey eyes regarded Benedict's brother.

Wisely, Francis chose to disregard him. "And Beatrice seems to have sloped off too. More's the pity. Old Tuffy danced with her twice this afternoon and found the experience most satisfying. He's of a mind to call on her once we're back in town. About time both of them settled down. It's her fourth season, isn't it?"

"Third, I believe," answered Benedict with a pleasant smile. "And last I heard; she and Mrs de Villiers were discussing the advent of liberal Toryism while perusing the cheeseboard." He paused a beat. "And you know how tempting cheeseboards can be... I'm not sure she'll have eyes for anything else."

"Cheeseboa...oh, lord. Really? Our Beatrice and Mrs..." Shaking his head, Francis wiped his brow. "*Really?*"

Benedict gave his shoulder a kindly pat. "'Fraid so, brother. Break the news to young Tuffy gently, won't you?"

"And in words of one syllable," added Tommy.

"Right ho." Francis examined them both. "Seems I'll have to make do with you two then. That or track Lyndon down. At least he'll still be up for another round of something alcohol-related." He frowned. "Mind you, he was surprisingly sober last time I spotted him. He's off to Norfolk again tomorrow. He was telling me he's of a mind to turn the often-waterlogged fields to the south of the property to mustard and radish. Apparently, they suit damp soil. Good for him!"

A weary footman passed by, proffering the last of the champagne. Accepting a glass, Francis turned to Benedict and Tommy, who had both declined.

"Don't tell me you're not imbibing either. It's my wedding night!"

"And a very warm and happy one," agreed Benedict, "during which I have drunk, danced, and been merry. And considerably increased your annual allowance in order for you to keep the newly minted Lady Fitzsimmons in the manner to which I expect she will very much want to be accustomed. Thus, I feel my participation in the day's festivities has been well and truly filled and is now over."

Giving him a final embrace, Benedict stepped away from his youngest, most beloved brother. "Now, if you'll excuse us, Tommy and I quite fancy a walk before bed. We're off to admire the begonias."

*

WATCHING OVER THEM, the moon was a serene presence, daubing the dewy grass in a pale, white-gold glow. Ashington's extensive gardens boasted hidden corners only known to three inquisitive small boys, now all fully grown. Tugging Tommy by the hand, Benedict led him down towards the boating lake, through the fronds of a willow, across a patch of mossy grass (where the gardeners heaped up twigs and fallen leaves), and then out of sight.

They settled against the trunk of an old beech. With his arms wrapped around his lover, keeping him warm, Benedict contemplated the stars. If he were a cleverer man, he'd have come up with something romantic or profound to say about them to share with Tommy, who would laugh and tease and love him, regardless. And then maybe share something of himself back.

Perhaps next time. He'd work on some ideas in the interim.

"They shine brighter out here than in town," remarked Tommy. "I noticed when we visited the lodge."

"They do," agreed Benedict. "Not all things about the country are bad." He squeezed Tommy a little tighter. "Especially when everything blooms and the evenings are long, like now during the summer months."

He stayed quiet for a few minutes. The country was also better than town for quietness, too, in his opinion, not that he'd ever persuade his lover.

"I like the summer months best," said Tommy, his soft voice fracturing the quiet. "I dislike being caught in the rain, and I detest feeling cold. Too much of my life used to be spent shivering in inadequate clothing. Though I'm not scared of thunderstorms."

Benedict hardly dared move. Minutes of silence filled the spaces between Tommy's raw words, a silence so deep, it was a poem in itself. His heart thudded in his throat.

"I like crocuses," Tommy conceded, "but I prefer dandelions and...and simple daisies. They were the only flowers I knew by name as a child. They grew up with me, between the dry cracks in the streets. Horses trampled them, mud and leather boots crushed them, and still, they never gave up."

In the circle of Benedict's arms, his fair head tilted back to rest on Benedict's broad shoulder. Benedict buried his nose in the fine hair, not trusting himself to speak.

"I…I do not have a favourite dessert," Tommy continued, "except I often purchase a quart of sherbets or barley sugars. They live in a jar on the corner of my desk. Red ink is an affectation, nothing more, nothing less. Though I find any errors in the calculations in my ledgers are clearer with it."

He held up his left hand and pulled back the cuff. A faded, jagged crescent disrupted the pale, smooth skin of his slender wrist.

Benedict swallowed. It was the only one of his questions left unanswered. Half of him wished he'd never posed it. "You never need tell me the story about that if you don't want," he whispered. "If it is too much."

"I will, one day," said Tommy with a smile in his voice. "But not yet. Perhaps to pass the time during a long ride, when we have exhausted all other activities to occupy us." He shook down his cuff. "It is nothing really. Simply the opening sentence of a romantic story about a poor young man who fell in love with a rich, handsome rake."

Benedict chuckled and hugged Tommy closer, like the rare, precious gift he was. "Does this romantic story of yours have a happy ending?"

A foolish question, one to which he already had the answer.

"Of course, Your Grace. Like all the best stories do."

Acknowledgements

I'd like to thank my publisher, NineStar Press, and above all, my editor, Elizabetta, for her endless patience and encouragement.

About the Author

Fearne Hill is a Lambda Literary finalist. She lives deep in the southern British countryside, a stone's throw away from the private country estate providing her inspiration for Rossingley.

When she is not writing queer romantic fiction, Fearne works as an anaesthesiologist.

Email
fearne.hill@fearnehill.com

Facebook
www.facebook.com/fearne.hill.50

Facebook Group Fearne Hill's House
www.facebook.com/groups/1172459269938382

Twitter
@FearneHill

Instagram
www.instagram.com/fearnehill_author

Other NineStar books by this author

The Last of the Moussakas

Rossingley Series

To Hold a Hidden Pearl

To Catch a Fallen Leaf

To Take a Quiet Breath

To Melt a Frozen Heart

To Mend a Broken Wing

Regency Rossingley Series

To Tempt a Troubled Earl

Coming Soon from Fearne Hill

To Beguile a Banished Lord

Regency Rossingley, Book Three

I must not swive the stable boy (again).
I must not swive the stable boy (again).
I must not swive the stable boy. (again).
I must not…

"Crocodile tears won't save you this time, Master Rollo."

Pritchard's lisping note of triumph was unmistakeable. "No matter how prettily you shed them, you've pushed your Papa too far. He is provoked beyond measure."

"He'd be his usual fine and dandy self if you hadn't gone running to inform him."

"My primary role in the Rossingley household is to serve the earl," answered Pritchard, as prissy and prim as ever. "Not his licentious offspring."

Rollo harboured an ugly notion that his father's valet had been waiting a long time for this moment, possibly since when Rollo, at age four, had sprinkled rich, resinous lily pollen amongst Papa's meticulously folded white linens. It had been the opening salvo of a rather jolly dislike of each other.

"You're relishing this, aren't you, Pritchard?"

"Tremendously," Pritchard confirmed.

Escape flitted across Rollo's mind, but only for a second. One step ahead, and perhaps recalling the time Rollo had feinted past him and sprinted away across the lawns, Pritchard had brought along reinforcements in the form of two burly footmen stationed either side of the library door. The window, alas, was closed.

Rollo shot a pleading look towards Kit Angel — Papa's divine and terribly understanding paramour — currently decorating the settee, who shook his head. Everybody was loyal to Papa to a fault, and it was damned annoying.

"Sorry, old chap." At least Kit sounded genuine. "For what it's worth, I tried to talk your father out of it. Some of us enjoy having you around."

What did he mean by *having you around*? Rollo wasn't planning on going anywhere, unless swallow diving headfirst out of the nearest window and running for the hills until Papa had calmed down counted. And talk him out of what?

Before he could further parse Kit's words, Papa himself swept into the library, dressed in his favourite chartreuse silk banyan and pearls. Rollo coveted both immensely. As always, the eleventh earl was impeccably turned out, though this morning, his flamboyant attire sat at odds with the discomfiting, frigid set of his mouth. Rollo barely dared meet his pale eyes; when his mouth looked as grim as that, his gaze could freeze a lake.

"Rollo, my darling."

Rollo winced. Only a fool would mistake the endearment for anything other than an affectation.

"Yes, Papa."

The ice-chip eyes glittered. "You know why you're here, I assume?"

"Yes, Papa."

Experience taught Rollo that short answers tended to be met more favourably. Unfortunately, his smart mouth had a lamentable tendency to act independently of his mind. "Writing out *I must not swive the stable boy* one hundred times was a significant clue. The lack of hot water in my room this morning more subtle. But no less vexing."

The faintest ghost of a smile twitched his father's lips, gone in an instant. Even in the midst of a scolding, Rollo still appreciated he had the best of fathers. Most would have introduced his arse to the switch long ago.

"Do you have anything to say for yourself, Rollo?"

Rollo straightened his shoulders. Might as well be hanged for a sheep as a lamb and all that. The importance of standing up for himself had been instilled in him from a young age; Papa could hardly complain now he was reaping what he'd sown.

"Yes, Papa. Several things, actually."

Papa sighed. "I'd expect nothing less."

"Firstly, my wrist aches." Rollo waggled it to demonstrate. "I have indelible green ink stains on my second favourite blush waistcoat, and I'm still frightfully chilly. And, for the record, Ellis was an able, willing, practiced, and—dare I say—extremely encouraging participant."

"Naturally, he was; you paid him two pounds!"

"And it was very well deserved."

"And then a further crown, on account, for future favours!"

Goodness, Pritchard had been busy. Rollo shot him an evil

look, though in having his financial transactions laid out so bluntly, his bravura hung by a thread.

"At risk of repeating myself," Rollo ploughed on, "I considered it money well spent. Ellis has several strings to his bow."

"Evidently."

His father's fine blond brows knit together. The line between standing up for himself and cheeking Papa was a fine one; Rollo had a sneaking suspicion he might have tiptoed across it.

"Darling Rollo," began his father, a layer of frost coating each syllable. "For all I care, our stable boy could have the whole string section of London's prestigious Philharmonic Society tucked behind the fall of his breeches. And you could have twanged every single instrument."

Rollo had been on his knees attempting exactly that until he'd been discovered by the second groom, who'd blabbed to the head groom, who'd gone tittle-tattling to Pritchard.

"Nevertheless, as you are well aware, there is nothing I detest more than fortunate, well-heeled members of society taking advantage of those in their employ." With an irritable flick of his hand, Papa waved away Rollo's attempt to defend his actions. "That Ellis was willing is an irrelevance. You placed the man in a devilishly awkward position, and I simply will not tolerate it. Have I made myself crystal clear?"

"Yes, Papa," he replied meekly. "Sorry, Papa."

"And so you should be."

Yet to be mollified, his father folded his arms and began pacing in front of the fireplace. "The simple truth remains. Our loyal servants are out of bounds. I distinctly recall this being made perfectly clear to you when you returned from Eton last year. Did I not?"

Rollo hung his head. "Yes, Papa."

"If it was your first demeanour and you were totally in the dark, then, of course, I would instruct you on how a Duchamps-Avery should behave. It would be remiss of me not to. But, as it is, the fact that you stand here, arguing the point after all I've…"

Ahhh, to begin the day with one of Papa's sweet lectures. Rollo didn't need to tune in for the rest; he knew how things ran. Their disputes were well rehearsed operatic duets, composed of increasing exasperation on Papa's part, Rollo feigning abject apology, a discourse on how a Duchamps-Avery should conduct themselves, ending with a loving embrace and a promise to do better. As usual, Pritchard and Kit had been making a fuss over nothing. Rollo would bow his head a few times, continue to appear suitably repentant, and ride this one out.

Content in the sure knowledge he was loved, Rollo's thoughts drifted. In a few moments, Papa would fizzle out and decree his penance. Idly, he wondered what it might be. Papa was nothing if not creative. Over the years, Rollo's punishments had ranged from counting all the earwigs in the orangery (aged five, he was discovered hiding in the coal cellar after two hours of searching) to scrubbing the scullery steps with a toothbrush (for convincing his brother, Willoughby, that eating ground up pinecones would allow him to see better in the dark). Willoughby casting up his accounts the next morning during the church sermon aside, some of Rollo's so-called punishments had turned into rather good fun. Like the time he was consigned to digging over the vegetable patch and unearthed an adder, which had slithered over Pritchard's foot.

"To that end, Rollo, it is high time you had a firmer hand.

My own father, rest his soul, oft quoted that a rose bush must be heavily pruned in order to produce the best blooms. And, on this occasion, I believe he was speaking the truth. Don't you agree?"

Papa's lecture appeared to have taken a horticultural detour. "Er…yes?"

"Excellent." His father clapped his hands. "Therefore, Dobson will accompany you when you depart for your trip to Norfolk this afternoon, see you safely settled in, and return to collect you in three months' time."

"D-Dobson will…what?" Rollo's happy flights of reminiscence screeched to a halt. *Did…did he…did…?* "Sorry, Papa, I must have misheard. Did you just say Dobson's accompanying me to *Norfolk*?"

"Got it in one, darling. You are clever. To Goule Hall, to be precise. On the edge of the Broads, between some hellish backwater named Stokesby and another provincial bog going by the name of Wroxham, I believe. A delightful, if not a tad isolated, property belonging to the Ashington estate. The duke's twin brother, Lord Lyndon Fitzsimmons, remains in residence after spending an enforced period of seclusion there a couple of years ago, whilst he…ah…reflected on several episodes of…ah…poor behaviour in and around the *ton*. I shall spare you the details. Suffice to say that in comparison, dear boy, your antics are those of a rank amateur."

CONNECT WITH NINESTAR PRESS

WEBSITE: NINESTARPRESS.COM

FACEBOOK: NINESTARPRESS

X: @NINESTARPRESS

INSTAGRAM: NINESTARPRESS

BLUESKY: NINESTARPRESS

THREADS: @NINESTARPRESS

www.ingramcontent.com/pod-product-compliance
Lightning Source LLC
Chambersburg PA
CBHW060232100726
47907CB00003B/605